### Praise for *Summerlong*

"Peter Beagle's novel *Sum........................................*ead that
moves through a finely det*......................................*; old and
as urgent as language. Its st*....................................*ds of the
tale and try to pull it into w*..............................*g passion,
comedy, love, despair into a study of life on the B-flat harmonica,
accompanied by a soundtrack of wind and waves, and, always, good
smells from the kitchen."
—Patricia A. McKillip, author of *The Riddle-Master of Hed* and
*Dreams of Distant Shores*

"Best-selling fantasy-author Beagle crafts a tantalizing picture of an
atypical Pacific Northwestern couple whose lives are inter-rupted
by myth and mystery. When Joanna and Abe meet a young waitress
named Lioness, they are immediately drawn to her *primavera* aura
and offer her a home in Abe's garage. Life on Gardner Island blooms
in an endless summer during Lioness' stay. The couple's lives and their
relationship continue as usual until Lioness' attempt to run from her
past begins to unravel when her mother and husband arrive in town.
As Lioness struggles against her fate, her restless and defiant energy
touches Abe and Joanna, who find new passions—and, unexpectedly,
new intimate partners . . . Themes of love, loss, nurturing, and
adapting are wrapped up in this deliberate and bittersweet tale of
what it is to love in your own time, in your own way."
—*Booklist*

"In his first new novel in more than a decade, Beagle creates an intimate
drama . . . beautifully detailed fantasy."
—*Kirkus*

"*Summerlong* is myth made flesh: a novel that makes real not just the
force of gods and powers, but the hair's-breadth between them and

fragile, mortal things—and how the transfigurations they visit can grace us, destroy us, and ultimately push us into blooming again. Soft, suffused with awe, and wryly, unflinchingly honest about the human heart, *Summerlong* is beautiful in its love for our messy complexity; for the first step into cold water, for the death that lets us grow again, and the ways we learn to love each other—and ourselves—wiser and better."
—Leah Bobet, author of *An Inheritance of Ashes* and *Above*

"If you like mythical fantasy, it is a wonderful treat. Even if that's not a genre you're familiar with, you'll struggle to find a more absorbing, beautiful novel this year. 5 out of 5 stars."
—*Bastian's Book Reviews*

"It's been three years since Peter S. Beagle released a short story or essay, and longer than that since his last novel. That's a long dry spell, especially for someone whose writing was such a big part of my childhood. Fortunately Beagle's latest novel, *Summerlong*, is due out this September, and it's absolutely worth the wait."
—*Pixelated Geek*

### Praise for Peter S. Beagle

"One of my favorite writers."
—Madeleine L'Engle, author of *A Wrinkle in Time*

"Peter S. Beagle illuminates with his own particular magic such commonplace matters as ghosts, unicorns, and werewolves. For years a loving readership has consulted him as an expert on those hearts' reasons that reason does not know."
—Ursula K. Le Guin, author of *A Wizard of Earthsea*

"The only contemporary to remind one of Tolkien."
—*Booklist*

"Peter S. Beagle is (in no particular order) a wonderful writer, a fine human being, and a bandit prince out to steal readers' hearts."
—Tad Williams, author of *Tailchaser's Song*

"It's a fully rounded region, this other world of Peter Beagle's imagination."
—*Kirkus*

"[Beagle] has been compared, not unreasonably, with Lewis Carroll and J. R. R. Tolkien, but he stands squarely and triumphantly on his own feet."
—*Saturday Review*

"Not only does Peter Beagle make his fantasy worlds come vividly, beautifully alive; he does it for the people who enter them."
—Poul Anderson, author of *The High Crusade*

"Peter S. Beagle is the magician we all apprenticed ourselves to. Before all the endless series and shared-world novels, Beagle was there to show us the amazing possibilities waiting in the worlds of fantasy, and he is still one of the masters by which the rest of the field is measured."
—Lisa Goldstein, author of *The Red Magician*

"Peter S. Beagle would be one of the century's great writers in any arena he chose."
—Edward Bryant, author of *Cinnabar*

### Praise for *The Last Unicorn*

"*The Last Unicorn* is the best book I have ever read. You need to read it. If you've already read it, you need to read it again."
—Patrick Rothfuss, author of *The Name of the Wind*

"Almost as if it were the last fairy tale, come out of lonely hiding in the forests of childhood, *The Last Unicorn* is as full of enchantment as any of the favorite tales readers may choose to recall . . . a delicate, sensitive, yet powerful rendering of all the intangibles that make a fairy tale unforgettable."
—*St. Louis Post-Dispatch*

"*The Last Unicorn* is one of the true classics of fantasy, ranking with Tolkien's *The Hobbit*, Le Guin's Earthsea Trilogy, and Lewis Carroll's *Alice in Wonderland*. Beagle writes a shimmering prose-poetry, the voice of fairy tales and childhood."
—*Amazon.com*

## Also by Peter S. Beagle

### Fiction
*A Fine and Private Place* (1960)
*The Last Unicorn* (1968)
*Lila the Werewolf* (1969)
*The Folk of the Air* (1986)
*The Innkeeper's Song* (1993)
*The Unicorn Sonata* (1996)
*Tamsin* (1999)
*A Dance for Emilia* (2000)
*The Last Unicorn: The Lost Version* (2007)
*Strange Roads* (with Lisa Snellings Clark, 2008)
*Return* (2010)

### Short story collections
*Giant Bones* (1997)
*The Rhinoceros Who Quoted Nietzsche and Other Odd Acquaintances*
(1997)
*The Line Between* (2006)
*Your Friendly Neighborhood Magician: Songs and Early Poems*
(2006)
*We Never Talk About My Brother* (2009)
*Mirror Kingdoms: The Best of Peter S. Beagle* (2010)
*Sleight of Hand* (2011)

### Nonfiction
*I See By My Outfit: Cross-Country by Scooter, an Adventure* (1965)
*The California Feeling* (with Michael Bry, 1969)
*The Lady and Her Tiger* (with Pat Derby, 1976)
*The Garden of Earthly Delights* (1982)
*In the Presence of Elephants* (1995)

**As editor**

*Peter S. Beagle's Immortal Unicorn* (with Janet Berliner, 1995)
*The Secret History of Fantasy* (2010)
*The Urban Fantasy Anthology* (with Joe R. Lansdale, 2011)

SUMMERLONG
PETER S. BEAGLE

Beagle, Peter S.,
Summerlong /

2016.
33305236675215
sa            09/19/16

# Summerlong

## Peter S. Beagle

TACHYON
SAN FRANCISCO

Summerlong
Copyright © 2016 by Peter S. Beagle

This is a work of fiction. All events portrayed in this book are fictitious and any resemblance to real people or events is purely coincidental. All rights reserved including the right to reproduce this book or portions thereof in any form without the express permission of the author and the publisher.

Interior and cover design by Elizabeth Story
Cover art "The Prayer" copyright © 2013 Magdalena Korzeniewska

Tachyon Publications LLC
1459 18th Street #139
San Francisco, CA 94107
415-285-5615
www.tachyonpublications.com
tachyon@tachyonpublications.com

Series Editor: Jacob Weisman
Project Editor: Rachel Fagundes

ISBN 13: 978-1-61696-244-9

Printed in the United States by Worzalla

First Edition: 2016
9  8  7  6  5  4  3  2  1

*To Peggy Carlisle,*
*who earned it all*

# 1.

# FEBRUARY

W ith so many flights coming in, from so many different points of the compass, he had no way of knowing certainly whether this one was hers. All the same, when he heard the airplane he stopped working and went out to the woodpile, away from the trees, watching the 767 crawl across the gray sky, beginning to circle for the descent into Sea-Tac. *She'd be making her final walk-through, reminding people to return their seatbacks to the full upright position.* He went back inside and called her number, leaving a message for her to come home to.

"Del, hi, it's me. I'll catch the five-forty, and we'll hit the Ethiopian place. Love you, cookie."

Sitting at his worktable, once again trying to play "Midnight Hour Blues" on the A-flat harmonica, he could see the two great blue herons stalking the shallows, dividing the rocky shoreline between them in silent, professional cooperation. He leaned on his elbows, watching the birds, marveling as he always did at the perfect stillness that attended their daily hunting. He had seen them stand as long as half an hour, waiting for prey to forget they were there. Far beyond them, two sailboats were racing down the Sound, the one in the lead canted over so far that its bowsprit was nearly touching the water. *I always think I'm going to like sailing,* he thought, *and I never do. What the hell am I doing, living on an island?*

On the ferry, he stayed below decks because of the wind. He drank a weak beer and read the paper without looking up, finishing as the first warning horn sounded. His car was parked on the left side of the boat, making it easier to turn onto First Avenue in the Friday rush-hour traffic. He got all the way to Denny without hitting a single red light, which was rare enough to be taken as a good omen. First to Denny, Denny to Aurora, get over and hang a fast right—careful down the hill, watch out for the skateboarders from the schoolyard across the street. The elderly station wagon coasted smoothly into the one vacant space of the three allotted to visitors by the condominium Homeowners' Association.

Joanna Delvecchio was shooting hoops by herself: even before he saw her, he could hear the basketball pounding harder and harder against the backboard mounted above her garage door. When she came to meet him, he said, "Must have been a real stinker. You're going to knock that thing loose again."

"It snowed in Chicago, and there were seventeen planes ahead of us to get de-iced, and we had a reserve because Tamara was out with some kind of family crisis, and there were these huge college kids who wouldn't stay in their damn seats, and I'm so glad to see you." As soon as the door closed behind them, she hugged him so hard that her chin dug painfully into his collarbone. "God, I really don't know if I can hang on another three years—"

"Well, four, practically. Because of that leave you took—"

"Right, when Lily was so sick. So, four more years of being a head waitress in a flying Burger King, training gravel-brained girls to tell the difference between tonic water and ginger ale." She widened her eyes and let her mouth go slack, miming bewilderment. "Smiling at people who know it's my fault that we've been sitting on the runway for two hours. I'm never going to make it, Abe."

He loosened her grip slightly as he kissed her ear. "Yes, you are, Delvecchio. You're going to serve the full twenty-five-year sentence, no time off, and then you're going to start traveling every which where they fly, and for free. And that will make it a whole lot easier for a retired elderly gentleman, barely scuffling along on a professor's pitiful pension, to accompany you, which is good, because you always overpack." He kissed her properly this time, easing her toward the coat closet. "But right now you're being taken out to dinner, because you're starving. Your blood sugar drops like a rock, and you get all glumpy. I can always tell."

But she pulled away, shaking her head. "I don't want to go out. I don't want to go anywhere, ever, in my whole life. I'll do spaghetti, you throw one of your salads together. It's all in the fridge."

"I hate making salads," he grumbled.

She laughed for the first time. "I know. That's why they're so good. There's new dill coming up in the window box." She hesitated for a moment. "Make it a big one, with everything. Lily said she might be coming for dinner, if she gets off early at the station."

"She won't show," he said. "Give you four to one."

But he made the extra salad. Joanna reheated the spaghetti when it became obvious that her daughter was not going to join them. Over dinner she asked him about the book, and he shrugged. "No word from the NEH, and they'll be announcing any day now. John Ball and the Peasants' Rebellion are just not grant material these days. I knew that when I applied."

"Well, but you've never been writing it just for that. I mean, not just to get a grant."

Abe blinked at her. "I'm not? Boy, shows you what I know. I could have sworn—"

"You're doing it because John Ball matters to you," she said. "Seven hundred years, or whatever it is, and he still matters to one crabby old fart out on Puget Sound. You wake up thinking about him, and you'll go on doing it, grant or no grant. Beats the hell out of waking up thinking about Burger King."

He patted her arm. "When I wake up in the morning, the first thing I think is, *I have to pee.* The second thing I think about is you. I don't get around to John Ball until after I've had my English muffin. Sometimes not until after coffee."

Joanna's butterscotch-brown eyes, very slightly mismatched, turned up at the corners when she smiled. "For a crabby old fart, you've still got some moves on you. Practically worth breaking out the Vouvray."

They cleared the table, washed the dishes in companionable silence, and went to bed. In the night he woke to the bedside lamp and saw her standing naked at the full-length mirror. He said quietly, "Mirrors lie. This is a scientific fact."

"So is a double chin," she said. "So are stumpy Sicilian legs and spider veins. Not to mention a butt that's practically got skid marks, it's dragging so low. God, my body's really gone south this last year—I mean, look at me, Abe, really look." She turned to face him, spreading her arms wide. "The tits are still okay, just barely, but look at that belly, you'd think I'd had a dozen babies instead of only one. I never used to look this bad."

"Come here, Del," he said; and, when she shook her head, "Right now. You want an old man to have a heart attack, you standing there like that? Come here, damn it."

She came back to bed then, feeling smaller than usual when she curled in his arms. He said, more harshly than he meant to, "You listen now. At this very moment, I promise you, both of my exes are out there growing meaner and uglier by the day, just like me. You, you just keep growing prettier as I look at you, and I've been looking at you for a really long time. You want to know what you look like, you ask me. I'm ten and a half years older than you, and I know I'm still hot stuff because you tell me so. Same thing, exactly."

"No, it's not," she mumbled into his chest. "You're so much better-looking than you were twenty years ago, with that cool white beard and everything, and I've turned into this walking *mess*. My crew, they're all little bunnyrabbits, all of them, the men too. I should have gone for international, day one, before Lily was born. Europeans don't care if you look like the *Night of the Living Dead*. And at least I'd have seen Florence."

But his hands were slipping down her back, pulling her close. She resisted at first. "Ah, you're crazy. Wait, wait, I'll get the light."

"No way, lady. Us old guys need all the stimulation we can get."

They slept late, and wound up taking the noon ferry to Gardner Island, using both cars. On deck they watched for orcas, and Joanna talked about Lily. "She's got such lousy taste in women, that's what gets me so pissed at her. I don't care that they're usually grocery clerks or construction workers—hell, the lawyer was the worst of the lot—but they treat her so badly, Abe. I know, I know, she practically asks for it, and it's her life, not my business. I know all that. It shouldn't break my stupid heart, but it does."

"I should talk to her," he said. "We used to have such long, serious talks when she was little. About death and sex and dinosaurs, and why some people can raise one eyebrow and some people can't. It's been a while since we had one of those."

"She always liked you." Joanna's voice sounded determinedly toneless. "You never disappointed her. Unlike me."

"Come on, I never had a chance to disappoint her. I've been Uncle Abe almost all her life. Uncles get away with lots more than mothers. Uncles go home."

The ferry turned slowly into the wind, approaching the island. It was a curiously warm wind, surprising Abe with its unseasonal caress, but Joanna shivered and shoved her hands deep into her jacket pockets. "Lily was born disappointed in me. They put her into my arms, and we looked at each other, and I knew right then: I'm never going to please this one, not ever. Everything she does, every dumb choice she makes, it's all got to do with that very first disappointment. Does that sound absolutely weird?"

"No, just absolutely vain." He put his arms around her from behind, nuzzling into her hair. "God's sake, give the kid some credit, let her be independently dumb. You can't be snatching all her idiocy for yourself, that's just plain greedy. Think how dumb her father was, ditching you for a real-estate agent. It's in the genes, cookie."

"Don't call me cookie," she said automatically, but she pressed herself back against him. "I thought of a way we can prop up that saggy porch of yours. I'll show you when we get there." The arrival horn sounded then, and they went below to their cars.

Following the tomato-red Jaguar—her single luxury—off the dock, he paused at the lone traffic light of Marley, Gardner Island's only real town, then turned up into the green-shrouded hills. *Sixteen years. Sixteen years I've known I don't belong here, and there's still nowhere else I want to be. Somebody else . . . that's another matter.*

He thought about Lily as a child, playing contentedly with skeletal horses twisted out of pipe cleaners. An undertow of memory caught him there, summoning the night drive sixteen years before, and the blood that had looked so black on Joanna's new skirt. *Another girl, it would have been. Lily wanted a sister so much.*

The Sound came into view at the top of the first ridge, then vanished again behind the shaggy hemlocks that had long ago replaced the logged-off pines and Douglas firs. Ahead of him, the red Jaguar handled the turns with autopilot ease, just as he did making the run from the ferry to Queen Anne Hill. He saw two deer browsing in someone's tomato patch—they never looked up as he passed—and a family of raccoons prowling the roof of the elementary school. *I wonder if they crap up there, the way they do on my beach stairs. Probably.*

The last descent to the coast road always felt to him like tumbling straight into the gray sky and the gray water below. He could see her riding the brakes, as he was forever telling her not to do. He ordered himself not to say anything about it, though he knew he would. She turned left at his battered green mailbox, crept down the steep driveway—paved once again last year, and already fracturing like arctic ice in the spring—veered sharply right at the fork, and nosed the Jaguar into her favorite space under the burly wisteria vine. He parked by the woodpile, and they stood silently together, regarding his house. Turk, the neighbors' enormous hound, dimwitted to a point of near-saintliness, came and barked savagely at them, and then settled down to insistently snuggling his head between Joanna's knees.

Abe said, "The porch isn't that saggy. We could go another year, easy, without messing with it."

"What's that thing on the roof?" She pointed to a peculiar bulge near the attic window, barely visible beneath a winter's humus of hemlock needles. He blinked, then shrugged. "What? It's always been there, you just never noticed it before. Doesn't leak or anything."

Joanna was looking at the little one-car garage, down a slight slope to the left of the house. She said, "You know, a really good spring project would be to clean out that dump so it'd be fit for a self-respecting car to live in. It wouldn't take that long, two of us working."

"Del, that's where I keep stuff, we've been over that. That's my reference library." She laughed in his face, her warmly derisive, anciently bawdy Mediterranean laugh. After a moment he joined her, as he never could resist doing. "Okay, it's my *stuff* library, but some of it comes in useful sometimes. I made that choice way back, keeping the car dry or my papers."

"Well, if you ever looked at those boxes, you'd see the mildew all over them, never mind how many old bedspreads you cover them with. What's wrong with moving them to the basement?"

He sighed. "Because that's where I've got all my beer stuff— my boiler and my carboy, all my bottles and yeast and malt and everything. Give it up, Del. I know you're right, no question, I'll deal with it. Summer, I promise, after we get back from the rain forest."

About to continue the argument, she caught herself and laughed again, but it was a different sort of laugh. "I didn't think I did that so much anymore, nagging you to change the way you live. After knowing you all these years. I'm sorry. You never do that to me."

"Ah, I do too," he said. "Getting on you about leaving lights on, not soaking sticky dishes, living on banana-pancake mix half the time. Making fun of the way you scour the whole bathroom whenever you shower—"

"Just the bathtub, come on—"

"Point is, we both do it. That's how you tell we're practically in a relationship." He put an arm around her shoulders. "Look, I tell you what. We go inside—you unpack—I salvage my leftover meatloaf for sandwiches—we maybe take small nap afterward—we work on the porch, or the attic, or the garage, or nothing at all, whatever you like—and tonight we go out to the Skyliner. All Sicilians love the Skyliner Diner."

"Deal," she said instantly. "But if I do want to make a start on the garage, that's what we do. Fair enough?"

"Understood." But in fact they spent the afternoon peacefully accomplishing nothing of any importance. Joanna dozed, shot desultory baskets into the hoop she had nailed too high on a huge hemlock, threw a pointedly playful fit over a discovered Rosh Hashanah card from Abe's first wife ("I thought you said she'd found Jesus big-time—what's she doing sending you High Holidays stuff?"), and sang "Your Cheatin' Heart" in the bath. Abe hosed raccoon droppings off the stairs that led down to his stony sliver of beach, and loudly searched his sagging bookshelves for a nineteenth-century monograph on fourteenth-century agriculture ("It was *here*, it's *always* here, I never move it!"). The meatloaf was still edible, the nap sociable; the attic, porch, and garage left alone; and four hands of a card game called "That's All" ended, as usual, in a mild dispute over exactly how many consecutive wins that made for Joanna. Later he washed clothes, while she became entangled in a long, repetitive telephone conversation with Lily that left her depressed, and angry with herself for being so. "Damn her, she pushes buttons I didn't even know I had—every one, every time. And then she touches my heart, some way, and I say exactly the wrong thing, and I always wind up feeling like such a fool."

"Well, the buttons work." He knew better than to say it, and he was unable not to. "If they didn't work, she'd quit manipulating you the way she does. She's been doing it to you since she was a child."

Joanna looked at him for a long time before she spoke again. Her voice was quiet and even, completely unlike her normal tone. "Thank you. I can't tell you how much I needed to hear that."

He spread his hands. "Come on, you want the truth or you want comfort? You know I always tell you the truth."

"Yes," she said. "You're the only man who's ever told me all the truth, all the time. In my life. You're also the only man I've ever wished would lie to me, just now and then. Might show you actually care what I think of you."

The calm remark caught him amidships, blindside on, and he

found himself gasping for words. "I do care, for shit's sake. Twenty-whatever years, of course I care what you think, you damn well know I care. I just hate to see the same thing happening to you with her, over and over, every time." He gripped her wrists, and while he could feel her resistance, she did not pull away. "Del, I'm a mean, cranky, solitary old Jew, and I know it, and I like it, and if you didn't put up with me, who would? You ought to get combat pay."

"Don't flatter yourself, you're not *that* much trouble. I've had *cats* whose company manners mattered more to me than yours." But she smiled a little, and moved against him. "See, Lily would notice if I was gone—if I just disappeared—because then she wouldn't have anyone to yell at, anyone to fail her. You, I sort of wonder. Twenty-whatever years, I don't know if you'd be anything but inconvenienced."

He stared at her, amazed to find himself outraged, afraid of spluttering like an aggravated cartoon character if he even opened his mouth. He managed at last to blurt out, "Inconvenienced? *Inconvenienced?* You really mean that?"

"I don't know," she said. "I told you, I don't know."

It rained that evening—a Gardner Island rain, soft as snow, seeming to blow from all directions, capable of turning to a razor-edged mist within hours—but they drove down to the Skyliner anyway. The diner looked like an old streetcar, sidetracked onto a bare, windy bluff overlooking the Sound. There were no other buildings nearby, and the dark little parking lot was as rutted and potholed as the gravel driveway itself. Even so, the Skyliner was bursting and humming with light, like an acacia tree in spring. They heard music from within, and Abe growled, "Rats, they've got the flamenco guy back. I had my face fixed for the trio."

"Since when don't you like flamenco?" she asked. "First I've heard of it."

"Since it became music to eat arugula by, that's when. California cuisine is corrupting everything light beer missed."

They went in, greeted Corinne, the manager—a dainty retired detective who had always wanted to run a restaurant—and were seated in their usual booth, in back, by a window. The guitarist was flailing doggedly away at a *soleares*, candles were lit on all the tables, and both Abe and Joanna agreed that the paintings on the walls this month weren't nearly as horrendous as last month's exhibit. Abe stole a glass of ice water from a vacant table and let it sit untasted, as he always did. He said, "You look nice."

"Thank you. You're cute too, except the beard needs trimming. I wish you'd lose that shirt."

"Last time, I promise. How's the bald spot doing?" He bent his head forward for her to inspect.

"You'd have to be looking." She ruffled his hair, then shook her own head in something more than mock irritation. "Rats, I wish my hair would do that, turn all Spencer Tracy white like yours. Mine's just going this old-soap gray, just like my mother's. I think the coloring's making it worse."

He touched her hair gently. "Del, I keep telling you, just don't color it then. United doesn't care. They're not allowed to care anymore."

"The bunnyrabbits care," she said grimly. "I know it shouldn't bother me, I know it makes me a bad person, but I'm not going to have them grinning at me, calling me Mom. Lily doesn't call me Mom, why the hell should they? *She'll* probably be calling me Mom too, by the time we get to the salad."

Abe looked up at the girl standing patiently by their table. "Would you really do that?"

"No," the girl said. "I would just call her ma'am, and I would say, 'I'll be your server tonight. May I tell you about our Special of the Day?'"

She was tall, almost as tall as Abe, and slender, and her voice was low and clear, with the slight, warm hint of an accent. Thick and heavy and desert-colored, her hair caught the candlelight and gave it back with the added rawness of a living thing when she turned her head. But her tanned, slightly freckled face—a trifle long by current standards, cheekbones more than a trifle heavy— was at once thoughtful and merry, and her eyes were dark green as elm leaves, and shaped like them, tilting up slightly at the outer corners. She said, "The special is blackened snapper in a ginger-mango sauce, over a jasmine rice pilaf. I really recommend it."

"Primavera," Abe said softly. "Primavera, by God." She looked blankly back at him. Abe said, "Actually by Botticelli. It's a Renaissance painting of a young girl who represents spring—that's *primavera* in Italian. You remind me of her."

The waitress did not smile, but a shadowy dimple appeared under one cheekbone. "Perhaps she reminds you of me. I can also recommend the pan-seared scallops."

When she had gone to fetch their wine Abe said, "California. Santa Cruz, maybe San Diego. They're all moving up here. Unbelievable."

"She's not from California," Joanna said. "You know she's not from California."

"Greek, maybe. Balkan somewhere. The accent could be Greek."

Joanna patted his hand. "Listen to you. We used to have a captain who always came on the P.A. like that, talking in little tough grunts. Sweets, that child just knocked you on your ass, and you're hoping I won't notice. Forget it, she knocked me on my ass too. How old do you think she is?"

"Nineteen. Eleven. One hundred and twenty-six. I have no idea." He realized that his voice was shaking, no matter how level he tried to keep it. "Del, I taught European history until last spring. People really do look different in different times, that's just something

I know. You look at the paintings, the statues—faces change, it's genetic and cultural and spiritual, all together. That look—Del, that model got discontinued a very long time ago."

"Well," she said, and the light-brown eyes that he knew so completely widened in teasing affection. "Sometimes maybe one slips through."

The waitress brought their drinks, took their entrée orders, and came back with those in smiling silence. Abe and Joanna ate and talked and laughed quietly, and never quite took their eyes from her. She returned once to ask them whether everything was all right; for the rest, she had two other tables to serve, and it was plain that the cook was tired and slow that evening. Once they heard him cursing her in the kitchen, and the guitarist stopped playing for a moment and half-rose from his stool. Joanna said, "He's in love with her."

"How can you tell?" Merlot always made Abe benignly argumentative, dogmatically broadminded. "Just because he can't keep time for shit, that's not necessarily love. Rhythm's a lot rarer than love."

"When she looks at him, he smiles. So sweetly, so hopefully, it could break your heart. Sometimes she smiles back, sometimes not. Abe, you can't miss it."

"I could miss it." Abe turned his head as the waitress came out of the kitchen with a tarry smudge of grease or oil on her forehead. The guitarist resumed his questionable *bulerias* as she passed, playing with renewed flair, but she never looked at him. Joanna said, "There."

"Doesn't break my heart. Just proves she's got a half-decent ear. You want to split another bottle?"

Joanna gave him what he called her downtown-Palermo look. "So you can have that child bring it over here? Sure, why not? I just don't want you to think this is all going unobserved."

"I never do." He raised a finger to the waitress, who was helping an elderly couple gather their leftovers and struggle into their heavy, damp coats. When she came to their table he ordered the second bottle of Merlot, but it was Joanna who asked, "When you have a little time, would you come and sit with us? We'd really like that."

The waitress considered them gravely. "Because I look like a painting?" Her low voice was amused, but not mocking.

"No," Joanna said. "Just because we think you'd be nice to talk to, that's all." She nudged Abe, who nodded and added, "Please."

The waitress's eyes were tired, but clear as a spring-fed pond. She said finally, "I have one more table. When they're gone."

All but a few booths had emptied, and the guitarist had smiled one last wistful smile at her and slipped away into the rain, when at last she returned to sit down between them, folding her arms before her. She said, "My name is Lioness. Lioness Lazos. Who are you?"

They told her together, oddly hurriedly, for all the world like immigrants hoping to be allowed to remain on the Aegean island where she told them she had been born. Joanna asked, "Forgive me, but Lioness is a Greek name? One more thing I never knew."

The girl laughed very softly. "My mother wanted to spell it *Lyonesse*, with a y and a couple of esses, but my father wouldn't let her. That's what she told me, anyway. I never knew him."

Abe never took his eyes from her face. He said, "That was an enchanted country, Lyonnesse. Did you ever hear of it?"

The waitress's expression did not change, but she shook her head. Abe began to recite, his voice slightly rasping, and more than slightly Newark, but as plain and casual as though he were the one taking her order for the Special of the Day.

> *When I set out for Lyonnesse,*
> *A hundred miles away,*
> *The rime was on the spray,*

*And starlight lit my lonesomeness*
*When I set out for Lyonnesse,*
*A hundred miles away*

*What would bechance at Lyonnesse*
*While I should sojourn there,*
*No prophet durst declare,*
*Nor did the wisest wizard guess*
*What would bechance at Lyonnesse*
*While I should sojourn there.*

A door slammed behind them: a weary busboy returning from heaving an evening's trash into a dumpster. Lioness Lazos did not turn, but her face tightened with the effort of not turning, and Joanna saw this and knew that she had been seen in turn. Abe finished the old Thomas Hardy poem.

*When I came back from Lyonnesse*
*With magic in my eyes,*
*All marked with mute surmise*
*My radiance rare and fathomless,*
*When I came back from Lyonnesse*
*With magic in my eyes!*

The green eyes had a brown shadow to them in the candlelight. The waitress said, lightly and carefully, "Well, I haven't any magic, nor any secrets. I am just a lady lion, a long way from home."

Her father was a Greek businessman, she told them—powerful, mysterious, even dangerous; her mother, a landscaper and nursery-woman, had left him when Lioness was an infant. She had brought her daughter to America, raising her in a series of small upstate New York and New England towns, remembered now mainly by their gardens. There had been high schools and, in time, community colleges, from the last of which Lioness had dropped out to go skittering through an equally anonymous run of dead-end jobs, this being the latest. "I've only been working here a couple of weeks, less. I like it a lot, the people, but the rain!"

Abe told her, "Lioness, there's a saying that on Gardner people don't tan, they rust. You'll get used to it."

The elm-green eyes changed then, becoming momentarily soft and unfocused, an old woman's eyes, not seeing either of them. Lioness said quietly, "I don't mind the rain. It's the cold. I never could bear the cold."

Joanna asked, "Where are you living? Are you on the island?"

"There's a room, right in back." The girl pointed. "I can stay there as long as I need to—Corinne likes having someone here at night. It's not a bad room, really, and I borrowed a sleeping bag." Something came loose in her face; something held too closely slipped free. "But I have to find a warm place, soon. I cannot be cold again, not again."

Joanna touched Abe's wrist without looking at him. "You know, there's a little garage—actually, it's not that little, and it stays pretty warm if you plug in a heater. And we never use it for anything."

She felt his arm tighten under her hand, and braced herself for protest. She was genuinely startled to hear him grumble to Lioness, after a long moment, "You could come out tomorrow and take a look, see what you think. It's not as though . . . I mean, I guess I could move a couple of things."

Lioness regarded them both in silence, her out-of-time face utterly unreadable. She said finally, "I will come tomorrow afternoon, after we serve lunch. Thank you." She rose abruptly and moved away, swiftly collecting glasses and dishes from other tables as if she were picking flowers. Abe and Joanna looked after her without speaking.

When they left the Skyliner, it was still raining lightly, but the air had turned curiously gentle. The rain itself felt almost warm on Joanna's skin, which would have been unlikely for Gardner Island in July, let alone February. Driving home, Abe told her, "It's your fault, I just want you to understand that. When she mugs me and takes off with all my priceless little treasures, then you'll be sorry."

"You don't have any priceless little treasures. Just your beer things and me. Anyway." She was fiddling with her safety belt and the window handle. "Anyway, I couldn't let her be cold. I couldn't, Abe. I don't know why."

"Coming from somebody who always steals all the blankets, every bloody night." The car skidded momentarily as the mud dragged at the tires, and he took his hand off hers to turn the wheel and keep them on the road. "Yeah," he said. "I don't know why either, but yeah, me too. And when you think about it . . ."

The sentence, unfinished, trailed into silence. Joanna eventually asked, "When you think about it, *what?*"

"Isn't that odd?" Abe asked softly. "Look, here we are, the two of us, people of a certain age and a certain . . . wariness, right? We don't pick up hitchhikers, we hang up on people who want to sell us timeshares over the phone, and we never buy anything that's advertised on TV. Aronson and Delvecchio, they've been around the block, right?"

"I bought a thing that makes grilled-cheese sandwiches. Years ago. I never told you."

"So here we are, and we meet this girl in the Skyliner, looking like she made it to Woodstock a day late, and the next thing you know you're offering her my garage—rent-free, I have no doubt— and I'm letting you do it. Just what the hell happened back there, Del?"

The Sound filled Joanna's window, black as onyx, but dancing with reflected light from the Seattle side. A ferry was heading out, itself bright as a birthday cake, and Joanna could see another sparking off toward Vashon Island. She said, "I don't know."

# 2.

# FEBRUARY

Cleaning out the garage took less time and involved less effort than either Abe or Joanna would have imagined. Lioness came to help whenever she was off-duty, pedaling the uphill miles from town on Corinne's rusty green bicycle, usually clinging with two free fingers to some plastic-bagged dish from the diner. She always leaped to the ground while the bicycle was still freewheeling down the ruinous driveway, instantly ready to do barehanded battle with the most cobweb-rich corners and window ledges; to stagger up to the house, her arms piled full of dankly melting cardboard boxes, and then to set them down as carefully as though they all held crystal heirlooms instead of ragged, mysterious, overstuffed, illegibly-labeled manila envelopes. She would arrange them so precisely on the basement floor that access to all brewing equipment somehow remained possible, and hurry back for more. "I ought to be doing this myself," she protested in her faint accent when Abe or Joanna aided her with a load. "You should not have to work to give me a place to sleep."

Abe patted an overburdened arm. "Listen, you've already turned up a whole manuscript I forgot I wrote, and you've found both my divorce decrees, not to mention an entire box of Chess 45s. Believe me, the very least I can do is carry something." And Joanna, bringing sandwiches and apple juice, said, "Lioness, sweetie, you could turn out to be a crossdressing cannibal, and it would still be worth it, just to have that dump sorted out. As far as I'm concerned, you can have the house—we'll sleep in the garage and feed you breakfast in bed."

Lioness shook her head until the coarse tawny mane swung across Joanna's eyes and her own, stinging their faces and making them both laugh. Joanna continued, "No, I'm serious. I haven't gone in there for years without a whip and a chair. It's even starting to smell better, for God's sake. Used to smell like a sex club for weasels."

"It will stay warm at night, I can tell." Lioness's voice was low, almost a mumble. "I'm sure I won't be cold." She knelt to lift a box spilling over with old looseleaf notebooks and faded yellow legal pads, stacked another on top of it, and started back toward the house. Joanna gingerly picked up something that looked like a gargoyle done in green bubble gum, and followed her.

Lily Delvecchio came to visit one afternoon, unannounced, when Joanna was gone for two days on the Chicago run. Abe, submerged in the economic patterns of fourteenth-century England, was unaware of her presence until she burst into the house and his workroom, panting as though she had run all the way from town, as she sometimes tried to do during the periods when she was running. Short and dark as Joanna, but squarely made, without her mother's distinctive tilted eyes and thoughtless athletic grace. "Who is that out there? Hauling stuff out of the garage? Who is that?" she demanded hoarsely.

"Nice to see you too, Lilsville." Abe didn't turn his head. "I'm fine, thanks, can't complain. Your mom's in great shape, never saw her looking better." He finished a paragraph, promptly crossed it out, and skidded his swivel chair to face Lily. "That out there is Lioness. Miss Lioness Lazos. She's going to be living in my garage for a bit, just until she finds someplace better."

"She is gorgeous," Lily wheezed. "She is utterly fucking gorgeous." Catching her breath, she regarded Abe suspiciously. "Does Joanna know about her?"

"It was Del's idea, kid." He leaned back precariously in the chair, propping his feet on a box of books. "Abandon hope. She's not your type."

"No?" Meant as defiance, the single syllable instead came out with a flatly pained sound. "And why would that be, Uncle Abe? Too pretty for me?"

"Nobody's too pretty for you." His voice was gentle, again seeing the sunny child turned gradually morose by schoolyard battlefields and heartless loves. "I just think she's seriously straight."

"Well, I think we'll just let her decide that for herself, shall we?" Suddenly cheerful, she came over to hug him, briefly but strongly. "I forgot Joanna was flying today, but I'm off at the station, and the weather's so great I'll hang out for a while anyway. Maybe take a blanket down to your squeeny little beach. I utterly cannot believe this sun, it is fucking freezing in Seattle."

Fifteen minutes later, by his ancient pocket watch, she was trailing Lioness past his workroom window, struggling with a box that completely blocked her vision, and chattering blithely all the same. Lioness was smiling, replying too softly for him to hear. Lily stayed for Indian takeout.

"I'd guess you're about to start seeing more of your daughter," he told Joanna when she called from Chicago the next evening. "She is definitely much smitten with our new tenant. It's quite something."

Joanna was silent for what seemed a long time. "Is the tenant smitten with her?"

"What do I know? On Lily it looks good. I like watching her

being happy, even if it doesn't come to anything. It's been some while since I've seen her really happy."

"God knows." She paused. "So what about the tenant?"

"Lioness? Fantastic. She's got the garage practically finished— even doing a bit of decorating already . . ." It took him a moment. "Del, for shit's sake, are you out of your Sicilian mind? Jesus flipping Christ, woman, I've got corns older than she is!" Having marveled just that morning over the springing flex of Lioness's hips as she bent to lift a disgracefully shiny exercise bicycle, he was greatly enjoying his feeling of virtuous outrage. "Cookie, even I have some small sense of shame."

"Don't call me cookie, I've told you, damn it." Her voice was warm with amusement. "You know, when I offered her the garage, it never once occurred to me that she's young and great-looking, and that she'll be here alone with you while I'm off serving bad booze to strangers. I didn't think about it for a minute, and I was married to a man who taught me to think about things like that. How do I know you're not going to run off to Bali with this child?"

"Because I'm sixty-five years old, with hair in my ears. Because you know every one of my limitations in bed. Because I can't afford to run off anywhere we can't walk to. Because she'd pull really important muscles laughing. Because I happen to be exhaustingly involved with a cranky, contrary, insomniac basketball freak of a Sicilian flight attendant. Pick any one of the above. Very carefully."

Joanna was laughing herself now. "None of the above, although I do have my favorite. The fact is that I trust the girl with you, the same way I'd trust her to treat Lily kindly. And I don't know why. I don't know a thing about her but that, Abe, you come right down to it. But there it is."

"Yeah, I don't know anything, either." It was not entirely true by then. Lioness always brought her own meals, and ate them at work, only coming to the house on occasion for a glass of water, or to use the bathroom. She never disturbed him when he was writing, except to ask if he and Joanna would mind her weatherstripping a window, or whether something that looked like garbage really was garbage. On his part, Abe made a conscious point of keeping their conversations brief, and of never sitting down when they spoke together.

The Primavera face had nothing to do with it, nor did the way in which she flung back the Sahara hair when she turned on her knees to smile at him as he passed the garage where she was scouring and scraping and deodorizing. "It's the air," he explained to Joanna, three-quarters joking, "it's something that happens to the air around her. Like when you're looking across a hot stove or a steam radiator, and the air seems to be rippling, distorting things, just in that one place. With her, I think the molecules turn sideways, or get on edge or something—they start dancing, boogieing, rubbing up against each other, they get all sort of warm and sweaty, and the air just changes. Probably accounts for the weird weather."

The day that Lioness invited him to share her Japanese bento-box lunch was an unseasonably mild one: clear enough that Seattle seemed closer than it was, and they could make out sandpipers scurrying along the lee shore of Bainbridge Island. Abe commented on it as they sat outside on his ancient lawn chairs, eating sushi and daikon radish. "This is not right. I love it, but it's simply not right, and I know we're going to have to pay for it. The Pacific Northwest is very Calvinist."

Lioness chuckled into her salmon roll without replying. Abe expanded. "See, pleasure ends in retribution, always. We're overcharged for happiness, and we deserve to be. There'll be an earthquake—we get them, you know—maybe a flu epidemic, maybe a storm down from Canada, Alaska. You'll see. Calvin's God always balances the books."

"Oh, I don't like that," Lioness said. She sounded like a child.

"No, that isn't right, that isn't the way things go together. Pleasure is the one thing the gods don't charge for—they can't, they love it too much themselves." She stopped, peering at him almost slyly, as though she were pretending to be a spy. The look was so comical, so foreign to her naturally candid expression, that it was all he could manage not to laugh. She said, "The sushi's good, isn't it? I just love sushi."

"You get it at the place by the ferry terminal?" She nodded. Abe said, "Try to time it for when Wakatsuki's in the kitchen. This is okay, but Wakatsuki's an artist."

Lioness had turned away and was gazing out over the water, seemingly watching a pair of kayakers gliding close to the blackberry shore. One paddler was a man, the other a woman; they kept their crafts as close together as courting birds. Abe said, "Gods. That's plural?" When she did not respond, he went on, "Good, I like that. My folks got stuck with that one desert psychopath, and wished him on everybody else. Him and his loony cousin Allah. No court of appeals, no plea-bargaining, nothing but tantrums and boasting and endless demands for love. I always envied the Catholics— at least they have saints to pray to, they have the Virgin. Forget monotheism, humans are too much for one measly god. We need pantheons, we need a million gods, like the Hindus. I'm telling you, we need bloody mobs of gods."

Lioness did not take her eyes from the two kayakers as she brushed away a few grains of rice and abruptly stood up. "You wouldn't like them. They walk the streets, talking to themselves. They smell bad." She started back toward the garage and Abe ambled carefully after her.

Watching her kneel on the gray floor and begin to scrub at a stubborn oil stain, he discovered that he was shivering slightly, in spite of the warm noon. He took hurried refuge in the Peasants' Rebellion, but found himself leaning on his desk, scratching his bald spot, staring at nothing and getting nothing done, until he saw her pushing her bicycle up the driveway in the dusk. She wore a thin blue cardigan over the faded, ill-fitting flower-print dress she always wore in the Skyliner; he doubted that she owned another. He called to her, offering a lift into town, but she only waved and shook her head. A moment later she had vanished behind a hemlock grove.

At Joanna's apartment, the next night, he related the conversation while making minestrone and garlic bread. "It was just the one line, the way she said—*'You wouldn't like them.'* The way she looked when she . . . ah, you had to be there. You really did hadda be there."

Joanna sampled the soup. "Another tomato wouldn't hurt. I'll cut one up. So. What are you telling me? You think we've got an axe murderer on our hands?"

"No, Christ's sake, of course not. Taste."

"You left out the oregano."

"Did not either. I'll put some more in."

She leaned against his back. "You've got a nice nape. Vulnerable, like a little boy's neck. Never did discuss rent with her, did we?"

"I think we owe her for upgrading the garage. I can't imagine charging her, Del. I just honestly can't."

"Me neither. Stir it a bit." She wandered in a small circle, fiddling absently with spice jars and silverware. "I was thinking, maybe we could ask Corinne what she knows about her."

"Already did. *Bupkes.* Corinne doesn't know a thing more than we do. Kid shows up out of the rain, asks for a gig, Corinne's shorthanded, she puts her on shift the same day, and the rest is history. Absolutely no complaints, most efficient waitress she's ever had. Taste. Perfect, yes?"

"Perfect. A little Parmesan, and we're in business." She grated and sprinkled, while he took the garlic bread out of the oven and set it on the table. He said, "I'll tell you what's weird, though. What's weird is, Corinne obviously doesn't want to know any more than we do—and you know Corinne, for God's sake. She was a detective, she always asks questions, it's just what she does. Not this time, boy." He leaned on the table with both hands, glowering over it as though it were a lectern. "The one thing she'll say is that the kid must have worked on her bike, oiled it or something, because it's running like a dream, like new. Oh, and you're right about the guitar player."

"So." Joanna got the expensive Amarone out of the hutch. Her mother had fought her own sister to grim and permanent silence over that hutch. She handed the bottle to him to open. "So what do you think?"

"I think I forgot the Swiss chard. Hell with it, too late now. I think I have to get up early tomorrow and take the car in for an oil change. I think she doesn't have any more earthly possessions than a sleeping bag and the clothes she stands up in. Maybe an extra blanket, maybe a Sunday dress, that's about it. Our Lioness definitely travels light."

She threatened him with the cheese grater. "You're stalling, Aronson."

"Yeah, of course I'm stalling. I'm an old man, and I'm hungry, and you know I can't think when I'm hungry. All I'm sure about is, I like her voice. Nice voice. Also, go figure—I hate raccoons, but I like to watch her leaving the last of her sandwich for them. For the rest . . . for the rest, it feels all right having her around the place, Del. It feels good. Rent or no rent."

"Next time you make this, make extra," she said. "What the hell."


There was more baggage than Abe had suggested, but not very much more. The extra blanket and the change of clothes were supplemented by a flannel nightgown, two towels and a washcloth, two copies of *House & Garden*, a frayed satin pillow, a few cheap scarves and an ancient stuffed camel, all crammed into a battered blue duffel bag. On the garage walls—first asking permission— she put up a Miss Piggy calendar, and a couple of wayworn travel-agency posters of the Greek Islands. The only other decorations were flowers: daffodils in wine bottles, pansies floating in discarded Skyliner saucers, geraniums and petunias putting out thready roots in soft-drink containers. Her sleeping bag lay unrolled in a far corner, with only a gaunt air mattress to cushion the cement floor. A school notebook lay by the pillow, along with a few colored pencils.

Joanna offered a thick slab of packing foam, which was politely refused. "I'm used to sleeping like this. Good for the back." The grubby purple parka was accepted, however, and the clatter of Abe's old portable electric heater could often be heard up in the house. The sound troubled his sleep until he grew used to it, but Joanna found it oddly comforting. "Like when Lily was still home, and I'd wake and hear her little stereo playing really softly in the middle of the night. As though she were singing the lullaby now, not me."

The weather had held extraordinarily fine all through Lioness's relocation, but she was barely established in the garage before Abe's predicted out-of-season Alaskan storm slammed into the island, snapping trees, flooding roads, snatching shingles off roofs, and inevitably taking out all electrical power. Seattle itself came to a complete stop: the Weather Channel spoke raptly of record wind velocities and equally unheard-of low temperatures, before it went out with the cable. Abe and Joanna, veterans of legendary Gardner outages, built a fire, made tea and cocoa over it, and eventually found the flashlights that Abe had stored in a safe place he couldn't remember. Two had gone dead ("Those damn batteries were *new*, I swear!"), but the big Maglite was functioning well enough for him to grope his way down to the garage, bang on the door, and yell for Lioness. There was no response, though he stood calling until Joanna summoned him back to the house, her voice barely audible above the wind. They sat up silently by the fire for some time before they finally went to bed. The electric blanket was as dead as the telephone, but they knew how to compensate well enough.

Joanna was already asleep, and Abe involved in a foggy half-dream that somehow connected John Ball with Frederick Douglass and Sarah Silverman when the pounding on the door finally roused him. He put on a bathrobe, grabbed a flashlight, and stumbled downstairs.

Lioness blew into the house like a dead leaf, the wind slamming the door behind her. She was soaked and shaking, her eyes blank with fear, and she seemed not to recognize him when he spoke to her. She could not speak at all herself, even when Abe drew her to the fire and brought her a towel. "Dry your hair," he said, not sure that she understood him. "I'm going to find you a robe." Beneath his hands, her own fingers felt like smooth stone.

Joanna woke and came down to them. Lioness was standing where he had left her, still trembling so violently that water flew from her hair. Abe felt it on his face. Her lips were moving, trying to form words, but making no sound. Joanna took one swift look at her, and told him, "Get the fire going. I'm getting this dress off her."

Crouched before the hearth, raking the ashes in search of a few live coals, he heard Joanna gently coaxing, "It's all right, it's okay, honey, just raise your arms and stand still a second. That's good, there we are, now put this on, it's the warmest, fluffiest robe you ever wore. Wait just a minute, your back's all wet, poor thing." *This is how she is with passengers*, he thought, *with children flying alone, this is what she's been doing all her life, before I ever knew her. For* his part, he tenderly coaxed flames up out of embers, and Joanna brought Lioness to stand as close to the fire as she could endure. "Turn around now—keep turning around, that's it, just like a hot dog, there you go." Close behind him, Lioness's skin smelled incongruously of very new spring grass.

"Cold," she managed to whisper at last. "So cold, cold." Her hair was swathed in a beach towel, and the robe was Joanna's thickest, but it appeared to have no more effect than the fire itself. When Joanna put her arms around Lioness, Abe could see the girl's convulsive shivering actually rocking her own body. Nevertheless, she held Lioness tightly, and very gradually the trembling slowed, though it never seemed quite to cease. Lioness said, "I thought it would be all right, truly. I thought I could bear it without troubling you." Her soft, shaky speech was more formal than that of the Skyliner Diner waitress, and her accent slightly more pronounced. "I did think so. Please forgive me."

Finding his voice was harder than remembering where he had hidden the flashlights, but Abe eventually managed it. "Jesus Christ, what forgive? There's a storm, it's bloody freezing, the power's out—of course you came to us, you'd be a lunatic if you hadn't. At least we've got blankets, quilts, we've got a fire, we'll keep you warm. Del, you work on her, I'll make coffee."

He was already blundering toward the kitchen when Joanna came after him. Her voice was low, as intense as her grip on his arm. "Forget the coffee. Forget the fire, the fire isn't doing it. Abe, she's frozen right through to the bone—you'd think she'd been locked in a glacier for a million years, like a mammoth or whatever. All the quilts in this house aren't going to touch that kind of cold . . ." She stopped abruptly, but she did not release his arm, nor his eyes. Her dark-olive skin had gone pale as ice itself, and her eyes reflected the flames, and he thought he had never seen her before. She said, whispering herself, "This is what it means—*stone cold.*"

"What should we do?" he asked. "What do you think we should do?"

"Body heat," Joanna said. "Help me get her upstairs." When he only blinked at her, she grew instantly impatient, snapping, "Come on, I know what I'm doing. Come *on!*"

Lioness made an effort to climb the stairs, but in the end he had to carry her most of the way. Her body was as heavy with cold as a child's with sleep, and when he lowered her onto his bed she lay without stirring or opening her eyes. He stretched, rubbing the small of his back with both hands. "Okay," he said. "I'll get a couple of cushions and curl up in front of the fire. Call me if you need me."

Joanna was already taking off the white robe he had stolen for her from the best hotel in Seattle. She shook her head, pointing to the bed. "I said body heat. That's you and me, buddy. Get in there."

She slept on the wall side, with her arms around Lioness, under a snowdrift of quilts. He lay wide awake, with his back to them both, feeling his body very slowly drawing the girl's terrible trembling into itself, as the storm continued to rattle the windows and grieve in the chimney. *In bed with two women, classic porno fantasy. Everything in life happens a little too early, or a little too late.*

Sometime in the long night Lioness put her arm over him, without waking. Instantly frozen himself, ready to yelp for Joanna, he heard the soft, blurry mumble, "Hunting . . . he knows . . ." When he turned his head to hear better, his cheek came against an unfamiliar and distinctly warming breast, and he nearly fell off the bed in alarm. Lioness said clearly, "He *knows*," and nothing more until morning.

# 3.

# FEBRUARY

The storm took another full day to blow itself out. Lioness stayed by the fire, most often sleeping as close to the hearth as she could get, but occasionally sitting up to drink bowls of Abe's cocoa, staring silently into the flames. Most flights out of Sea-Tac were still grounded, and Joanna spent the day watching over her guest, entertaining her with tales of the multitudinous Delvecchio clan, especially the legendary Aunt Carlotta: Cicero shopkeeper, black-eyed siren, despiser of bootleggers and Prohibition agents alike, inventor and surreptitious marketer of what the family referred to as Instant Muscatel. "She ran Frank Nitti out of the store with a curling iron once. Didn't like his manners."

Lioness's laughter was almost a whisper. "What did she think of Abe?"

"Oh, she loved him. He taught her to curse in Yiddish, and he let her sneak Sicilian slang into Scrabble games. She always warned him never to marry me, because I was a smart-mouth child who wouldn't ever give him strong sons. Which was true enough." She was quiet for a time, while the rain shook the windows and wind sucked flames up the chimney. In his workroom Abe rattled pages with stiff fingers, dropped books on his table, and periodically recalled another few words even Aunt Carlotta had never learned. Joanna said, "But we've been together for twenty-two years, give or take. Him here, me there. It works out better."

Lioness turned to face her directly for the first time. "I thought you were married," she said. "I was sure you were married."

Joanna's own laugh was the rough Sicilian one that usually came out only with Abe. "Maybe that's because we're not." She raised her voice for the benefit of the next room. "He's vain, he's fussy, he absolutely hates change, he's got a maddening habit for each one of those elegant silver hairs—I mean, we are not talking about your average garden-variety pain in the ass here." There came a dry chuckle from the workroom, but no other response. Joanna went on, "And I'm flaky, moody, highly changeable, a world-class disaster as a mother, and when I'm not being a flying waitress I rollerblade and shoot hoops, and collect kitschy salt and pepper shakers. Married? It's a miracle we even agreed on where to eat, the night we met you."

Lioness suffered a sudden new spasm of shivering and moved closer to the fire. Joanna threw more wood on it, though she herself was sweating, and took Lioness's hands between her own. She went on talking, almost in the same rhythm with which she rubbed the thin, rigid fingers. "'Che gelida manina!' Big aria from La Boheme. I have got to be the only Sicilian who can't stand opera. He loves it, of course, but we made a deal about stuff like that a long time back. I don't go to operas or baseball games, and he doesn't come to flea markets, antique stores, or garage sales. We're both really good at making deals."

She felt the momentary convulsive tremor in Lioness's hands and held them against her own body as she studied the pallid face. "You know, you really could be allergic to cold. I've never seen anyone react to a storm the way you have. Does it always get you like this?"

The look in the green eyes haunted Joanna long beyond its swift fading: it made her think of some small, draggled thing hunched in a net. But the voice did not match the look at all: it was fiercely faraway, saying with a kind of soft defiance, not to her, but to the fire, to the cocoa-skim in her bowl, to Abe's books along the walls, "There is cold and cold."

Joanna stood up and stretched, glancing at the windows. "Letting up some. They'll be flying by midnight—I'll have to catch the four AM ferry." Turning, she called loudly, "Which means there'd better be a few boiled eggs and a honeydew in the fridge, come dawn. You hear me?"

A bellow from the workroom, "Honeydew? Where the hell do you imagine I'm going to find a honeydew in this weather?"

"Hamaguchi's market. On the Point. He's got a generator." Joanna put the back of her hand against Lioness's cheek, then her forehead, and nodded with satisfaction. "Like thawing a steak. I'll put a smidge of brandy in the cocoa next time."

When Joanna came downstairs at a little after three in the morning, power had been restored, the rain and wind had died away, and there were four boiled eggs and a melon in the refrigerator, and a pot of oatmeal on the stove. But the fire was a single orange spark in the ashes, and Lioness was gone.

The storm was the last of the season. From the following day, the Gardner Island weather turned almost alarmingly gentle, bringing geese and butterflies back unseasonably, summoning rhododendron and magnolia blossoms not due for a month or more. There was rain still, but it was of a docile, almost absent-minded nature, barely remembering to start and stop, or to agitate windshield wipers. The *Seattle Times* ran a short, jokey editorial on the unusual mini-climate across the Sound, and Mr. Nakashima, the retired postmaster, with whom Abe sometimes played Go in the little waterfront park, told him, "Chinooks. Down from Canada, chinook winds. Happened just like this in '51. Gonna be a mean winter next year. Nineteen fifty-one, same thing."

Joanna put in a field of new bulbs on the lee side of the house, and found a combined salt-and-pepper shaker in the Pike Place Market in the shape of a plump, smiling sow and her piglets. Abe wrote a chapter on fourteenth-century tenancy and freehold customs, and learned to play Sonny Boy Williamson's "Goin' Down Slow" on the harmonica. The great blue herons now prowled the shoreline by solitary turns, which meant eggs in the alder-tree nest; and the serenely brainless Turk waded hock-deep in the freezing Sound to bark at herring, arrived early to spawn. And Lioness Lazos bought a new dress.

It looked a good bit like the old Skyliner dress, a long cotton print with imitation Georgia O'Keeffe flower patterns from modest collar to hem. But it was a deep green, almost matching the color of her eyes. Its length made her look as though she were barefoot, and where she walked it seemed to turn the air green around her. Corinne raised her pay by five dollars a week.

Lily Delvecchio, who came to the Skyliner every Saturday, and often during the week, shyly brought her a burgundy velvet dress, "just to rotate, to save wear on that pretty new one." Lioness declined gently, saying, "I like wearing the same thing to work all the time. It brings me luck." But she held the dress against her cheek before she handed it back to Lily, and Joanna saw it in Lily's closet many times thereafter. She never wore it herself, but it never went back to the store.

"One thing, anyway," Joanna said, on an afternoon when Abe was staining the beach stairway with one more useless raccoon-repellant and Lily was lying on her stomach in the soft new grass, writing a press release for her public radio station's current strike. "She is definitely on the run, hiding out. I make it financial stuff—bills, credit cards, collection agencies, bankruptcy even. Lots of people just disappear when it gets to that point."

"Abusive boyfriend," Lily said without looking up. "Husband. A man, anyway, you can't miss it. That's why she's got all those little twitches—that's why she's always looking over her shoulder, jumping at sounds, noises. She keeps thinking he's found her, poor baby. I know a ton of battered women like that. You can't miss it, once you know the look."

Abe began to sing the parody of "Smoke Gets in Your Eyes" that he always sang on this particular job.

> *They asked me how I knew*
> *Raccoon shit was blue,*
> *So I smiled and said,*
> *"Please don't lose your head—*
> *Raccoon shit is red . . ."*

He sat up, considering. "Me, I'll bet on drugs or politics. Maybe both. A little dealing to help with the tuition—a little property damage to help the redwoods, Iraqi children, whatever. So she's gone to ground in Bigfoot country, vanished into the great gray Northwest. Very sensible, with Canada so near."

Lily said, "I don't care. Whatever she's done." She did raise her head then, and her eyes were shining in a way that always twisted Joanna's heart, and always meant trouble. "I don't care."

"Oh, me neither," Abe agreed. "FBI's loss, our gain, no question. But I can't help wondering." He knuckled his mouth thoughtfully. "I keep wondering what her real name is."

Joanna said, "What? Why? I mean, suppose she turned out to be Jane Schwartz from East Oshkosh? That would make a difference?"

Abe shrugged. "I'd just like to know." But after a moment he nodded slowly. "Yes. Actually, it would."

The orca came very early one morning. Abe was down on the beach, digging clams for dinner with Joanna in Seattle, when he saw the two-foot-high dorsal fin drifting just beyond his next-door neighbors' crumbling boat dock, where the bottom shelved away abruptly. There was a resident pod in the Sound—he had glimpsed orcas from friends' fishing boats, and even once from the ferry— but they never came this close to land, even when the salmon were running. He walked slowly toward the water's edge, saying softly and absurdly, "Well, hey there, sweet thing. Hey there, brown-eyes."

The orca rolled partway onto its side, showing a flash of white belly and a single round eye—not brown, but black beyond blackness—and then flopped back again, so close inshore now that Abe feared its stranding. He took a few steps into the water, making vague shooing gestures and talking as he would have talked to a dog or cat. "Go on, already, get out of here, go on, you'll get hurt. Beat it, okay?"

The squeaky, rubbery sound that answered him—like a child playing with a toy balloon to drive its parents mad—made him laugh, but the orca's aimless, constricted movements concerned him, and he waded out farther, hoping to frighten it back into deep water. But the orca only whimpered and squeaked, threshing as though it were indeed stranded, eyes rolling almost out of sight in the great piebald head. The tail flapped listlessly; the tall fin seemed to be wilting in the morning sun. Abe said, "What? What is it with you?"

Behind him Lioness's voice said, "She is lost."

Abe turned to see her standing at the foot of the beach stairs, wearing a garish old Hawaiian shirt of his—damn, Del finally had given that one away—and a pair of ragged gray cutoffs. Her legs were slender and pleasant, and he was embarrassed to find himself looking at them, or even thinking about Lioness having legs at all. He said, "What lost? Orcas don't get lost. They've got natural e-mail or something."

"She is a baby. She should be with her mother." Lioness waded into the water beside him, smelling of sleep and oranges. "There's nothing wrong with her, but she is frightened and crying. She is too young to be alone."

Abe became aware that he could not feel his feet. He backed away, saying, "Christ, it's freezing, orcas don't cry, what are we doing? How do you know she's a she?"

Lioness did not answer. She moved past him until the water was above her chest, resting her arms on the surface. The orca turned sluggishly to keep her in view, but showed no interest otherwise. Lioness stood quite still, and began to speak.

It was a language that might have been Greek, or might not, her voice slow and soothing, so soft as to be almost inaudible at times. He wondered whether the orca felt the words slipping over its skin, warmer than seawater, as he did. One word that sounded like *cazha* kept repeating itself, and each time the orca seemed to respond, either with a slow, almost splashless flap of its tail, or with another weary attempt at a side-roll, as though it were trying to turn over onto its back. The three-inch-long teeth showed occasionally, but more in an exhausted grimace than in menace. Abe stepped farther back all the same.

"They're not really whales, you know," he said. "They're really a kind of super-dolphin."

Lioness was half-crooning now, and gradually the creature began to react more and more strongly, the rubber-doll squeaks growing louder, the huge mouth opening and closing rapidly, the body rocking like that of an excited infant in a crib. Slowly it heaved itself backward, away from the shore; then, with a sudden rough grace, wheeled and glided out toward deeper, bluer water, never looking back. Abe and Lioness watched silently until the dorsal fin submerged to pass under a tourist cruise boat.

"Well," he said. "I guess you told her where to find her family. And probably where to get a home loan, and maybe a perm. Very impressive."

Lioness shook her head, still gazing after the orca. She said in a flat, distant voice, "Of course not. All I did was to calm her a little, so she could remember herself. You can't think when you're so frightened." She turned abruptly and started back to shore.

Abe stood where he was, thinking that he could see the water closing behind the black-and-white body—like a living yin-yang symbol—then followed her on feet so numb that he could not even feel the stones and shells he stumbled over. Yet Lioness showed no sign at all of being aware that she was soaked from the shoulders down. *There is cold and cold.* Shivering on the beach, he asked, "What does *cazha* mean?"

Lioness looked momentarily startled, as though he had caught her in some private, pointless lie. "It means little one," she said. "Little sister, really."

"Greek?"

Lioness shook her head again, smiling. "I must change and go to work," she told him, and walked away. Abe watched her climb the stairs in her wet shorts and his old discarded shirt. He was certainly staring; but it may be said in his defense that he was staring neither at her legs, nor at her behind, nor thinking at all of her hair, nor of her slim, straight back. His mind was occupied entirely with the single question it had skirted from the evening Joanna and he had met the woman he still, in himself, called Primavera. *Who are you?*

Lily Delvecchio gave a dinner party in her Wallingford walkup, and invited Lioness, along with Abe and her mother. There were three other people present in the tiny apartment, all from her public radio station: one was the program director; one was a shy young intern who kept asking what she could do to help; and one was the lead investigative reporter with whom Lily had been spasmodically entangled for the better part of a year. She had a child's round-faced, unformed prettiness, except for a carnivorous crescent smile. As always, she insisted on sitting next to Joanna, making great play of seeking an older woman's wisdom on every possible occasion. Joanna, who loathed her, was more polite to her than she ever was to anyone else.

Abe rather enjoyed the evening, partly because Lily was quite a good cook, and partly because an academic career had left him with a delicate taste for tension, and a trained eye for vicious courtesy. Thus he understood that the program director's lavish congratulations on the meal were more than offset by her praise of the young intern's recent work, with the specific intent of keeping Lily anxious about her own. He saw the intern make a silent point of catching Lily's eye, half-preening, half-wincing, each time her boss complimented her. And he carefully observed Lily's sometime lover ignoring her almost completely, either to flatter Joanna further or to study Lioness Lazos as though she were the dessert course. *Beware the wrath of an uncle, you nasty little twit. I taught that girl you're messing with to sing "Ukulele Lady."*

Lioness herself ate everything set before her, went back for seconds, offered to wash the dishes, and listened with properly mild interest to the after-dinner conversation, while taking almost no part in it. She was curled on Lily's cherished blue-corduroy window seat, wearing her new green dress and a cheap glass necklace that glittered in the candlelight, serenely flaunting its tackiness. When Lily's lover asked her—pointedly, but in caramel tones—"Did you say you work as a waitress?" Lioness smiled and nodded without answering. The woman said, "But that's not your real job."

Lioness's expression did not change, but the long dimple that Abe and Joanna had seen on the night they met her, and rarely since, appeared under her left cheekbone. "Well, the food is real. The customers are real. The pay is real. So the job is probably real too?" There was the faintest upward lilt at the end of the sentence.

"But that's only what you do," Lily's lover insisted. "That's not what you are. You're studying something—you're preparing, getting ready for something. The look is all over you." Consciously or not, she was beginning to ape Lioness's speech patterns, and even her accent, as she leaned intently toward her across the intern. Abe was certain that she must have done the same thing with Lily once.

The dimple deepened. Lioness said, "That is very clever of you."

"Perceptive," the program director said. "Most perceptive person I've ever known, this one." Lily was looking from one of them to the other. Abe's stomach hurt for her. He asked if he could have another cup of coffee, and she hurried away to fetch it.

Lily's lover never took her eyes off Lioness. She said, quite slowly, "You are really a mystery, a riddle, aren't you? And you enjoy it. You are one of those people who can turn the currents in a room toward them or away from them, as they choose, isn't that so? And you enjoy it. About such things I am never wrong."

*Christ, you probably came on like this to Lily, and it probably worked.* Abe looked on with a mixture of scholarly detachment and prurient interest, as Lioness looked directly back at her challenger, herself smiling and still. She was holding a half-full glass of wine, and her legs were folded slantingly under her, in the manner of a sleeping deer or goat. She replied quietly, "You are not only wrong, you are silly. You are really a silly woman."

The gentleness of her voice and the courtesy of her manner belied the laughter under the words. Lily's lover stared, plainly uncertain whether she had been insulted or not. Joanna became earnestly interested in her wine, looking as though she were fighting back a sneeze. Lioness gestured lightly toward her, saying, "I told my friends Abe and Joanna when I met them, I have no secrets, no magic, nothing up my sleeve. I am exactly what I seem—an ordinary waitress in a nice little restaurant on a pretty commuter island. I have no special ambitions, I am not in training for any great mission, I am not studying anything but how to move between Table Three and Table Five without stumbling over the broken tile. And I am very glad of it—of all of it." The last four words held a sudden unexpected force that stirred the hair on Abe's wrists.

Lily came out of the kitchen holding Abe's coffee cup very carefully in both hands. Her eyes were dry, and not at all red, but to Abe they looked muddy with old unshed tears. Lily never cried, had not cried since her earliest school days. The intern and the program director were gaping at her lover, apparently waiting for some cue to respond, while the woman herself continued to flounder for a reply, as though bobbing for apples at some emotional Halloween party.

Lioness looked across the room at Abe, and he saluted her very slightly with his own wineglass. For an instant the long green eyes not only met and held his, but somehow surrounded them, drawing him first into a deepening garden of wildflowers whose colors he could not name, and then farther on and down to a lonely, freezing lair, leaving him tangled in bad shadows. He shook his head to break the spell, and Lioness turned away.

"Well," Lily's lover said at last, with some dignity, "I may be a little silly—I may be a lot silly, I'd be the last to deny it. But I know what I know, because this is my job. You are special, you are different from everyone in this room—" here her eyes rested briefly on Lily—"and sooner or later you will be found out. Sooner or later, I'm just telling you now."

The words were meant flirtatiously, and delivered with an archly crooked smile, but their effect on Lioness was startling. She considered Lily's lover with an expression that on another collection of features might have meant fear or trapped anger; but to Abe the Primavera face appeared rather to become almost savagely thoughtful, focusing on the woman as though there were no other object in the room or the world remotely worthy of its scrutiny. Lily's lover actually seemed to shrink away into her chair momentarily, before she shook her head, as Abe had done, and mumbled, "What was I saying? Cheap red always gets me." She excused herself then and went into the kitchen, murmuring something about crème brûlée.

The intern and the program director were left staring at Lioness, who ignored them and nodded almost shyly to Lily. Lily gave Abe his coffee, with a quiet light in her own face that Abe had never seen, and went to sit beside her. Joanna was watching them, but Abe could not read her look. The program director said, "She shouldn't drink, I've told her," and the intern whispered, "She doesn't mean you're a spy or anything. She just can't stand it when she can't figure people out."

"But there is nothing to figure out. Nothing at all." Lioness's voice remained patiently amused, but her eyes had darkened past green to the shade of a different evening, filling Abe's mind with panthers and greedy vines and slow bronze rivers. She bent her gaze on the two young women, one after the other, and Abe saw each grow still, their own eyes slightly too wide. They were both leaning toward Lioness in an oddly awkward, unbalanced way, as though the room had begun to move.

Lily was staring too, though Lioness was not looking at her. She appeared more curious than entranced, but Abe found himself growing nervous even so. He spoke up, announcing loudly, "Yes, well, what I want to know is how Lioness was able to clean out my garage, or how on earth she manages never to lose her temper with the cook at the Skyliner." The intern giggled. Abe went on, "If that's not scientific evidence of otherworldly origins, I don't know what would be. In the immortal words of Groucho Marx—" he picked up his venerable leather backpack by its fraying strap and plopped it on a side table—"I rest my case."

His words broke the moment, as he had intended them to do. The program director blinked, shivered, and asked Joanna, "Is he like this a lot?"

"He's gotten worse since he retired," Joanna said. "Full-moon nights, he's just impossible."

The intern burst out uncharacteristically, "He's so cute! I wish he were my father."

Joanna kicked Abe's ankle, hard. "We'll talk. Give me a call." Then Lily's lover returned with the dessert, and Joanna, avoiding it, moved to the old upright piano that had been her housewarming gift to her daughter. Self-taught, thumpingly dauntless, she played for the rest of the evening, leaving the choosing to her hands, one tune slipping into the next: from Broadway music to the Beatles, to the silliest of television comedy themes; and at last, not quite consciously, to the folk lullabies that she had sung to Lily long ago, in another world, where even grief was safe.

> In Scarlet town, where I was born,
> There was a fair maid dwelling,
> Made every youth cry Welladay—
> Her name was Barbara Allen . . .

Lily came to the piano to join her, singing in the tender soprano that made such a surprising contrast with her normal speaking voice, which was startlingly low and rough, and was often taken for a man's voice on the phone. The three women, after a suitably polite silence, began talking among themselves again; but Lioness leaned forward in the blue window seat, setting down her wineglass and listening to the old song as though she had never heard it before.

*Father, oh Father, go dig my grave,*
*And dig it deep and narrow.*
*Sweet William died for me today—*
*I'll die for him tomorrow . . .*

That night, in Joanna's kitchen, preparing her predawn breakfast, Abe asked her whether she had observed the other guests' briefly bewildered reactions to Lioness's attention. "They looked absolutely hypnotized, did you notice? I knew a guy once who could hypnotize chickens—it was sort of his big party trick. They looked like that, just for a moment."

Joanna shrugged impatiently. "I was just watching Miss Thing, the bitch. I cannot believe my idiot kid could be breaking her heart over someone like that. Idiot, idiot kid." She grinned fiercely. "Lioness got her number, anyway. That was something to see."

"I really hope Lily doesn't fall in love with her." He had not known that he was going to say it, and after he had spoken the words seemed to hang ponderously in the air. Joanna laughed. "Bit late in the game, isn't it? That whole dinner was for Lioness—it wouldn't have mattered if no one else ever showed up. Anyway, aren't you the one who's always telling me not to worry so much about Lily?"

"I'm not worrying about Lily," he said slowly. "As you're always saying, she could do way worse."

Joanna turned to face him, all Sicilian mother now. "And so could Lioness, buster. Lioness could do a damn sight worse than my idiot kid."

Abe put his hands on her shoulders, stroking her, helplessly moved by the familiar sweetness of her bones. He said, "I know, Del. She'd be lucky. She would be."

# 4.

# FEBRUARY/MARCH

Joanna was genuinely ashamed of herself for immediately detesting the new copilot on Chicago 2712. He couldn't help looking like an Eddie Bauer mannequin, any more than he was responsible for being named Kyle, or for the deep, lazy Southwestern warmth of his voice. The well-trained handlebar mustache was certainly real, and the tan could well have been; and it couldn't be considered his fault that his features were as neat and even as though they had been stamped in a mold. Nor was there any justification for blaming him because the other four flight attendants tended to collapse into steamy little puddles when he spoke to them, or smiled. "But I even hate his teeth," she confessed to Abe. "How can you hate somebody's teeth?"

"Doctor Fell Syndrome," Abe suggested. "You know—'I do not like thee, Doctor Fell, the reason why I cannot tell—'"

"Yeah, yeah, yeah," Joanna finished the doggerel with him. "'But this I know, and know full well: I do not like thee, Doctor Fell.' No, I think it's more me, getting so I hate everybody." She patted his arm. "Except thee, of course."

"Just for that, you can have the rest of the lox." They were eating a drowsy dawn breakfast on Abe's swaybacked front porch, having spent the night celebrating nothing at all with an impromptu Kurosawa film festival, fueled by a two-year-old black lager of Abe's brewing that Joanna called Nameless Evil, and combined with a good deal of what she also called "interspecies fraternization." Abe had sustained a slight muscle pull.

"Well, he tries," she said. "Ah, they all try, really—they're all so nice to me, so thoughtful, so considerate, you could scream. I mean, sure, I'm crew lead, and they'd damn well better be nice to me, but it's like what that actress—Dietrich or somebody—said about getting honorary Oscars. She said when they gave you one of those, that meant they figured you had six months to live. I'm really starting to feel like that lately. Very depressing."

Abe patted her thigh and reached into his bathrobe pocket. "All is not lost. Listen to this." He dug out his harmonica—a warworn B-flat Hohner that he would have saved before his manuscripts had a fire broken out—and began to play Little Walter's "Quarter to Twelve." It was a slidey, brooding tune: not exactly mournful, but hardly suggesting that all was right with the world. Joanna stopped him with a look halfway through. He protested, with only mild indignation, "I just finally got it right—took me forever. I was showing off for you."

"I know," she said. "And God knows I know how important it is to let one's man show off—it's already cost me a marriage, two boyfriends, and a father. But I can't hack Delta blues this morning, I'm sorry. Play a polka or something, sorry."

Instead he put the harmonica away and asked, gently enough, "What's the matter, cookie? Work?" Joanna did not reply. "Lily? Come on, you've been glumpy a whole lot lately. Talk."

"It's going to be on your tombstone, you know that," she threatened him. "'He called her 'cookie' one time too many.'" Abe repossessed the plate of lox. Joanna said, "I don't know. Too early spring, maybe. I guess I wasn't ready for all this, all at once." She gestured vaguely toward the blossoming rhododendrons that framed the kitchen window, and the grass already deepening toward a summer greenness. "I don't know—it's as though my skin just won't fit right. Everything's all prickly and itchy underneath, only I can't ever scratch. Like that." Her voice wavered toward a question without quite getting there. "Can't be the change, unless you can do that twice. Can't be depression, because I'm not especially depressed—I'm not—just glumpy. Call it premature spring fever."

Abe patted her again and glanced at his watch. "Tell you what. You don't have to be at work until five, right? Look, I'll take the day off and we'll do whatever you like. Go for a hike, putter in the garden—hit the nursery and buy some plants, that always cheers you up." He took a long, determined breath and added, "There's a garage sale in town, I saw a sign. Looked like a big one."

Joanna smiled at him. "I appreciate the gesture. You're a brave and selfless person, Aronson, but that's not what I want. What I want—" and she drew a breath herself—"okay, what I really want, I want to go kayaking."

Abe's eyes widened. "What? Del, half the time you get seasick if we go up on deck on the ferry. I'm always braced in case you have to run to the head—"

"That's the ferry," she said firmly. "That's every boat I've ever been on—high over the water, so I always feel dizzy looking down and the waves make me squirmy just watching them. But the kayaks . . . Abe, sometimes when they're passing just to the right of the dock, there's an angle when you can't really see them at all, and the people look as though they're sitting on the water like birds, just gliding by with the tide, part of all of it. I want that, Abe, I do, I don't care how stupid it sounds. I want to know what that feels like, being a bird on the water."

Abe was silent for some while, musingly devouring the remaining lox and refilling his coffee cup until the carafe went dry. Then he stood abruptly. "Well, get dressed, we'll go see about it."

It was Joanna's turn to gape. Abe said, "Kayaks. There's a place down by the ferry terminal. Sale or rent, one-holer or two-holer. Like outhouses. Let's go."

He took her hands and began pulling her to her feet, as she protested, "Abe, God's sake, I was just talking, I didn't mean going kayaking right now, this very minute—"

"Yes, you did," he said. "I know when you're joking. Let's go, Del, seize the day."

Before Joanna quite knew what was happening, she was showering, dressing ("Wear your Aunt Carlotta's capris, you know they drive me wild"), and on her dazed way into town. Abe was outlandishly encouraging, saying, "I wish you'd told me sooner, who knew?" and "I've always had a bit of a thing about kayaks myself. Listen, this is an adventure, we have serious decisions to make. River, oceangoing—wood or fiberglass, what do you think? I'd go for walrus skins myself, but I don't think they let you do that anymore."

Only at that point was she able to tell him, just as the Skyliner came into view, "Abe, I'd have to do it alone. If I ever did it."

Abe's foot slipped off the accelerator as he turned to stare at her, and the station wagon almost skidded into a ditch. He cut the engine, let it coast to a stop on the shoulder of the road, and said quietly, "You can't swim."

Joanna did not look at him. "I know that."

"I tried to teach you. Twice. You were too scared."

"If I did it, I'd wear a life jacket. Flight attendants know that stuff."

Abe started the car again, but sat still, his face expressionless. "What life jacket? I'd be there, the pride of the Second Avenue Y. Swimming like a senile alligator."

"No, you wouldn't," she said. "I'm sorry, I'd be alone."

"Jesus fucking Christ, Del, this isn't ego! This is not ego—this is just you can't swim, and I've got every right to be worried about you. Life jacket, for shit's sake. Jesus Christ."

"Let it go," Joanna said. "It's not going to happen, let it go. Let's go home."

Abe turned the car and silently headed it back the way they had come. He said nothing more, nor did she, until they were at the house and he had parked as always at the woodpile. "It isn't ego, Del." Putting a hand on her arm as he killed the engine, he felt her muscles tense, briefly and startlingly, before they eased under his hand. "You're a grown woman—you'll do what you bloody want, same as you always have. I'd just feel a whole lot better if that water weren't so cold."

Joanna patted his hand. "Never mind, it's not going to happen. Forget it, all right?" She got out of the car, not realizing that Abe was not following, until she looked back and saw him still in the driver's seat, leaning on the steering wheel and looking straight ahead.

They did very little together for the rest of the day. Abe, in time, drifted inevitably back to his workroom and his book; but Joanna, after a couple of abortive attempts at the basket and the back garden, finally wandered out to the porch, where she sat doing British crossword puzzles with an irritable skill until it was time for her to leave. Abe walked with her to her car and said, as usual, "Look out for the crazies." She said she would.

"I'm sorry about the kayaking thing," he said. "I guess it just took me by surprise."

"That I'd want to do it? Or that I'd want to do it without you?" Her voice was level; her eyes were focused slightly to his left.

"Both. Both, really."

"Well, I shouldn't have brought it up," she said. "It was silly, don't worry about it."

He was reluctant to see her drive away. "You'll call when you get in?"

"Don't I always? Don't worry if I'm late, okay? O'Hare's getting worse by the day." He watched the red Jaguar scrambling up the driveway—mud-clumps, pebbles, and bits of crumbling pavement flying from the wheels—then turned slowly back toward the house. *I must be upset, my stomach feels funny. How else do I ever know?* But Joanna and he had been miffed at each other often enough over two decades; why should the back of his throat taste hot and rancid this particular time?

He went to work—until the harmonica, there had never been any other sanctuary for him—but the sourness continued in his mouth and his mind, until he gave in to it and put on one of his oldest blues albums, sprawling adolescent-style on the floor as Big Bill Broonzy sang:

> *"Can't stay here, ain't no place I rather be,*
> *can't stay here, ain't no place I rather be—*
> *Ain't nobody put me here, can't no captain set*
> *me free . . ."*

"Yeah," he said aloud, in the best weary Delta growl he could manage. "Tell it, old Bill." But his own weary honesty compelled him in time to get up and turn off the stereo. *You don't have the blues, son, you have a vague malaise. Middle-age, middle-class malaise. There's a reason you never hear anybody singing the malaises. Hell with it.* Giving up all pretense of work, he put on clothes suitable for a retired history professor, and drove into town to have dinner at the Skyliner Diner.

It was Lioness's day off, which left him feeling at once relieved not to have to deal with his motives for going, and annoyed that he should even be considering this. Corinne's surprised expression when she greeted him made him aware that he had never been to the Skyliner without Joanna, and he stumbled through a clumsily pointless explanation for her absence. He made a point of sitting in a different booth than the one they always took, and of ordering a drink and an entrée that he wouldn't ordinarily have considered. Even so, virtuously alone at his table, he felt as uncomfortable, as drearily traitorous, as though he were somehow betraying Joanna with himself in a cheap motel.

*You need guys*, he told himself sternly. *You need a circle of male intimates, just a small one. Guys to have lunch with, guys to hang out with in your special hangout—you need a regular poker night, a gym partner, something like that. Monday Night Football, Super Bowl parties. A treehouse.* But at sixty-five he knew his own nature too well to pay any heed to the old refrain. Beyond Joanna, there was only a younger sister in Wisconsin, a younger brother in Texas; they usually called each other on Thanksgiving. He was vaguely but genuinely fond of the Yandell family next door, but could count the times he had actually set foot in their house. Old Mr. Nakashima in the park, the couple who ran the bookstore in town; the few professional colleagues infrequently re-encountered at those historians' conventions he bothered to attend . . . beyond Joanna, there was finally nothing but work and the harmonica. On nights like this, he felt that it should definitely bother him more.

Waiting for the meal to arrive, he read conscientiously from a biography of Wat Tyler, until—sourly set for the flamenquista—he was jarred to attention by the throaty snarl of a chromatic harmonica playing "Georgia on My Mind." A tall, gaunt, floppy-haired young man wearing jeans, a black waistcoat, and a black cowboy hat was sitting on the guitarist's stool, his eyes shut tight and his cupped hands fluttering as he leaned into the vibrato. Abe's book fell shut, and he never noticed that his order had been placed before him as he stared. The blues harp moaned on, its cry sometimes thinning to a pinpoint peak, repeating a four-note riff over and over; then swooping and squeezing down into a growl that rattled forks on the nearest tables. By the time the man finished the tune, Abe was applauding wildly, amusing and annoying the other diners, and ignoring both reactions. The cowboy bowed graciously to him, said clearly, "Man, they let just anybody in this place," and launched into a cheeky arrangement of "Rhapsody in Blue." Abe got pesto sauce on his tie.

The cowboy came over and sat with Abe during his break, having closed the first set with a wrenchingly drawn-out "All Night Long" that brought applause from the kitchen, if not from anyone else but Abe. His first words were, "Let's see it, daddy. Whip it out." Abe silently handed over the old B-flat Hohner. The cowboy inspected it with his fingers, grinning slyly over it, shaking his pale forelock out of his eyes. He asked, "How many others you got at home?"

"An A and an E-flat." Abe felt oddly embarrassed. "That's all."

"Good start," the cowboy said. "I'm Billy Masters. Twelve-Bar Billy, most folks call me."

Abe grinned back at him. "Which folks? Your mother?"

"Just my band, so far. But it's getting around." He tried a quick, stinging lick on the Hohner, then wiped it and gave it back. "Nice tone. You want to blow some?" The look on Abe's face made him snicker. "Man, this is the Skyliner Diner, ain't nobody listening but the cook, 'cause he's a fool for mouth-organ blues. Get up there and blow for the cook."

The temptation was great—*hell, you've got "Goin' Down Slow" practically perfect*—but Abe shook his head. "Thanks, but I'm just good enough to know I'm not good enough. No chance."

"Come on, man," Twelve-Bar Billy coaxed him. "They're bound to fire my ass anyway, I got to load up on the free booze while I can—come on, do me a favor." Abe stood firm, and the cowboy finally stood up, shrugging without malice. "Damn, most folks, they just fight to get onstage, nine out of ten times they can't blow for shit. Ninety-nine out of a hundred. And here you are, you're probably real good, and you won't do it for me. Ain't that the way?" He fumbled in the black waistcoat for a battered business card, and shoved it into Abe's hand. "We're Seriously Blue, out of West Seattle, and we're gigging down at Chance Encounter next Saturday—come catch us, and stick around after. I mean it, I'm really looking for some backup."

"I'll be there." Abe put the card carefully into his coat pocket. "But I promise you, I can't play for shit either."

Twelve-Bar Billy smiled and slapped his shoulder, turning away. "We gonna see about that later, daddy. I promise you." He shambled back to the stool, sat down with one foot on the floor and the other propped on a rung, yelped sharply, "Brace yourselves now!" and went into "Nobody Knows You When You're Down and Out." Abe sang along with him, inaudibly, blissfully.

He never remembered exactly when the Hohner came unbidden out of his pocket a second time; only that he did not play "Goin' Down Slow," but improvised a countermelody on either "Make Me a Pallet" or "Richland Woman." Twelve-Bar Billy whooped his delighted vindication, beckoning Abe to join him with a nod of his head, but Abe remained at his table, settling his bill and leaving quickly after the two numbers, though Billy called after him to stay. He drove home very slowly, almost on the shoulder of the road, singing to himself in a peaceful murmur.

Joanna would have called from Chicago, left a message, and undoubtedly gone to bed by now; he'd call her suitably late in the morning. The night was warm and clear, and nearly starless, owing to the steel dazzle of the full moon, and from the top of his driveway he could see the full spread of the Sound and all the golden walkway to Saturday Seattle. He was about to start the wary descent when he saw the fins.

There were a dozen of them, at least, cruising so close inshore that, even from such a distance he could make out individual nicks and scars in the moonlight. They passed back and forth like shining sailboats, like dancers: unhurried, unthreatening, not drifting but waiting. He could never have distinguished the rescued young orca of a week before from the rest of the pod, but there was no mistaking the slender figure poised on the slanting bluff that had long since been Joanna's daffodil bed, before a tremor had sliced it in two. Lioness Lazos was standing there, not at all like a witch, arms raised to order tides and powers to her bidding, but as calmly as the great dorsals themselves: greeting, perhaps, but never commanding, even seeming at one point to wave them diffidently away. And still the orcas danced for her.

By the time Abe had parked and hurried around the house, skidding on the gravel he had put in to keep the weeds down, she was gone, as he had known she would surely be. The orcas were still there, however, weaving their phosphorescent paths, and sometimes—unusual for killer whales—slapping their tails on the water to scatter the glitter back to the moon. He knew no parallel for this, for a pod risking stranding to pay some sort of tribute to . . . to what? To whom? He stood considering the matter for some time, watching the orcas, before he went inside to make himself a drink. When he came back out, they had vanished.

# 5.

# APRIL

By mutual agreement, Abe always made his Christmas beer early in the spring. It was an annual and reliable source of sorrow: the black, strong, malty homebrew that he hunted like the Snark each year invariably eluded either his skills or his ingredients and equipment, which he made a principle of never blaming. Joanna loyally drank what she could manage, usually slipping the rest of her share to an air-traffic controller friend who actually liked it. Abe himself took it like medicine, proudly and stubbornly, but unable to get through a glass without complaining. "It's just a dark lager, for God's sake—I've been making perfectly decent lagers forever, I don't know why the hell I can't ever get a *Schwarzbier* right. A kid could make the stuff at a sidewalk stand, like lemonade."

"Maybe it's the yeast," Joanna would suggest dutifully. "Maybe it's the water. Your tap water's so hard."

"There's nothing wrong with the fucking water. Nothing wrong with anything but me." And Abe would slouch and growl off to his study to spend the rest of the day blowing Junior Wells blues and writing evil letters to newspapers. Getting this long-established ritual over with during the usual wet, windy Gardner Island spring was distinctly easier on Joanna, who was fond of Christmas, and made the rest of the year's brewing a downhill run, by contrast, for Abe. Even his occasional failed attempts at a Belgian-style lambic could be discarded without rousing more than a sigh and a shrug as he turned the remaining cherries or raspberries into preserves. And his English barleywine improved every year; even Lily, who detested all beer, agreed on that. The barleywine was always a comfort after the *Schwarzbier*.

But this spring the Christmas batch turned out right. It turned out better than right—it turned out better than Abe could ever have fantasized, back in the days when his dream of brewing the perfect black beer was almost as young as his relationship with Joanna. After two decades of disaster, he found this sudden triumph curiously alarming, which was hard to explain. "I haven't done a thing differently—nothing, you understand? Same hard water, same hops, same bottom-fermenting yeast, high-temperature mash . . . if it was wrong then, how come it's perfect now? It doesn't make a damn bit of sense."

Joanna offered the strange mild weather as a possible factor, but he dismissed the idea before she was done proposing it. "Nah, we had that nice little spring three years ago, and the *Schwarzbier* was just as rotten then." But in fact they had never had a season like this one, and Abe knew that as well as she. Fawns and flowers were the least of it: early whales, geese, and lawns could be rationalized, unlike warm night rains, absurdly golden morning clouds, windless wine-soft twilights, and backyard vegetable gardens exploding in such riot that the hungriest deer could not keep up with them. There was no Gardner Island precedent for such bounty. The Seattle newspaper ran a small but prominently featured article on the subject; and Mr. Nakashima, stretching out his ribbed neck in the improbable sunshine like an ancient turtle, told Abe, "Earthquake weather. Watch the birds."

Joanna did watch them, always, in the uniquely wistful way of someone who spent her working days passing far beyond their sight, slogging back and forth through their air. Sometimes she donned a life jacket, borrowed Abe's binoculars and the dank little rowboat that the Yandells kept for their children's use, and drifted out onto the Sound for hours at a time, studying the sky through a pair of inadequate field glasses. There certainly seemed to be more birds than usual for the time of year, but it was the variety that struck her, not the number. Fumbling through Abe's battered field guide, she noted, beside the resident loons, herons, cormorants, and scurrying terns, two species each of shearwaters, puffins, and fulmars—all of which she most often confused with each other— as well an astonishing assortments of murres and murrelets; and, once, a dark, wicked-swift something that she kept telling herself couldn't really have been a skua, down from the Arctic. But even that was more likely, more comprehensible, than her two visions of great, unflapping white wings, surely less substantial than the wind that bore them, or the clouds that mirrored them. Both times she rowed frantically back to shore and ran into the house to tell Abe; both times the white wings were gone when he came outside.

"Wandering albatrosses," he told her. "The big ones, gooneybirds. You get them up here once in a hell of a while." He thought for a moment. "No, make that wondering albatrosses. Just circling and circling, wondering, 'Who's that pretty person all the way down there, wondering up at us?' A whole new species, probably." But he took her to dinner in Seattle for each sighting, claiming that it could only mean good fortune to have a girlfriend who saw albatrosses over Gardner Island. She knew he was teasing her, but the wings still rode her mind as they did the wind, and the restaurant was her favorite.

She never looked at the shop near the ferry terminal, and she changed the subject whenever Abe pointed out kayaks gliding past the house. Even so, home between flights, she found herself accumulating brochures concerning kayaking tours of Alaska's Inside Passage, the coast of Maine or the Fijian islands. Waiting eternally on the runway for clearance, she soothed passengers while debating the issue of single- or double-seating, sit-on or sit-in; rollerblading down Queen Anne Hill, she balanced wood against polyethylene, fiberglass against both; basic knee straps against the deluxe version, an expensive flotation device against a compass and a folding anchor for the same money. Sleek, needley boats meant for running wild rivers held no interest for her; the models she studied were all designed for ocean cruising, whether "flat water, mild swells" or "surf, high waves." Of those that lured her, most were reassuringly out of her price range—but a few, two or three . . .

At that point, she always tossed the catalogue aside and went out to shoot baskets, wishing earnestly that she had never mentioned kayaks to Abe—or, worse, to herself.

As Abe had predicted, she saw much more of Lily in those days than she had since her daughter left home. She knew beyond illusion that Lily came as often as she did solely to spend as much time as she could with Lioness Lazos; but she also knew Lily regarded her as a reasonably acceptable backup if Lioness should be unavailable. In such cases, they usually left Abe in the fourteenth century and walked the road above his house that led to town in one direction, and up into the hills in the other. The island's highest ridges were a ragged, foggy tonsure where only owls and eagles nested, and where a few overgrown dirt paths still opened out into wide lawns and stone houses: last survivors of Gardner's great lumber days, now inhabited by fourth-generation website designers and financial planners. Joanna and Lily never walked that far.

One afternoon during that long Lioness spring, as they halted to catch their breaths, Lily abruptly asked, "Who was Gardner, anyway? Some old robber baron?"

"Virgil Gardner," Joanna said. "No, he was a Tlingit Indian. They used to have their summer lodges here, the same way people do now. Because the fishing was good, and it was a lot less buggy than the mainland. Anyway, Virgil Gardner was the last Tlingit chief on the island. The lumber people named it after him when they pushed the Indians out. Abe says it's what we always do—kill people off, and then stick their names on streets and parks and towns. Like trophies. Animal heads."

Lily looked sideways at her. "Useful, carrying on with a history professor all these years." But her voice was gentle, and barely mocking.

"Yes," Joanna said. "Just as useful as it was when he was practically doing your homework for you—and I'm talking college, not third grade. We do remember?"

Lily nodded, smiling a bit sheepishly. They began walking again, more slowly now, as the grade steepened. A deer stood motionless in the shadow of a hemlock, not stirring even when they had come within a few steps' distance. Only when Lily reached out a hand did it turn and saunter slowly away into deeper shade, lifting its feet like a queen crossing a muddy street. Lily said, "I can't believe I'll ever be with anyone the way you're with Uncle Abe. Just not going to happen."

"You don't know that." Joanna was promptly indignant, both with the toneless resignation in her daughter's voice and with the world that had put it there. "You're a kid, you're twenty-eight, you think the world ends if you're by yourself for ten minutes. It doesn't work like that, baby. Trust me, it is not like that."

"Mom, listen to me!" Joanna was so startled by the word that she stopped in the road, and Lily took several steps onward before she realized that her mother was not beside her. She said, "Look, I can handle being alone. I always could, from way back. We do remember?" It was Joanna's turn to nod and look away. "There'll be others, other women, countless gazillions of them—I know that. I'm just not—I'm just not exactly looking forward to it, that's all."

Joanna would have hugged her then, but she knew much better. Lily went on, "I don't mind. I can cope, I don't mind. But it would be nice . . . sometimes it would be nice to hang with someone long enough to have a little history. Someone who understood my jokes, someone who knew I was weird and it was all right with her. That would be nice."

"You're not weird," Joanna said automatically. "Anyway, the grass is always greener. Abe and I stay together because we're too old to split up, that's all. Nobody else in the world would have either one of us." She had meant to make Lily laugh, but had no luck. They walked on in silence for some time.

"I'm crazy about her," Lily said finally. "I shouldn't be, but I am."

Joanna did not bother to ask whom she meant. "Why shouldn't you be? She likes you, I know that."

"Oh, for God's sake." Lily's mouth was held so tightly that tiny vertical lines Joanna had never seen before appeared on both lips. "Because wherever she belongs, it's not with me. I'm not nearly as dumb as I act sometimes." She did another rare thing then, putting her hand on Joanna's arm. "She's really good to me, she's better to me than anyone's ever been. I mean people I've lived with—people who said they loved me. But she doesn't want me. She doesn't want anyone, I know that." The last words came out in a sad small whisper.

"Maybe that's best," Joanna said hesitantly. "Falling into bed, that'll ruin a perfectly good friendship, nine times out of ten, take my word for it."

But Lily did not hear her. She said, "Listen, listen to this. You want to hear the way she's been to me? Listen."

She caught her mother's hand and drew her down by the side of the road to sit under a splitting, shedding old pine that had somehow escaped the loggers in its prime. Joanna brushed away the needles, leaned back against the tree for comfort, and hoped that whatever was oozing out of the bark would come clean in the wash. A ground squirrel scampered almost across her fingers, and a passing car slowed for its driver to stare at the two women sitting on the ground. The warm wind shifted a little, bringing her the sudden smell of the Sound.

"I made a pass at her," Lily said. "At the diner, a couple of nights ago, after closing. I guess I'd had a few drinks, I don't remember. Not a big, wild pass—I just sort of put my head in her lap." Her voice was a child's muffled mumble again. "She turned me down, but she did it so it didn't hurt. So it didn't make me feel like a stupid, ugly dyke freak nobody could want, never mind her." Joanna felt her heart clench like a fist. She squeezed Lily's hand hard, but Lily pulled it away.

"And what she said—what she said was, 'You don't need me, sweet Lily.' She called me that, sweet Lily. And I blubbered, yes, I did, I really did need her, but she just shook her head and smiled at me—you know, the way she does?" Joanna nodded, seeing the long dimple. "Then she said, 'But if you ever truly need me, I will come to you. If you call to me, even just inside yourself, I'll hear you.' That's utterly what she said, Mom." Again the unlikely word in that soft childish voice melted Joanna's bones.

"Well," Joanna said. There seemed very little beyond that to say, but she tried it again. "Well. That was good of her. She's a kind person, I felt that right away, when Abe and I first met her." To herself she said, *You are a thick, insensitive moron, and you will go straight to hell for being an insensitive moron.* To her surprise, Lily responded eagerly. "Yes, yes, she is. And she would come, she would—but I'm never going to call her. Not like that, not the way she meant. Because you can't do that, when somebody makes you a promise like that. You can't take advantage."

Joanna did put her arms around Lily then, braced for rigidity, if not rejection. But Lily stiffened only momentarily before she relaxed, not merely enduring the embrace but actually pushing into it, taking comfort from the closeness of her mother's body. Joanna said into her hair, "No, of course you wouldn't take advantage. Not you." She could not keep from adding, "Hell, you don't even ask for what's there," but she mumbled that bit to herself, and never knew whether Lily had heard her. She asked, "Do you want to keep walking?"

Lily shook her head. Joanna got up, brushed herself off, and helped Lily to her feet. "Abe's got some Rocky Road in the freezer. I'll fix us a couple of sundaes."

They walked close together on the way back, hardly speaking until the house came into view, and Lily's car, parked at the top of the driveway. Lily stopped abruptly then, her face losing color. "She's down there," she said. "She's there, working in the garden. I can see her."

Joanna craned her neck and saw Lioness weeding the new garden, her face smudged, her hair sticking to her forehead. She looked up briefly to smile and wave a mud-caked hand, and after a moment Joanna waved back. Lily said, "I can't go down. I can't face her. You go ahead, I'll just take off. I'll call you later."

"Ah, baby," Joanna said. "Come on, baby—you told me yourself she was kind. You said she didn't hurt your feelings."

"She didn't. I hurt my feelings." Lily's eyes were very wide, and looked unnaturally dry. "Go on, I'll call. Go!"

Joanna started slowly away, and then turned. "No," she said loudly. "No, forget that, you're coming with me." Lily gaped, long unused to her mother raising her voice or giving orders. Joanna said, "You heard me, kid. I never made your excuses to your friends when you were little, and I'm not starting now. Anyway, you have to say goodbye to Abe. No more crap, that's it."

She began walking down the drive again. Behind her, she heard Lily's slightly dazed voice, speaking with a heavy mock-German accent, announce, "Und you vill fasten der zeatbelts, mach schnell!" But she also heard the footsteps.

Abe was in fact deep in a chapter on Parliament's fateful 1351 passage of the Statute of Labourers, and available for no more than a kiss on the cheek and a reminder to drive carefully on the way home. There was no further sign of Lioness, neither in the garden, nor in the garage, where Lily searched and called for her. Obviously bewildered and disappointed, she said only, "Okay, maybe we didn't see her. Shared hallucination, part of the bonding process." She hugged her mother quickly, refusing company back to her car. Joanna slapped Abe lightly on the back of the head—"No reason, just on principle"—and went to sit on the porch and read. She did not make herself a sundae.

A short while after Lily's departure, Joanna heard a child's laughter in the garden, and saw Alli Yandell, her neighbors' six-year-old daughter, pretending to be a horse daintily nibbling grass from Lioness's outstretched hand. She play-devoured a sizable tuft with every sign of enjoyment, kicked up her heels, and whinnied for more. Lioness, laughing herself, plucked another handful, which Alli mimed eating as well before galloping off to harass her brother. Lioness gazed after her for a long moment, and it seemed to Joanna that the tall, slender body slumped just a little, from the shoulders, and that the Primavera face looked older. She lowered her gaze to the book, oddly embarrassed to have seen her so; and when she looked up again Lioness was gone.

Lily telephoned late that night, as Abe was drowsily watching an old Barbara Stanwyck movie and Joanna, upstairs, was packing for the morning's Chicago run. Lily said without preliminaries, "Lioness was in my car."

Her voice was perfectly conversational, unsettlingly casual.

Joanna tried to keep her own voice sounding as normal. "Honey, she couldn't have been. I mean, I saw her in the garden right after you left—I don't know how we could have missed her."

"She was in my car," Lily repeated. "I smelled her." Joanna had no answer. Lily went on quietly, "You know I can tell people by their smells. Even in the dark, since I was little. She's never been in my car before, but I smelled her there all the way home. On the ferry, all the way home. I did, I'm not making it up." She sounded like a little girl. "I'm not!"

"I know," Joanna said. "I know, I know you're not." She realized that she was trembling, and sat down on the bed. She said, "Baby, listen, let's figure this out—"

"And I'll tell you something else." Lily was silent for an instant, during which Joanna could distinguish, not only her breathing, but the crackle of ice in a drink and the chiming of the kitchen clock that Joanna had given her on her last birthday. Lily said, "I heard her. I was driving home, and I heard her voice in the car."

"No." Joanna realized that she was suddenly angry, aching with fear and raging pity. "Uh-uh, no, I'm sorry, baby—no, you didn't. You thought you heard her—that I believe, I do believe it. Lily, honey, I'm sorry, let's try to keep some perspective on this. You couldn't have heard Lioness talking to you. Just no."

"I heard her." Lily maintained her troubling calmness. "I'll tell you what she said. Just if you want me to."

Abe came into the room then, as though summoned, announcing happily, "I would watch Barbara Stanwyck read the *Journal of the American Medical Association*." Joanna waved him fiercely to silence, at the same time beckoning him just as urgently to sit beside her. She said into the phone, as evenly as she could, "Yes, I do. Tell me what Lioness said to you."

Lily's voice was clear and strong enough that Abe could hear her words without putting his head against the telephone. "She told me, 'Lily, never be afraid of sadness. Sadness is your friend. Remember.' I heard her say that."

Joanna did not answer. Abe saw her eyes close, only for a moment, and her teeth shut hard on a corner of her lower lip. Lily was half-singing as she went on. "I don't even really know what she meant, and it doesn't matter. I heard her. I'll know." She said goodbye then, and Abe and Joanna sat together on the bed for a long time without speaking.

# 6.

# APRIL

Everard Yandell, the telephone lineman who lived across the little creek from Abe's house ("You can call me Ev, or you can call me Yan, like that Chinese cook on the TV—just not Everard, okay?"), hated harmonica playing with the passion he usually reserved only for television evangelists, California tourists, and the New York Yankees. Abe quite liked his neighbor, but he found it absolutely irresistible to sit on his back steps in the cool, promising mornings, working on a practically original arrangement of Big Walter Horton's "Walkin' by Myself," visualizing the sound invading Ev Yandell's dreams and waking him with steam already oozing from his pores. This would last until Joanna's cry of "Aronson, get your ancient ass inside, and leave that poor man in peace!" and an apologetic phone call to Janice Yandell, who found the whole thing absurdly funny. Janice found most things funny, and wished her husband would grow a beard too.

But on this particular Saturday morning Joanna was already on her way to Chicago, and Ev Yandell was sitting on the step beside Abe, dolefully shaking his head and dramatically covering his ears.

"I do not get it. I absolutely do not get it. How a civilized man—a university professor, no less—can sit there day after day, making that awful noise, just as happy as a little pig in shit. How that nice woman puts up with you." He offered Abe a crumpled paper bag. "Here, I brought you a couple those doughnuts you like. Anything to shut that thing up."

Abe broke off abruptly, shoved the harmonica into his cardigan pocket, grunted, "Gimme," and snatched the bag. He sampled a chocolate-covered doughnut, with sprinkles, and remarked scornfully, "Feh, day-old," but kept eating. Ev demanded, "Why couldn't you take up the piano, like your girlfriend plays? Or the—what is it?—the cello, there's a nice instrument for a retired gentleman like yourself. Now I could live with a nice cello next door."

"Strings are for sissies," Abe announced. "Harp's the only instrument that ever let me express my true feelings about being alive at this moment in this world. A person plays the harmonica from his belly, you understand?"

Ev snorted. "If that racket's your true feelings, I'm selling my house." They sat in reasonably companionable silence while Abe finished the doughnuts. Ev said then, "That girl you got living in your garage?"

Abe regarded him slantingly. "What about her?"

"Nothing. Just a real looker, is all."

"So she is indeed. So is Janice." Abe lifted the harmonica threateningly. "You know I'm not afraid to use this."

"Put that thing away," Ev pleaded. "I just said she was a looker. Can't help noticing, can I?" He sighed, resting his chin on his folded hands. "She's way too young for you, and I'm way too married for her. Life is flat-out unfair."

"No argument, son." Abe dug for leftover chocolate crumbs in the wrinkles of the bag, but his neighbor went on staring down toward the garage. There was no sign or sound of Lioness.

"Tell you something funny," Ev said at last. "Not because I've been spying on her, nothing like that—it's just I couldn't help noticing, like I said. My kids."

Abe waited, but Ev did not continue. "What about your kids? Jesse wants to be a professional wrestler. Alli wants to be a horse. That's all I know about them. Sum and substance."

"Well, they been hanging out at your place a lot lately. You know that, don't you?"

"They have?" Abe scratched his head, nodding slowly. "Oh, right, I see them once in a while when I'm working. Only from the window—I guess they talk to Del sometimes, but they don't ever come inside." He caressed the Hohner absently, thinking about an entirely different introduction to the Horton blues. "They don't bother anyone, if that's worrying you."

"No," Ev said. "That's not it." He was silent for a little while longer, clearing his throat and running his hands aimlessly over his face and neck. Then he said, "Okay, what it is, it's them with her, Lioness. You really never seen it?"

Abe looked at him. Ev said, "She teaches them stuff." About to continue, he turned his head sharply, then suddenly nudged Abe's shoulder. "There, look, there's Jesse. Little rat promised he'd clean out the boat first thing after breakfast." Abe could see Ev's blond, skinny, tireless nine-year-old son at the garage door, raising his hand to knock, and then sprawling on his seat, laughing with surprise and delight as the door opened before he touched it. Lioness stood there.

She was barefoot, wearing the older of her two dresses, her hair wrapped in what looked like a dishtowel, as though she had just washed it. She held out a hand to help Jesse up, and when she smiled at him the physical shock of it jarred Abe to the roots of his hair. He felt the smile, and he seemed to hear it as well, like the first whisper of summer rain. Beside him, Ev was breathing shallowly, and had turned quite red. When he saw Abe looking at him, he laughed himself, shaking his head, but it was the thin laughter of an embarrassed boy no older than his son. "Watch now," he said. "Just watch them."

Lioness was still holding Jesse's hand, but the boy was already tugging her toward a slight depression just down the slope from the garage. Like an echo of his father, he was chanting, "Watch me, Lioness, watch me! Look, I can do it! Look!"

And with that, Jesse Yandell knelt, plunged both hands into the damp earth, joyously embracing dirt, stones, and snails to the fullest extent of his reach, and rose again with his arms full of flowers.

On the back steps Abe stood up himself, and then sat down again. Beside him Ev mumbled weakly, "Oh, oh, Jesus." Jesse's left cheek was smudged, but his eyes and his grin were shining, and he held the flowers out to Lioness as proudly as though he were bringing her the golden apples of the Hesperides. Lioness clapped her hands like a child.

"I saw Alli doing that," Ev whispered. "But just once, and just a couple flowers. I thought she was picking them at first. Then I thought—I don't know—maybe it was like bulbs or something, could be like bulbs. But this . . ." His own eyes appealed for reassurance they did not expect, ever again. "I mean, bulbs grow in the ground, don't they? Open, I mean."

"Everything opens in the ground," Abe said. "Buds." He tried hard to keep the shakiness out of his voice, and was irritated when he could not. "But camellias, maybe not. Gardenias—dahlias— hollyhocks—begonias . . . what do I know? Del would know."

Jesse's overspilling armload was no properly arranged bouquet, but a glorious clashy hodgepodge of unrelated blooms, all due at different times of spring and summer, all requiring different soils and angles of sunlight—even Abe knew this—and none of them planted in that particular spot, which Joanna had recently cleared for a fuchsia bush. He said, slowly and carefully, "They really see a lot of her—Lioness?"

"Well, they like her," Ev said. "They talk about her all the time, like some kind of movie star—I mean, every night you got both of them going on about something Lioness said, Lioness did, something she told them, something Lioness always has for breakfast—whatever, every night. And that's all fine—she's real sweet to them, it's cute, I got no trouble with that." He gripped Abe's arm, seemingly unaware that he was doing it. "She came over for dinner a couple of weeks ago, Janice invited her. And it was real nice having her, really comfortable, you know? Like she'd been coming to dinner for years. Only we were out of bottled water one time, and Alli started fussing how the fruit juice tasted so crappy. I mean, she didn't say crappy, she wouldn't do that, but that's what she meant. Because Janice had to make it with tap water, right?" Abe nodded. Gardner Island water—the residents' one common topic of conversation—was drawn from a system of wells owned by a Seattle company, and its capacity for turning clothes green and coffee into asphalt kept the Marley supermarket forever short of self-styled mountain spring water. It was a particularly sore point during Abe's beer-making season.

"So Janice apologizes, because she forgot to get the bottled, and the juice does taste like moose pee—Jesse calls it that when he thinks I'm not listening. And Lioness just says, nothing to apologize for, she didn't even notice the taste. But the kids are looking at her—okay, I know how weird this sounds, but they were both of them looking at her, not talking, just sort of catching her eye and smiling to themselves, like they expected she could fix it. Fix the water. Like they'd seen her fix other stuff before, no problem, Lioness'll take care of this too. Abe, you understand what I'm saying? Could you please tell me you understand what I'm saying?"

"Fortunately, I speak fluent figment," Abe grunted. "So. So

Lioness snapped her fingers and right away the concentrated grape juice started tasting like champagne. Have I got that?"

Ev was shaking his head before Abe finished. "Uh-uh, no, nothing like that. Nothing changed—nothing—not then. Except ever since." He paused, glancing sideways at Abe, hands quarreling in his lap. "Except ever since, from that day on, our tap water's been tasting like bottled. Exactly the same, no difference, absolutely. You notice anything? I mean, you got to have noticed."

"'I never drink water,'" Abe said. "'Fish fuck in it.'" His W. C. Fields imitation was by far the best of a limited repertoire. Lioness was patting Jesse's shoulder, plainly praising him, but the boy was just as obviously crestfallen as she spoke. Abe strained to eavesdrop, tuning out Ev Yandell's voice in the process. He heard Lioness, soft but clear, and quite firm: "Put them back, Jesse. Put them all back now and cover them."

"But I did it right." Jesse's face looked as though he were about to cry. "Didn't I do it right?"

Lioness soothed him. "Yes—yes, you did it just right. But now you must give them back, and you must never do this again. Promise me, Jesse." Her tone was not at all commanding, but Jesse nodded sadly, bending to the shallow trench he had gouged in the dirt. Lioness said gently, "Oh, this is my fault. I should never have shown you and your sister." Abe almost missed the words altogether, because Lioness half-turned from Jesse, and seemed to be looking directly at him and Ev Yandell, though she made no sign that she saw them.

"I'm glad you showed us," Jesse said stubbornly. He was shoving the flowers down out of sight, scooping the earth back over them in great frustrated sweeps of his arms. He said, "I love your magic tricks, and Alli does too. I don't want you to stop doing them. The water tastes a whole lot better now."

"Jesse," Lioness said, and though her voice had not changed, the boy paused to look at her. Lioness said, "Those are not tricks, and I am not a magician. The earth is the only magician, always. There is no other. Do you understand me?"

Jesse's nod, from that distance, seemed small and grudging. Abe heard him say, "But how do you make the earth do all that stuff?" Lioness's laughter made the towel around her hair come partly undone. She removed it altogether, and Abe felt his cheeks flushing with an embarrassment that he had not known when she slept naked between him and naked Joanna. She said, "No one can make the earth do anything, child. But if you speak to it properly, it will sometimes do you a favor. Sometimes. No, cover them all," for Jesse had set a few flowers away from the trench. "They aren't for keeping. Cover them."

Jesse sighed as dramatically as any frustrated nine-year-old, but he obeyed. When the last flower was reburied, and the ground more or less smoothed over them, Lioness put her arms around him. He leaned against her, closing his eyes. Lioness said gently, "Thank you, Jesse. Tell your sister." He nodded, but did not answer her.

Everard Yandell said, equally quietly, "You're an educated man. Lousy harmonica player, but an educated man. You tell me what we just saw."

When Abe did not turn his head, Ev pressed on. "She's living in your damn garage, man, you deal with her every day. You got to say something." He clutched Abe's arm tighter, forcing him to face his neighbor's bewildered eyes. "Who is she, and what the hell is going on, and what the hell should we do about it?" His hand was cold, but his sweaty hair was sticking to his forehead.

"I don't know," Abe said. "Nothing. When Del gets back." He tried to make a joke out of it. "I never make any decisions except in the presence of a Sicilian." Ev did not laugh. Abe tried for his classroom manner. "Whatever she's done, or hasn't done, she hasn't harmed your kids. Does Jesse seem even the least bit scared?"

"Maybe she's a witch," Ev said. His East Texas accent had grown distinctly stronger. "Don't you look at me like that, man! It ain't all science out there, it ain't all universities and—and *reason*. There's all kinds of craziness everywhere—there's *stuff* out there. You saw!"

Both Jesse and Lioness turned at the sound of his rising voice. Jesse started toward them, while Lioness nodded and smiled briefly before she walked back into the garage and closed the door. Abe took the harmonica out of his pocket. "Go on home, Ev. Don't make me use this."

Ev stared at him for a moment longer; then turned to put an arm around his son's shoulders and led him away. Jesse squirmed against the tight grip, but he looked back to wave to Abe, who called, "See you, Captain Wheelie," a nickname that the boy had long since earned on his spectacularly battered bicycle. He blew a fast lick from Jesse's current favorite pop horror, and was rewarded with a sudden delighted laugh that reminded him, with a sudden piercing ache, of Lily at nine.

When everyone was out of sight, he got up and walked down to the cleared place where Jesse had first dug up the flowers. The boy had done a better job of covering them than he had thought: the soil was almost perfectly level, and only a little darker and damper than the surrounding earth. Abe looked around, shrugged and stooped; then straightened with a self-mocking snort and started back to the house. Before he had gone three paces, however, he turned, dropped stiffly to his knees, and began digging.

At first he scratched rather fastidiously at the dirt with his fingertips, but in a few moments he was raking hard enough to break nails, muttering to himself in something more than simple disbelief. Eventually he scrambled upright to stand gaping down at the reopened furrow, his eyes as wide as Ev Yandell's eyes had been. The buried flowers were gone.

———

Joanna made the Chicago run twice a week, on Mondays and Thursdays, and usually took the next day totally off from the world, doing nothing but writing letters and watching old black-and-white movies on television. But waking before dawn on a spring Friday morning, once again restless and fretful in her skin, she indulged herself as she had not done in some while, and drove down to the Pike Place Market. She did not invite Abe.

The Market had been Joanna's private comfort ever since she had arrived in Seattle as a college student. Cocooned by crowds, insulated by noise, she moved easily in her own warm silence, deliciously alone, perfectly content to wander aimlessly between the iron-columned arcades above ground and the subterranean dress and antique stores, nibbling on a Chinese pork bun or a chunk of frybread as she studied the boat traffic on Elliott Bay and the vendors arranging their displays. Sometimes she bought produce, sometimes fresh-cut flowers or handmade jewelry as a gift for a friend; sometimes only a crumbling paperback mystery to read in the Chicago hotel where her flight crew always stayed. Later in the morning, when the tourists started arriving, she would stand with them at one of the fish stalls, marveling at the king salmon and steelhead trout tossed showily but unerringly from seller to wrapper, never dropped, never plopping into the wrong hands. Later still, she might walk down the hundred-and-sixty-nine steps to the waterfront aquarium, or drift out to tiny Steinbrueck Park, barely more than a patch of grass just north of the Market, and lie on the ground to watch the Asian kites flashing overhead like the fish. By now she recognized longtime strollers and local vagabonds alike, as well as vendors, and wondered about them; some smiled or nodded as she passed, and she smiled mysteriously back, rather hoping to be wondered about a little herself.

On occasion, she did go there with Abe, did meet friends for lunch at Rachel, the big bronze piggy bank under the clock at the south entrance. But the Market was hers, and she was happiest alone, as now, roving the deepest levels with the smell of basil and garlic and coffee and salt water in her nostrils, and the sound of the ferry horns in her ears. As Abe had said, quite early on, gracious in defeat, "I know another kingdom when I cross the border. Nice little place you got here, Your Majesty."

The morning was cool, even chilly, and wet without being exactly rainy, and she once again pondered the difference between the weather here and that of Gardner Island, a few miles across the water. She was coming out of the Athenian Inn, having spoiled herself further with a late breakfast of a chicken-liver omelet and two mimosas, when she saw Lioness.

There was no mistaking the tawny, willful hair, or the grace with which Lily's faraway princess sank to one knee to help a child tie her shoe. The little girl was sniffling tentatively, clearly considering whether a bruised shin and a deformed balloon animal were worth a scene, while Lioness laughed up at her, teasing, "Ah, come on, very short person, how bad can it be if you can't decide how bad it is? Look, here's your shoelace properly tied, and here's your pretty giraffe, all better—" and so it was, Joanna saw, proudly stretching up its neck between the child's hands to nuzzle her cheek—"and there's your mother, and so all's well." She kissed two fingertips and touched them to the injury. "Go now, and tell Mother you've suffered greatly, and can only be restored to health by a serious ice-cream transfusion. She will understand." The approaching woman nodded curtly at her and swooped her daughter away, warning her loudly not ever to talk to strangers, even the nice ones.

Lioness looked after them, smiling as the little girl waved back to her over her mother's shoulder. Joanna had opened her mouth to call to Lioness when a strange thing happened: the Primavera face went completely still, all expression instantly gone. It appeared to Joanna that only Lioness's shadow showed any emotion, at once yearning forward and cowering against her as she stared at something beyond Joanna's left shoulder. Joanna did call then, but if the words reached Lioness, they never touched her. Nothing touched her in that moment.

There was no one behind Joanna when she spun round; and when she wheeled again Lioness had vanished, leaving only a child whining in her mother's arms to indicate that she had ever been in the Market at all. Joanna ran a few dazed steps forward, and then stopped, having no idea of where to look or what to imagine. Slowly she moved on, almost unseeing, through the tiled aisles, past the vintage fabric shops and the booths that sold clay ocarinas, turning every couple of minutes from a vague, curiously hopeful sense that she was being followed, as though Lioness were playing a joke on her.

Musicians were setting up their hammered dulcimers and their amplifiers now, and both the Market itself and the brick sidewalks of Pike Street were growing steadily more crowded. At times she was forced to a complete halt, waiting until a knot of sightseers ahead of her decided whether or not to enter a boutique or a restaurant. Her feet hurt, and she could feel her heart thumping behind her eyes, yet she stayed stubbornly on the trail—if not of Lioness, then of whatever had frightened her away. *We were right, all of us. Somebody's after her.*

She did not realize that she had long since given up on finding Lioness, until she suddenly recognized her, only a little way ahead, certainly hurrying, but not quite running. Joanna called her name loudly this time, but Lioness did not turn; if anything, she seemed to quicken her familiar swift, self-contained stride. Joanna lengthened her own pace to catch up with her, and touched her shoulder from behind, saying, "Hi, remember me? How soon they forget."

The woman who turned was as tall as Lioness, but much older. She wore an unfashionable woolen shift dress, had a broad, large-featured, strong-boned face, long gray eyes on the near edge of green, and moved with the deceptive suppleness of a smaller woman. Joanna apologized and started to turn away, but was stopped with a half-raised hand and an anxious smile. "Pardon, I am so very sorry to bother you—but since we have met so, do you know, is there a shop where one could find the antique maps? Charts, is that the word? Of the old world—old maps, antiques?" Her voice was deep, and almost hoarse.

Joanna directed her to the lowest level of the Market, and had already forgotten everything about the woman by the time she called Abe from a pay phone. He had left his answering machine on, but he picked up the phone as soon as he heard her voice. She said, without preamble, "It's me. Could you come down here?"

"Where's here?" Abe had his interrupted-at-work growl on at full strength. She told him where she was. "Why?"

"Because I'm your sweet patootie and I need you, that's why." The silence that followed seemed so long, and the static crackling in her ear made her so edgy that she said after a time, "I think I'm going to require a response to that one."

"Sorry." Abe's voice was curiously quiet. "I was just thinking, that's the first time you've ever said that. Twenty-whatever years, and you've never said that to me."

"I have too. Lots of times, one way and another. Anyway, you don't like people needing you, that's been understood from day one." He did not reply. Joanna said, "Abe. Come down to the Market. Please."

"Meet me at the Copacabana. Order the ceviche." He hung up.

Rain had begun falling as Joanna started across Pike Street toward the little Bolivian restaurant that had become their particular Market rendezvous over the years. She walked slowly all the same, thinking, *she wasn't wearing a raincoat, she'll get wet*, without noticing that she had left her own raincoat at home.

The ceviche bowl was half-empty, and Joanna's aching head was resting on her folded arms, when she felt Abe's hand in her hair.

She looked up to see him smiling dourly, saying, "Not everyone would ditch an entire brilliant and insightful chapter on how come Wat Tyler never got to meet with Richard II, just because his sweet patootie wanted a little company. Hank Williams wouldn't have done it, I'll tell you that."

"Noted," she said wearily. "Duly appreciated." He listened without interrupting as she told him about seeing Lioness in the Market, and what happened then. She said, "I don't know what could have alarmed her. I don't know what she could have seen."

"Whom," Abe said. "That's a whom, has to be. Whomever she's running from, that's what she saw."

"But I didn't see anybody! And I turned right around, Abe, like a shot—I swear I did, and I kept looking. Nothing, nobody!"

"Yeah, well." Abe sat up straight, looking almost embarrassed, his hands flat before him on the table. He said, "Something I meant to tell you."

He recounted what had passed between Lioness and Jesse Yandell, from the boy's first joyous revelation of his new power to Lioness's insistence that Jesse put the flowers back where he had found them, and his own discovery afterward. Joanna, in her turn, said nothing until he finished. "You're sure you were digging in the right place?"

Abe looked at her without replying. Joanna said, "Then I think maybe we ought to be scared."

It was almost a question, but not quite. Abe asked, "Are you?" After a moment Joanna shook her head. "Me neither," Abe continued. "Do me something, it's still just Lioness."

"I'm not sure there *is* a just-Lioness," Joanna said slowly. "But whatever it is, Lily's in love with it. That I am sure of."

"And whatever she is, Lioness is not an *it*." His vehemence startled them both, and he took her hand to reassure her, and perhaps himself. "Look, as long as you've got me over here, let's do something nice for ourselves. You choose. Movie?"

"All right," Joanna said, but then she shook her head. "No, not a movie. Ballard Locks. The steelhead have started coming through."

"And looking at jumping fish always calms you. Right, right, I know." He sighed dramatically. "Well, I offered." He snatched the last of the ceviche daintily between two fingers. "Ballard Locks. Okay."

"And maybe we could just pop by Lily's place afterward. It's Thursday, she's not at the station on Thursdays." Abe looked at her. "In and out, I swear. If she's not there, we'll just go."

"No waiting around? Like last time?" But he took pity on the look she gave him, and pulled her gently to her feet. "Ballard Locks, then. And afterward . . . afterward, we can wait for her. A little."

"No," Joanna said. "If she's not there, she's not there."

# 7.

# MAY

Twelve-Bar Billy's Seriously Blue consisted of lead and rhythm guitars, drums, electric bass guitar, and himself on harmonica. The drummer was a fierce-looking girl of eighteen or twenty, who looked fifteen, and who slammed out her solos with grinning vengefulness. The bassist appeared to be taking his beat directly from the rhythm of the tides, and the lead guitar was having problems with his amplifier, his pinched and bronchial singing, and his obvious loathing of Twelve-Bar Billy. The rhythm guitarist was blind, stroking his Gretsch dreadnought with a mystically metronomic 4/4 beat, whatever was actually being played. His guide dog lay calmly at his feet through the rehearsal, with its own somber yellow eyes closed. Billy said the dog was meditating, trained to it by Tibetan monks. "Tantric mastiff, daddy—they breed them over there, up in the mountains." Abe found it at least as believable as the bassist.

For his part, Twelve-Bar Billy played for a rehearsal audience of one exactly as he had in the Skyliner Diner, or as Abe had lately seen him before a stamping, dancing young crowd at the Gardner Island Third International Beach 'N Blues Festival on the waterfront.

Black cowboy hat slipping down over his eyes, black leather vest showing darker sweat-stains at the armholes, harmonica whipping back and forth, almost touching the microphone, periodically crying out, "Brace yourselves!" he blew whooping Mississippi field hollers, Kansas City lost-love moans, boisterous Chicago struts and challenges, Louis Jordan novelty numbers, and the theme from *High Noon* with the same passion—so personal as to be almost indifferent—as though there were no one listening to him at all.

Except during his occasional vocals, he looked directly only at the other band members, nodding encouragement or commanding their solos. Beyond that brief contact, he seemed to Abe to be long gone away, dissolved into the music, leaving hat, vest, and boots on their own to suggest their human presence. Jesse Yandell's buried flowers had vanished no more completely than he.

Yet when the rehearsal was over, he jumped lightly down from the middle-school auditorium stage and ambled back to the rear row where Abe sat uncomfortably in a rumpsprung folding chair. Ignoring greetings, he said, "Dogshit acoustics, but once we got folks on their feet nobody'll notice. How'd it sound to you?" He grinned mockingly when Abe hesitated, "Be gentle, please, it's my first time."

"A bit disjointed," Abe said. "Scattery, as though everyone were playing something a little to the left of everyone else. You were fine," he added quickly. "You sounded great."

Twelve-Bar Billy waved praise aside as he had done with hellos. "Hard to get good help these days. Some nights they sound damn near like a real band—some nights I could pick a better one out of a police lineup. Never been the same since I lost my old bass player." He sat down beside Abe, rapping the harmonica against his palm to knock the spit out of the reeds. "Now, once I get you up there, whole different story."

Abe said, "Now *look*, damn it," and Twelve-Bar Billy grinned again. "See, daddy, what I need, I need like brackets. Two harmonicas, the way Grisman's always got two mandolins framing the music. Me on one side the stage, playing lead, you on the other, chunking away on chords—wouldn't matter what anybody else was doing, we'd be holding things together, you hear what I'm saying? Couldn't miss. Could *not* miss. Revolutionary sound." He leaned close, lowering his voice, prodding at Abe's coat pocket. "So, you got your harp on you?"

"No, I haven't." It came out more snappishly than Abe intended. "I left it home just so I wouldn't be tempted like this. I may be senile, sonny, but I'm not as senile as I look."

The cowboy cocked his head, the colorless hair falling aside to reveal fiercely blue eyes, with faint lines under them that Abe had never noticed before. "Daddy, don't you know about temptation? Only way to get rid of it is to yield to it. That's a true fact."

"Oscar Wilde," Abe said slowly. "Well."

Twelve-Bar Billy laughed fully then. "I been thrown out of some really good schools in my time." He reached into his own pocket and brought out a second harmonica, this one looking as though it had been thrown out of at least one car on at least one busy freeway. "B-flat. It's their best key. About their only key, come to that." He pressed the harmonica into Abe's hand, firmly closing his fingers around it. "You know 'Seventh Son'?"

"Yes," Abe answered. "And no. Totally not, not ever, no chance. Look, you haven't even heard me. I practice in my house, and I play on my back steps, and believe me, that is as far as it goes. I fart around with the blues, that's all. I can't play with you."

But Twelve-Bar Billy already had him out of the folding chair and was walking him toward the stage, somehow without seeming to drag or guide him at all. "Ah, daddy, come on, it's just a half-ass rehearsal. I swear, if you really can't cut it, the word'll never get out of this dump. Anybody talks, he's gone, okay?" His arm was around Abe's shoulders, his bony, urgent face leaning down close; he smelled incongruously of ginger tea. "But you're the one, it's your time, I don't need to hear you blow to know. Drag it on up there and let's us make some music." The rest of the band, plainly impatient for his return, had struck up a faltering rhythm-and-blues vamp, but he gestured them silent. Twelve-Bar Billy said quietly, "It's your time."

"Well," Abe said again. He looked helplessly back toward the auditorium entrance. "Well, damn," he said. "Maybe it is. What do I know?"


Lily knocked several times, but no one answered. The front door was unlocked, as Abe usually left it, out of cranky conviction: "A drunk munchkin could break that thing down in three minutes—why should I get robbed *and* lose my door?" Turk, who regarded Abe's house as part of his manor, to be patrolled and defended against all squirrels, crows, and fish, came and barked maniacally at Lily, and then trotted complacently after her as she walked quickly through to the study. She went straight to the window, leaning on Abe's worktable. There was no hint of movement in the garage, though she waited for a long while.

The hound eventually whined his puzzled boredom, and she turned to him, smiling crookedly. "Obsessive, much?" she asked. "You really think so?" She scratched his head as she started back toward the front door. "You and my mother." Turk barked once, and headed for home.

Lily closed the door almost stealthily, so that the latch barely clicked behind her. She stood motionless, eyes closed, hands still on the knob, until at last she forced herself forward, turning the corner of the house and moving toward the garage as slowly as though she were laying an ambush. *Junior high school*, she thought. Her heart was shaking her whole body, and her throat ached terribly. *Oh God, oh God, juniorfucking high school, following Marilyn Jacobs all the way home on the bus.* Spying a smooth, brilliantly black stone, the size and shape of a small bird's head, she stooped for it, brushed away the earth, and held it out in one hand while she knocked lightly on the door with the other. "I brought you a rock," she mumbled, as the door began to swing open. "It's pretty. I thought maybe you'd like it."

But the door was unlocked, as Abe's had been, and the garage was as empty as the house. Lily stood irresolute in the doorway, the sunlight cold on her shoulders. Twice she started to turn away, changing her mind each time and returning to peer forlornly into the garage and call Lioness's name. Finally, now clutching the black stone in both hands, she nudged the door fully open and walked in.

Kyle, the copilot, made his move in the Chicago hotel. Joanna was in the bar, indulging herself with a second vodka tonic, oyster crackers and brie, and reading a mystery novel, which she had picked up at the airport bookstore solely because there was a kayak in the cover illustration. She was still waiting for the kayak to show up when the copilot walked in with his arm resting lightly but possessively on the slight shoulders of little Heather, the youngest of the flight attendants.

Neither one noticed her as they took seats in a dim corner under the shelf where the stuffed bobcat sneered through bared fangs. The copilot was still in uniform—Joanna could not remember ever seeing him out of it. Heather shed her coat, smiling as shyly as though she were revealing intimate skin instead of jeans and a cable-knit gray-green sweater. She resembled Lily only in her vulnerability, but that by itself set Joanna's expression rivaling the bobcat's. When a waitress hurried over to take their drink orders, the girl giggled in some embarrassment as she asked for a chocolatini. "I'm sorry, it's the only cocktail I really like." The copilot blinked only briefly; then patted her hand and tipped the waitress in advance. He said, "Make that two, okay?"

Joanna was mildly impressed. From observation during flights, she had visualized the copilot's seduction technique as involving nothing much more complex than mustache-flexing, a lot of eyelash-calisthenics, and a lunge. *Takes his time—no big rush to get her drunk and upstairs. Got some style, I'll say that.* She nursed her own drink, and watched as Heather and the copilot chatted over their twin chocolatinis, which in time were refilled, and unhurriedly replenished a second time. Half-tempted to order one, strictly for research purposes—*but Abe would be ragging me about it forever*— she waited until Heather rose, excused herself with great dignity, and gravely requested directions to the ladies' room. She hardly swayed—and certainly did not lurch, blunder, or wamble in the least—as she set off.

Kyle saw Joanna almost immediately as she raised her glass to him, looking straight at him as she finished her drink. She came toward him then, taking her time herself to pick up her book, and sat down across from him, in Heather's chair. Amiable as always, the copilot saluted her with his own glass. "Nice to see you away from the office. Out for the evening?"

"No," Joanna told him. "And neither are you."

The copilot made no attempt to register either bewilderment or indignation. He said calmly, "She's a grown person, she's twenty-three years old. Twenty-four in September."

Joanna put her book down between them on the table. "There's twenty-three and twenty-three. On my watch, she's about fifteen."

The copilot thoughtfully licked the rim of his chocolatini glass. "Kind of addictive, these things, in a really weird way." He regarded Joanna levelly over the empty glass. She noticed for the first time the glint of gray in the perfect mustache. "So the Flight Attendants

Association actually takes an interest in consenting adults' off-hours? You being the union rep, of course you'd know."

Joanna shook her head, smiling warmly at him. "Can't honestly say, to tell you the truth. It's a complex matter—positions change hourly. But I do know what *your* union thinks about sexual harassment charges. Nothing complex about that one. If I may?"

She took the glass from him and tasted the remains of the chocolatini. "Mmm. The complete package—diabetes *and* a hangover. Very nice."

Kyle's expression had not changed. "Harassment? It's the other way around, if it's anything. She knows what she wants—you see it every day, don't tell me you don't. Okay, you don't like me, but give me that much of a break, Jo."

Over his shoulder, she saw Heather returning from the ladies' room, walking steadily enough, but touching the wall every now and then. She stood up, saying, "I don't answer to Jo. Never have. You can go right on calling me Joanna, like everyone else. Or Ms. Delvecchio, ma'am—that'd be all right too. Nobody calls me Jo." On a sudden anarchic impulse, she patted his cheek with her fingertips. "Go after Tamara, why don't you? I don't think she's had a really good laugh in months."

The copilot said quietly, "You're a mean old woman."

The words caught Joanna almost physically, knocking the breath out of her as though she had been struck in the stomach. She could only stare as Kyle repeated, "You come on like everybody's aunt, everybody's big sister, whatever, everybody's babysitter, but the fact is you're just plain mean and sour, just growling it out till you retire." The New Mexico accent, amiably reassuring over the public-address system, had broadened to suggest northern Louisiana. "Well, there's more people than me waiting for that day." He rose, bowed mockingly, holding her eyes with his own, and strode away, patting Heather's shoulder as he passed her.

Heather looked after him in some puzzlement before she plopped down heavily where he had been sitting. She said, "Well," and then, "I think I want one more chocolatini."

"No, you don't," Joanna said. "You want to go upstairs and take a nap. After that you'll call my room, and we'll have dinner. Sound like a plan?"

"Sounds like a *good* plan. Can Kyle join us?"

Joanna sighed. "You can ask him. I think he might be booked."

Late that night, on the phone with Abe, she demanded repeatedly, "Why should it bother me? What the frigging hell do I care for one frigging minute what a pig of a butt-pinching copilot thinks about me? Tell me that, Aronson, you're so smart."

"Is this a rhetorical question?" He was having his favorite evening snack of pickled herring bits on graham crackers: the unmistakable muffled crunch at once annoyed her and touched her with its comforting absurdity. "So is it the *mean* or the *old* that's gotten to you?"

"*Old*, I'm used to, I've told you that. Even *too old* I can live with—most of the time, anyway. But *mean*, even from him . . . sour . . ." Now she was annoyed with herself, suddenly deeply weary of the sound of her own complaining. "Abe, just tell me, don't make jokes. Am I really getting sour and nasty in my damn old age? Just let me have it, okay?"

"Hey," he said, two thousand miles away, with his mouth full of pickled herring and his voice so astonishingly gentle and caressing that she could have wept. "Hey, cookie, are you crying?"

"No, I'm not, and don't call me *cookie*." In fact, she was not crying at all, only burrowing into his voice as she would have done into the hollow of his implacably bony shoulder. "But I mean, what if he's right? I don't care about *him*, but what if that's really how the bunnyrabbits all see me? What if . . . Lily . . . ?" and she was still not crying, but her own voice had thickened in her throat. "Lily . . ."

"Delvecchio, your daughter may be as dumb as a rutabaga when it comes to lovers, but not when it comes to love. There's a difference. Sweets—*cookie*—Lily's like everyone else you look after, and take care of, and knock yourself out for every damn stupid day of your life. She knows . . . they all know . . . *we* all know." He coughed, apparently around a graham-cracker corner. "*I* know. You hear me, Del? *I* know."

"I hear you," she said. "Drink some water, you never chew your food enough. Goodnight, old man. Thanks."

"Goodnight, my old woman. My Del. Goodnight. Wait, wait— you want to hear something really wild?"

"You got the NEH grant for the book? Abe, that's great—congratulations! That's wonderful! I'm really happy for you."

Abe positively cackled with delight, a sound she had never heard in all the years of their relationship. "Nope—nothing to do with books, grants, nothing like that. You are now keeping company with the second harmonica in West Seattle's only blues band. With, I may add, all the rights and privileges appertaining thereto. How does that grab you, Tigress of the Skies?"

The announcement was so unexpected that she reacted as slowly as though she were translating from a language studied very long ago. "You're playing in a band?"

"Next Friday night. At that godawful chili joint, Tucker's. Wednesday after that, the Skyliner. You'll be in town, so don't tell me you can't make it, you and Lily. Seriously Blue, it's called. All-natural—no preservatives, no food coloring, no artificial ingredients. And two harmonicas, no waiting. When the wind's right, it's practically music." His voice lost its normal omniscient serenity, and became fifteen years old. "Del, I played with them! It was just a rehearsal, but I actually kept up! We did "Seventh Son," and we did "Goin' Down Slow," and I played lead, Billy let me play lead on "Key to the Highway." And I was good, Del—I was really good, I could hear myself being good. Unbelievable—like hearing somebody else playing." When he paused, she thought she could hear his heart beating through the phone, as though they were resting after love with her head on his gray chest. "Del, when I . . . I mean, to actually play real music with other people, good or bad—Del, that's the way I'm supposed to feel in temple—Rosh Hashanah, Yom Kippur, whatever—and I never, never do. Do you understand what I'm telling you?"

She thought of Kyle, the copilot, saying "She's a grown person . . . she knows what she wants." Now she said to a soaring, adolescent Abe, "Yes. Yes. I understand. It's what you've been wishing for, all these years."

Another maniacal cackle. "We can invite Ev Yandell. Janice'll *make* him come, it's the neighborly thing." Then, suddenly diffident, almost mumbling, "I think Lioness works the Skyliner on Wednesdays."

"Well. That'll be nice. We'll be your groupies." She hadn't meant it sardonically, but it sounded so in her ears. "She's never heard your band?"

"No. Just Billy, by himself."

A pause, long enough that she wondered momentarily if they had been cut off. She said, "You know, I've never really heard you play."

"What are you talking about?" Abe was genuinely astonished. "All these years of me wandering around practicing, blowing licks, working on stuff half the night, driving you crazy, aggravating the neighbors. Heard me play, for God's sake."

"No," she said. "No, that's not what I meant. I mean, I've never listened to you that way. The way I guess you wanted me to listen. All this time. I'm sorry."

Abe laughed in the old way then, the slow, growly chuckle as familiar as a nursery rhyme. "Don't be. Old white man, fooling around, pretending to play the blues, what was there to listen to? I can't believe somebody thinks I'm good enough to play with a band. Tells you something about the band, anyway."

"No," Joanna said. "No, it just tells me something about you. I'll be proud to be your groupie."

After they had said goodnight and hung up, and she was engaged in her usual battle with the hotel's huge, flabby pillows, she had a brief fantasy vision of herself briskly piloting a kayak between islands over a mirror-smooth Puget Sound, while Abe, in the rear seat, blew something like "Take Five" or "One For My Baby," out of consideration for her boredom with the Delta blues. The image made her giggle in the darkness as she fell asleep.

Lily had had an intimate understanding with Abe's garage since her childhood. At different stages it had served as playroom, theatre, bandit hideout, hermit's cave (for those times when nameless anger and grief turned even her own room into enemy territory); and—at fifteen, on a mildewy sleeping bag—as the seaport for her first voyage through the dazing wonder of a stranger's body. But Lioness's conversion of the little space was so thorough as to be almost disorienting: the concrete floor was several shades lighter than Lily remembered it, with almost every stain and tire-track gone, along with the oily-rag aroma that still flavored certain of her dreams. The garage now smelled to her faintly of wet earth, more of alyssum and mignonette, and most particularly of apple blossoms. But the only flowers in sight were a few fragile, nameless sprigs in a few mason jars.

*A meadow*, she thought, *she's got some kind of spray that smells like a meadow, a pasture.* She stood gazing for some time at the white hillside villages in the Greek island posters, and at the Miss Piggy calendar, which she saw to be a month short of being current. She thought of turning the leaf herself, to bring the calendar up to date, but decided against it. Lioness's few spare clothes were hung on nails driven into exposed studs in a far corner; the stuffed camel, its naked, threadbare humps the color of baby shit, was half-hidden under the satin pillow. Lily held the camel against her face for an instant, and spent several minutes afterward making sure that she put it back perfectly. A bit of the remaining fuzz had come off onto a sleeve; when she caught herself trying to replace it, her gasp of laughter sounded to her as raw and hungry as a seagull cry.

There were no toiletries visible—Lily knew that Lioness used Abe's bathroom morning and night—except for a toothbrush and a nail file perched atop a liquor-store carton, along with a small unlabeled cologne bottle. Lily picked up the bottle and snatched out the stopper, greedily inhaling Lioness. She shook a few pale-yellow drops into one hand, rubbed both hands together, and then spread the cologne behind her ears, under her blouse, hard across shoulders and breasts, until her palms were completely dry. She pirouetted slowly as though before a mirror—though there was none in the room—and said aloud, oddly breathless, "There, now I smell like you. I smell just exactly like you."

In fact, the scent was surprisingly faint, no more than a warm whisper of Lioness: a leafy rustle, fading quickly into her skin. Lily lowered her arms, suddenly acutely lonely, telling herself that she had no smallest right to feel disappointed in any way. *The woman owes you nothing*, she thought. *You've nothing to give her, you don't get to have her, and you don't get to be her. The one good thing you can ever, ever do for her is to leave her in peace.*

But she set the black stone carefully down next to the stuffed camel, all the same; and before she left the garage, she gently touched a single drop of Lioness's perfume to the place where her heart hurt.

When she closed the door, a shadowy stain in a far corner stood up and was Lioness. She held very still for a moment, her head tilted a little to one side, and her nostrils slightly dilated, as she gazed around the room as though she had never seen it before. Presently she noticed the small black stone by the stuffed camel, and she began to smile: the soft, faltering, hesitant smile of a young girl confronted by utterly unforeseen sweetness. She did not speak, nor did she touch the stone, but held her hands out to it, upraised palms open, in the cold garage.

# 8.

# MAY/JUNE

What Joanna most dearly wanted, exactly as Abe had joked—though it took her some considerable while to admit this to herself—was to put to sea in a walrus-hide kayak: the real Inuit goods from the dim old photographs and newsreels, totally bare of conveniences, good for nothing but hunting whales. She also understood just as clearly that she had no business on Puget Sound even in the Yandells' rowboat, let alone in a skin soap-bubble, and that her fancy of drifting silently over bright shadow, in and out of time and dream, leaving no trail, was one of the dangerous ones, the ones that took people with them when they left. Glider pilots had such visions; skydivers too, some of them. She, of all people, had no excuse not to know.

All the same, she went on reading the books and brochures and roaming the kayaking websites; making phone calls, wandering diffidently on the waterfronts of Ballard and West Seattle into windy boatyards and workshops whose smells made her cough. Sometimes she spent hours drinking coffee in the company of sturdy, solid, prematurely weathered young men and women, articulate about little beyond the superiority of one paddling technique to another, wood construction to plastic, carbon fiber to wood, lake touring to whitewater runs. Shy by nature, she had understood young that other people liked to be asked about themselves and their passions, and by now she was able to inquire almost knowledgeably about a kayak's volume and profile, about one- and two-piece paddles, made light or tough, set feathered or straight; to speak of things like coamings, spray-skirts, rudder kits, drysuits, and odd heavy mittens called pogies. She never imagined that these conversations had anything at all to do either with her dreams or with reality, but she took in what she could, even so.

When she did climb into a kayak for the first time—moored securely to a Ballard dock—the immediate sensation was of wearing the boat like a Victorian hoopskirt, at once awkward and strangely snug. She was in the cockpit of a touring craft belonging to one of the leathery young women: covered to the waist by the enclosed deck, with her legs stretched out and bent frog-style, so that the balls of her feet each pressed against a peg, while her knees were pushed up under the deck, cushioned by foam pads. Positioned so, the kayak was all around her, coming quickly to feel less like clothing than like skin or warm fur. *Now I'm sitting on the water, at last. Now I really am like a bird.*

She told Abe nothing of this, fearing his encouragement even more than she feared Lily's tolerant derision. If she knew him at all, she was certain, he would take over her adventure, earnestly enthusiastic, urging her further and faster than she might want to go; always with the unspoken assurance that he would, of course, be with her when she set out at last. *I'll tell him. He won't understand, but I'll tell him. There's time yet, there's lots of time.*

The weather continued benign, almost disturbingly so for Joanna on the days when she could look across six miles of bright water darkening into a summer storm raking Seattle. It seemed to her at those times that there was a kind of sheltering barrier around Gardner Island: a sunlit frontier no Alaskan gale could cross, no lightning ever breach. "Like a pentacle," she said to Abe. "A pentagon, a pentagram, one of those. The things sorcerers used to draw when they were summoning demons."

Abe, warily sampling his new summer ale, looked up to answer. "Thing to remember, you had to get it just so. A circle wouldn't protect you from demons, even one with a star inside it. It had to be an absolutely perfect pentacle, and too bad if you flunked geometry. Magic's picky."

"Well, Gardner's sort of five-sided, if you think about it," Joanna said lightly. "Maybe the whole island's the pentacle."

Even stranger than having their own exclusive climate was the fact that Joanna had no sense at all of the summer passing. Well into June and early July, the air still kept the soft green taste of April, and the constant smell of damp grass and earth, even when there had been no rain. The rain came as regularly as in Seattle, but on Gardner Island it fell at dawn, leaving the day glittering behind it, or in the night, steadily, but so lightly that the mist had all evaporated by morning. Leaves that should have begun to change color by now, and even to drop, showed no such inclination; the rhododendrons framing the Yandells' house were blossoming more explosively than ever, and Joanna's own new-planted fuchsia bush already looked as maturely established as they. Abe's blue herons, who never raised more than two chicks in a season, had not only graduated their first pair but hatched a second, while the raccoon family whose digestive processes centered around his beach stairway had doubled their number and brought their friends. The *Times* ran long Gardner features—only slightly facetious now—quoting studies on miniclimates, greenhouse gases, global warming, melting icecaps and glaciers, and the changed migration patterns of caribou. Two reporters interviewed old Mr. Nakashima, who told them that there was a tsunami coming, same as in '64, and then went to visit relatives in Spokane.

On one such balmy Wednesday night, Joanna came alone—Lily having unconvincingly pleaded a work assignment, lack of sleep, and a cold—to see Abe and Seriously Blue perform at the Skyliner. She left her car at home, and was grateful that she had, for the diner was packed that night as she had never seen it. Corinne had laid on extra chairs, even for the smallest tables, and extra waiters were lurching between them, dodging and tripping each other. Joanna wound up sharing a booth with five blues devotees from Tacoma— all white and young—who sang along with every number, whether they knew the words or not, and vied with one another in yelling "Get down with your bad self!" She had a headache before the band's third tune, but the only alternative would have been to stand, and there was hardly room to lean against the wall. And she could not have observed Abe from that angle.

Watching him so intently that by and by the noise, the headache, and the near-claustrophobia came to seem distant and irrelevant, she realized that she had never seen him joyous. Funny, certainly, always—even on the night when Lily's unborn sister had died, he had somehow managed to make her laugh, carrying her in his arms into the hospital emergency room—and peaceful as well, when he was working, or when they were curled mumblingly together.

But joy—joy untethered, joy wordless, ravenous, overwhelming— that, never; that was a face he had never shown her, and she found it wondrously shocking to see him so. Seated on the opposite side of the stage from Twelve-Bar Billy, and for the most part providing only a backing for Billy's solos against the hiccupy chugging of Seriously Blue, he closed his eyes, tucked the Hohner into his short white beard (trimmed much more closely than usual, she noticed), and blew to slam shutters and rattle bones, to freeze the heart, and melt and freeze the heart again. As though they had grown up playing together—instead of running through, by Joanna's count, no more than half a dozen rehearsals—he changed rhythms exactly as Billy changed, deepening and ripening the lead line with grittily alluring harmonies, now and then allowing himself a brief counterlick, never more than a couple of cheeky measures, often lifted whole from another tune. Once, in the middle of "Nobody Knows You," he slid into the opening bars of "Climb Every Mountain," which doubled Billy up with wild laughter that spluttered through his own harmonica and turned the song into a cascade of outlandishly dislocated quotations through which they chased each other, ending up with something that might or might not have been "Flight of the Bumblebee." Twelve-Bar Billy never stopped laughing and Abe never altered his expression.

Through the set, Lioness came and went at the corner of Joanna's vision, the tall, slender form flowing between the overcrowded tables, even when the aisles seemed completely blocked by large bodies jumping and shoving. The cheering had been continuous since the third or fourth number, coming even from the kitchen and the other waiters, all but Lioness courting disaster as they tried to applaud while juggling their trays. She herself seemed to pay no obvious attention to the music, nor to the fact of Abe onstage; serving Joanna's booth, Lioness looked directly at her several times without a sign of recognition. The merry Primavera face smiled and nodded, dealing with orders as expertly as it dealt with loud attempts at flirtation, but the green-brown eyes reflected nothing of the Skyliner Diner, or of Gardner Island, or of any world Joanna knew. Only when she said diffidently, "Lioness, hi," did the eyes make room for her among the bleak and formless mysteries crowding there. Lioness said, "Yes, I'll take your order now."

After the second set, Joanna signaled to Abe that she was leaving. They had not been able to meet during his first break, because the band had been surrounded by acolytes and new-made groupies;

and, as the oldest member by far, Abe was receiving the lion's share of reverent marveling. But he came to her quickly, saying, with surprising shyness, "I did okay, didn't I? I was okay."

"Yes," she told him. "You were really good. I never knew you were that good." It came out wrong, and he looked slightly hurt, so she corrected herself. "I mean, with other people. I'm used to you sounding good—great—around the house and things, but this was different, the way you said, and I really do understand what it means to you. Abe, I have to go now."

He stared. "You have to what? What are you talking about— you just got in. You're not staying the night?"

She had not planned to say it, or known that she wanted to say it before she heard herself. But she was committed, and she plowed on. "I can't. There's stuff I have to do at home." His bewildered annoyance emboldened her strangely, at the same time that it made her feel horribly guilty. She said, "Look, I'll call you tomorrow. It's no big deal."

"No," Abe said. "No, you're right, of course it's not. I just—" He stopped himself that abruptly, beginning to turn away from her, his motions as stiff and clumsy as those of a high-school boy mortally embarrassed at being denied a dance. She had never seen him that way, either.

"I really do have to go," she said. She started to add the alibi, "It's the union, I've got to write a report," but the lie stuck in her throat, though Abe was already looking back at her, waiting for it. She said loudly, "I'm tired. It's too damn noisy here, and I've got a headache, and I feel like being home by myself. I'll call tomorrow, I told you."

Abe's reply was drowned out by the growing clamor for the band to play a third set. Twelve-Bar Billy called to him, and he moved off through the crowd—walking now, Joanna noticed, with something of Billy's gangly amble. Unreasonably irritated with everything in the world, and equally irritated at her own unreasonableness, she headed for the door, pausing outside to check her makeup and pat her hair. Only when she started down the stony driveway to find her car did she notice Lioness leaning against a tree, hands behind her back and her eyes closed. Her hair, snugged into a heavy bun for the evening's work, was straggling loose down one cheek.

"Well," Joanna said. "Wild times on Commuter Island." Lioness nodded without opening her eyes. Joanna said, "Lioness, are you all right? What's the matter?"

The eyes did open then, too widely, truly seeing her for the first time that evening. They were shining with fear, brilliant with it, beautiful with fear. Lioness said, almost too softly to be heard, "Joanna. Please."

The crack in the low voice brought Joanna close to her, putting her hands on shoulders that felt like a child's. "What?" she said. "Lioness, what? Talk to me." The shoulders twisted, as though to turn away, but Joanna held on, staring into a known face turned finally foreign, suddenly become a stripped and barren land beyond her knowledge. Abruptly, no longer trying to free herself, Lioness pressed close against her, pushing into her arms like a child ferocious with need.

Joanna stroked her hair, crooning wordlessly, while Seriously Blue thundered on in the Skyliner Diner—at moments she could just make out the slyly moaning second harmonica through the din—and patrons coming and going peered curiously at them. Over and over, until she was half-singing it, she murmured the Eliot line that Abe had repeated constantly to her in the emergency room: "All shall be well, and all manner of things shall be well," until Lioness slipped from her, shaking her head until the desert-colored hair came altogether undone, all but hiding her face. She looked to Joanna like the Lioness she and Abe had warmed together one night: a Lioness frozen all the way through and all the way down.

"No," she said. "No, Joanna. What is coming has come again, and nothing ever can be well." Her voice was quite composed, even placid. She turned away from Joanna and walked swiftly toward the restaurant without saying anything further, or ever looking back. Joanna stood still for a moment, calming her own trembling, and then set off to catch the last Seattle ferry.

Marley's one street was lighted only by storefronts, but the summer dusk was as pale and lingering as in most northern climates, and Joanna was glad of the walk, and of the night's odd stillness. She met no one on the way, except for a couple of dog-walkers, nor were there any other foot passengers waiting with her at the terminal. Yet when the ferry glided silently into the slip and she stepped onto the deck, she was bumped from behind by a white-haired man in a remarkably flamboyant red waistcoat. He excused himself with an imperiously quick bow, and vanished below.

Defying seasickness, Joanna remained on deck, savoring the warmth of the evening and watching the gillnet fishermen, permitted to work the Sound on certain Wednesday nights, while the ferry captains looked bitterly out for them. The sky was nearly starless, but in the light of a waxing moon, the boat's wake glittered against the darker waters like a jeweled road back to the receding island, like the diamonds her grandparents and Abe's alike had dreamed of kicking up, walking the streets of the new world. She wondered whether he might still be playing in the Skyliner Diner at that moment. *I should have been more admiring. I knew the right things to say—why couldn't I say them? I was planning to stay over, same as always—new nightie in my bag and everything. Why didn't I stay?*

Abruptly aware that she was hungry, she remembered that she had ordered only a meatloaf sandwich at the diner, and that most of it, swathed in aluminum foil, was yet in her purse. As she fished it out for a cautious nibble, there came a sudden raking of wings against her face, an explosive shriek echoing her own, a dirty yellow flash just missing her eye, and a huge seagull perched on the deck railing, the sandwich in its beak. Joanna caught her breath, staring at the bird with a confused mixture of fear and wild outrage.

"That's mine," she said. The gull's warning squall only angered her further. She repeated, louder, "That's mine, you flying rodent." She began moving slowly toward the railing, and the gull squawked again and lifted its wings.

Behind her, a deep, precise voice said, "He will fly off if you take another step," and she turned her head to see the old man in the red waistcoat. He raised his arms a little, like the seagull's wings, smiling at her with small white teeth. "Back," he said. "Back away, and I will get your dinner for you."

Joanna backed carefully toward him as he in turn moved slowly forward, now holding one hand out to the watching gull. He addressed it in unaccented English, alien only in its formal clarity. "Brother, what you hold does not belong to you. You have strong wings, you can hunt and fish for your own meals—we can only pay others to hunt for us, and even to prepare the catch so that we can eat. It is unworthy, it shames you, to steal from such creatures as ourselves."

To Joanna's amazement, the gull stayed where it was, cocking its head like an inquisitive parrot and lowering its wings. When the man in the red waistcoat reached for the stolen sandwich, it dropped the foil package into his hands without the slightest protest. The man said, "Thank you, my brother. Go now, with my blessing."

The gull made a strange sound—for all the world like a croaky coo, Joanna thought—then flapped off the railing, gone into darkness within two wingbeats. The man in the red waistcoat turned to face her, holding out the sandwich.

"Seagulls are never sated," he said, "never satisfied. They would always rather have what anyone else has than anything they might catch alone." He was older and taller than Joanna had understood when he passed her on boarding the ferry—how much older, she could not be certain. His lean, lined face was distinctly pale; but it was a healthy pallor, she decided, somewhere between snow and stone. The white hair was thick, the eyes a lively striking blue that was almost black, the carriage would have been military but for its grace, and the waistcoat (and its matching red handkerchief) actually went quite well with the slightly worn tweeds, the perfectly polished shoes—*are those actually spats?*—and the expertly tied and plumped-out gray cravat. She took the meatloaf sandwich, thinking, *I ought to curtsy or something. The way Miss Finley taught us in the third grade.*

"Thank you," she said. "Look, he didn't even tear the foil."

The old man smiled at her again, inclining his head slightly. It wasn't a proper bow, but the smile was real. He said, "I am good with animals. Not so good with growing things, alas." The "alas" sounded real, too, as though he were accustomed to using such words, and suited the warm, woody texture of his voice. "My name is Mardikian."

"Last or first?" She felt absurdly playful, almost lightheaded, and could not say why. The old man bowed again, more deeply this time, and straightened. "Mr. Mardikian will do well enough. And am I entitled now to your name?"

"Delvecchio," she answered. "Either way." *Those are spats. I swear to God, those really are spats.*

In the moonlight he followed her glance as swiftly as the seagull had homed in on her sandwich. "You are looking at my shoes. Are they out of fashion? I'm afraid I don't get by here very often, but I do like to keep current. Tell me, please, and do not be afraid of hurting my feelings. I have none."

He said it so calmly and flatly that Joanna took it as a mild pleasantry from another time. Treating it as such, she said, "I believe that, or you wouldn't be wearing those things. They haven't been in fashion since—I don't know—Agatha Christie? The weskit, okay—on you, it looks pretty good—but the spats go. Trust me."

Without a word, Mr. Mardikian bent to his shoes in a single fluid motion, unbuttoned the spats and tossed them over the side, where they vanished like the gull. "I have no attachment to possessions," he said. "As your folk put it, I travel light." He frowned questioningly then. "Lightly?"

"My folk?" she asked, still feeling like laughing, for no reason. "So where are you from?"

"Oh, from very far away," Mr. Mardikian replied. "A very far country, farther than the Antipodes, Hyperborea, or the Grey-Amber Island. Farther than Huy-Braseal, even." The words, in his woodwind voice, made Joanna shiver slightly, and recall old maps and bad movies. Mr. Mardikian spent no further time on his origins: on the empty deck he spread his arms wide to Puget Sound and looming Seattle, spinning himself in the moonlight, like a child, to face her again. "Yet at this moment there's nowhere I would choose to be but here—here in this night, on this splendid ship, chatting with this strange young woman whose name is the same both coming and going." He beamed innocently at Joanna. "Now I myself am exactly like your name, for I've spent all today back and forth between land and island for pure pleasure, never stepping ashore either place. Delightful day—most delightful I've spent in . . . oh, who's there could ever know? Not I, surely." For a single moment the handsome old face turned somber and shadowy.

Beneath their feet the boat's horn moaned, not for arrival, but as a warning to a stubborn gillnetter. Joanna took a bite out of her Skyliner meatloaf and offered the sandwich to Mr. Mardikian, but he declined wordlessly. She said, "You mean you've been on the ferry all day and not gotten off once? I didn't think they let you do that." Mr. Mardikian winked at her. Joanna asked, "But why would you do that? What would be the point?"

"Ah," Mr. Mardikian said. "Yes, the point. Truthfully, there is no point, my dear Delvecchio. There will be one, as there must be—tomorrow, the next day—but just today . . . just today, you find me happily pointless, drifting between destinies, as we pointless folk do, never alighting anywhere, never settling, never choosing. Only savoring, savoring." He rolled the last word out with such deliberate languor that Joanna seemed to taste it herself, and she laughed with him. Yet she was close enough to see something in his eyes—themselves the color of the twilight—that she read as regret, and she said impulsively, "Would you allow me to buy you a way-too-salty cup of clam chowder? I certainly owe you that much, and we should have just enough time."

Mr. Mardikian considered the proposal, stroking his chin. Two family groups came chattering up on deck together, just behind them. Joanna and the old man stepped aside to let them crowd to the railing and hoist the smaller children up to view the Seattle skyline. The wind had turned colder, making Joanna turn up her sweater collar, but Mr. Mardikian seemed not to notice this at all.

"Clam chowder," he announced, as serious as though they had been debating a state treaty. "A fine thing, Delvecchio." She had been certain that he would bow once more and offer his arm, but instead Mr. Mardikian held out his left hand to her, in a move somewhere between the invitation of a lover and the challenge of a fencer. His palm felt light and dry as a dead leaf against her own, but the fingers were surprisingly strong.

As they started below, she said, "What the hell, my first name's Joanna."

# 9.

# JUNE

"Lacey."

"Lacey who? Sounds like a country singer."

"Lacey the town. Right near Olympia, come on."

"Oh. That Lacey." Abe smacked his forehead dramatically. "Sorry. I'd plead incipient Alzheimer's, except I've always been like that. Okay, not Lacey who. Lacey when?"

"Lacey next Thursday, Friday, and Saturday. Club called the Wretched Pitiful Dump." Twelve-Bar Billy grinned at him, lifting his glass. "Swear to God."

"Really? Some hope for humanity, anyway." They were in Abe's kitchen, sampling his newest try at a Belgian-style ale. "But I can't make Thursday or Friday, I'm sorry. Saturday, okay."

Twelve-Bar Billy was clearly distressed. "Say what? What's Thursday and Friday?"

"Thursday, Del and I have an actual dinner date with actual old friends. Hers, not mine, but what the hell. Friday, I've got a meeting in Tacoma with a couple of other historians. We're all working the same side of the street—late medieval, John Ball, Wat Tyler, Jack Cade, Richard II, like that—and we want to sort of check and make sure we're not writing each other's books. There's an editor from one of the university presses—he might be there too. I'm really sorry."

Billy slapped the table in unfeigned outrage. "And that shit's more important than making the gig? Hey, you're part of a band, daddy. Nothing's more important than making the gig. Musician's first law."

"I'm not a musician," Abe said. "And I'm not part of a band, though it's a sweet thought, and I thank you. I'm a geezer who sits home and sits in, once in a while. When he can. That's how it is, Billy." He poured fresh glasses of the ale—which had turned out startlingly better than he had expected—and regarded the cowboy speculatively. "By the way, do we know each other well enough now for you to tell me your real name, and where you're actually from? And never mind being born on your father's ranch in New Mexico. I've been to New Mexico."

Billy looked back at him, neither protesting nor responding, for a long time. The afternoon sun had passed momentarily behind a cloud, making his blue eyes appear almost black. He said finally, "East Stroudsburg, Pennsylvania. Bernard. Bernard Joseph Miljanich. You tell, you die."

"I'll die old and silent," Abe assured him. "What do you think of the ale?"

Billy shrugged amiably. "Got me buzzed in one. Can't ask more than that from a beer." The blue eyes narrowed as he leaned forward. "But what you're asking from your life, that's something else. You want to go on playing retired geezer, writing books, and brewing beer—hey, that's cool, but you're a fucking musician, and we both know it. I knew it before you blew a damn note. And I'll tell you something else, daddy—uh-uh, you don't ever get to sit in with me and my band. Amateurs, dilettantes—never think I know words like that, do you?—wannabes with a little talent, I let them in, not you. You, you make every gig, or forget it. That's how that is." He emptied his glass in one gulp and glared at Abe.

"My," Abe said thoughtfully. "My goodness." From the kitchen window, he could see Alli and Jesse Yandell squabbling about something, while Turk the hound looked on, occasionally barking anxiously. Abe said, "Look, I could maybe juggle Thursday. Friday I don't know about." Twelve-Bar Billy did not reply. Abe got up to put bottles in the recyclables bin and scoop newspapers off the floor, never looking at Billy. "Maybe I can work something out for Friday. I'll have to call you."

"You do that, daddy."


The copilot never filed a complaint, as Joanna had feared. He returned to treating her with his habitual affable disdain; and whatever he revealed of their hotel encounter to the rest of her crew, she could detect no change in their attitudes toward her. They still called her Mom, still asked her—late on the red-eyes— for a crone's wisdom regarding men, cooking, and herpes, and still said, "She's such an old sweetie" when they thought she was out of earshot. Heather, the youngest, began doing her hair rather in Joanna's style, but stopped when the others teased her.

The one complaint any of the crew made concerning Joanna had to do with her growing insistence on things being done the same way at the same time, on the ground or in the air. Absolute continuity, which she had scorned since childhood, now became almost desperately necessary to her as she sensed herself being dragged away from it—or it from her. Gradually she began, having always been slightly superstitious, to develop her own private observances to conjure constancy: all crewmembers, herself included, had to sign in for every flight exactly an hour and a half before departure, and she came to demand two passenger counts before takeoff, instead of the usual one. The final cabin walk-through had to be performed before the showing of the safety video—never after— and it always had to be little Grace, who monitored the available space in the overhead bins. Snugged with the others into her jumpseat as the plane picked up speed on the runway, she was perfectly aware of the foolishness of imagining them all protected simply because she had made sure that everyone took the same seat every time; but the sense of security was quite real for all of that, and honestly comforting. Yet as soon as she walked away from the plane, in Seattle or Chicago, the soft, sliding, shapeless, absurd alarm came sluicing over her, slyly stronger each time. She slept increasingly poorly, alone or with Abe, and drinking was no help.

Once she tried talking about it with Tamara, her unofficial lieu- tenant on the flight crew. Tamara was in her midthirties: black and slim, cool and controlled, and terminally exquisite—the sight of her always made Joanna feel like a walking landfill. She said briskly, "Half my friends are having panic attacks. The way I see it, if you're not panicking, you're not paying attention."

Joanna shook her head vigorously. "I just get nervous sometimes. That is not panic."

"You're nervous all the time," Tamara answered. "I work with you. Everybody's starting to notice."

"Oh, that's great," Joanna said in despair. "That's just really great. Everybody? Kyle?"

Tamara laughed. "Kyle wouldn't notice if we were being hijacked to Uzbekistan. No, I'm the only one you have to worry about so far. Listen, I can get you Prozac, Zoloft, all that stuff, all you want, no questions asked. I know more damn psychiatrists. Probably tells you something."

"I don't think it's a pill I need—" Joanna began.

"Honey, these aren't pills. These aren't tranquilizers, not the Mother's little helpers you probably remember from the Stoned

Age. Think of them as Therapy In A Box—Serotonins 'R' Us. What they do, they help regulate all that stuff the brain naturally produces—enzymes, endorphins, whatever—they just put things back in balance, that's all. So you can think straight. I'm on Zoloft, myself—every sister ought to be. Especially my mother."

"Tamara," Joanna said. "Did you ever go to the beach and stand right at the edge when a wave was coming in? Right at the edge of the land?" Tamara nodded, puzzled but attentive. Joanna said, "The wave breaks right at your feet, and the water rushes back into the ocean, and you can actually feel it sucking the world right out from under you. Surfers must feel like that—like going a million miles an hour, only backward. Do you understand what I'm saying?"

"I was raised in Santa Barbara," Tamara said.

Joanna patted her perfectly-manicured hand. "Well, that's the way I'm feeling a lot these days. Not a problem, really—I just don't think they have enzymes for that."

Tamara regarded her with something more than her usual offhand composure. "Premonitions? I had an aunt like that. We used to say she could smell disaster a mile and a month away. Never a good premonition, not one time. She said there wasn't any such thing."

"I don't know what this is," Joanna said wearily. "Premonition, intuition, good, bad—let it go. I'll try not to be so nervous, that's all."

Tamara checked her makeup, clucked her tongue in serious dismay, and headed for the nearest lavatory. Over her shoulder she said, "Tell you one thing I do know. Nothing in life's ever as bad as you thought it was going to be. Or as good. It'll work out."

The Gardner Island weather remained mild and springlike, unaffected by the turning of the planet. Lily was, to her own astonishment, made personal assistant to the program director at her radio station. Abe continued performing regularly as Seriously

Blue's rhythm harmonica in restaurants, small clubs, and high-school gyms in towns like La Conner and Darrington. Joanna began to take informal kayaking lessons off Ballard from a taciturn New Zealand woman older than herself. She did not mention these to Abe—even when they cut notably into the Gardner weekends—though she did describe odd Mr. Mardikian at some length, to make him laugh. She met the old man often on the ferry now, journeying merrily back and forth as routinely as she flew her Chicago run twice a week. "But I've never seen him get off, either side. I mean, he must, obviously, sometime or other—I've just never seen it."

"Maybe he lives on the ferry," Abe mumbled from the depths of the fourteenth century. "Maybe he's the Flying Armenian."

Joanna started to laugh, and then didn't. "That's almost not funny. Nothing about him makes any sense—nothing connects with anything else. He wears the same clothes all the time—the same, right down to his socks—but they're always spotless, absolutely immaculate, he could be modeling them. And he never eats or drinks on the ferry, I'm sure he doesn't. The clam chowder, the coffee, the hot chocolate, they're all gone by the time we dock—but Abe, I swear he never swallows a mouthful. I don't know how he works it, but I'd swear."

"Could be a stage magician, keeping in practice. Or a vampire. You notice if he casts a shadow?"

"Oh, stop it," she said, cuffing the back of his neck lightly. "Yes, he's got a shadow, and no, he's not afraid of sunlight or crosses— and if the ferry cafeteria ever used garlic in anything, I don't see him giving a damn." She sighed and flopped down on the ancient workroom settee, where she sometimes napped while he worked. "Nothing connects."

Abe had stopped writing, and was looking at her with his first real attention of the conversation. "It does give one to think.

Whom else do we know who doesn't exactly connect with much of anything?" Joanna stared back at him without speaking. Abe said, "Whom else do we know who doesn't quite seem to belong?"

"That doesn't mean a thing." Joanna found herself becoming curiously defensive, and even angry. "That's not evidence, that's not proof of—that's nothing! Just because he's a little strange, and she's—"

"Just Lioness." Abe put up both hands, palms out. "Forget I said anything. You need me, I'll be in 1379."

But after he had gone virtuously back to work, Joanna lay curled on the old couch, unable to fall all the way asleep. She did almost dream of Mr. Mardikian, who was almost stepping ashore, but not quite.

Lioness Lazos continued working at the Skyliner Diner, living in Abe's garage, and magically managing neither to encourage nor to dishonor Lily's adoration. But nothing about her had been quite the same since the night Seriously Blue played the Diner. The graciously removed air that had been so present that rackety night never really left again: she stayed more and more to herself when she was home, climbing the slope to Abe's house only to bathe or use the toilet, never simply to visit. Abe, who had grown accustomed to seeing her coming and going, whether in the garden, on the little beachfront, or skidding brakeless down the driveway on the old green bicycle, admitted to Joanna—under severe duress—that yes, if you looked at it one way, this could be said to count like missing somebody. And Joanna was pleased to hear it, and said so. "Humanizes you. I've never been sure you actually missed anyone in the world. Including me."

"Of course I miss you," he growled. "I like missing you—you always come back before it gets annoying. This is different, this is missing a person who's actually here. Senseless, pointless, gives me the fidgets. Silly, feeling like this." One undernourished buttock perched on his worktable, he scratched fiercely at his beard and glowered at Joanna.

"She's scared," Joanna said quietly. "I don't know what she's scared of, but it's nothing we ever imagined." She moved closer and leaned into his arms, taking comfort in the familiar sleepy smell of his skin. She said, "If I had to guess, I'd say she was trying to keep us clear of whatever she's mixed up in. So we don't become the well-known innocent bystanders."

"'Mixed up in.'" Abe grinned crookedly, shaking his head. "Nothing mixed-up about Lioness, cookie. *Up to* is more like it." He rubbed Joanna's shoulders gently, feeling her sudden silent wistfulness against him. He said, "Nothing we can do, I know that much. She wants help, she'll ask for it." Unconsciously, from old, affectionate habit, he ran a finger up and down around the rim of her right ear. "And we'll help her."

"Quit, that tickles," she said; and then, "Abe? Could we have her here for your birthday next week? While this weather lasts? I mean, not just her—we could have Lily too, and anybody else, really, anyone you want. Your band, all of them. Ev and Janice and their kids. We could do a cookout, a barbecue."

The snarl, "Barbecues—the ultimate goyish sacrificial rite," was promptly countered by, "Well, you always like them once we're having them, every time. You don't like thinking about them, that's all. Please, Abe." The last unplanned words startled him and alarmed her: she asked favors very rarely, and never begged for anything. But she did not retreat from her desire, nor mock the need she could not understand. She said only, "It'll be a good birthday. I promise."

"Just no damn presents," Abe grunted; and then, "The concept of the barbecue as we know it may not be ready for Seriously Blue. I'm just warning you."

In fact, the band behaved remarkably well, considering that one of its members was not only blind but alcoholic, and another two demonstrably certifiable. They ate whatever was set before them (the blind guitarist had a tendency to grab things off the grill, the fierce girl drummer off other people's paper plates), and expressed proper appreciation of Abe's beer-flavored barbecue sauce. There were no birthday presents as such, but Twelve-Bar Billy saw to it that each musician brought along at least one bottle, even if most of them had no labels. He also made the lead guitarist leave his eight-inch bowie knife in the van's locked glove compartment. Janice Yandell had some minor difficulty with the bass player, who took a determined fancy to her; but Billy led him down the stairs to the beach, to discuss arrangements, and brought him back in a bit, pale and overly apologetic. Otherwise, the barbecue went without incident.

Lioness, to Joanna's surprise, not only accepted the invitation without any coaxing or cozening, but went conspicuously out of her way to set Abe's guests at ease with one another. She treated Jesse and Alli Yandell as though they shared a deep old secret, and the Seriously Blue's drummer like a refound sister, instead of an angry orphan possessed by merciless rhythm. Joanna looked up from coals and kebabs at one point (Abe having no image of himself as any aproned, swaggering Grillmeister) to observe the lead guitarist tearfully explaining to Lioness that he only hated Twelve-Bar Billy because of the latter's maddening habit of stepping on his solos. Lioness soothed him, assuring him that Billy had matured remarkably in the course of the afternoon, and would never again interfere with his self-expression. She was also seen sitting beside the rhythm man, petting his dog, and listening as he explained to her about hearing Rasputin's voice in the night. She ate nothing herself, but appeared to be enjoying Abe's Belgian ale.

Lily arrived late and alone. She greeted her mother absently, and then drifted off to chat cautiously with Twelve-Bar Billy, who had flirted with her assiduously the one time she came to a Seriously Blue performance. ("So you're a butch dyke truckdriver lady, sugar? Well, I think that's just great, I think that's the only thing for a sensitive-type woman to be these days. I swear, I'd be one of those myself, if I were a lady.") Anyone else would have retired in disorder, badly in need of a kidney transplant, but Billy got away with things.

She made a pronounced point of not noticing Lioness's presence at all: Joanna, watching intently, noticed no haunted glances, nor even one choked-back greeting when they passed near each other. When Lily eventually wandered back to the grill, Joanna moved impulsively to put an arm around her shoulders. Lily slipped it, saying angrily, "Don't, I'm all right. And if I'm not all right, it's not her fault. I am too damn old for this."

Melting and helpless, Joanna said, "No, you're not. You're my lovely, lovely eight-year-old in the red sweater and your favorite bib overalls, and someone hurt your feelings on the playground, and you won't ever tell me what happened, and you won't cry, and you will *not* cry." But Lily was, fortunately, not listening: she was staring away at a tall woman who had just come around the corner of the house. Rather, she was staring at Lioness, who, on seeing the woman, had uttered a small cry that might have been of numb terror or equally paralyzing joy. It was that sound that made Joanna recognize the woman who had asked about antique maps in the Pike Place Market.

"If this were a movie—" Joanna never remembered whether she had actually spoken aloud—"we'd go into slow-motion right here." Indeed, as Lioness and the stranger walked toward each other, it did feel as though all other living action had been muted, the color abruptly wrung out of the moment, so that everything Joanna could see, except for those two figures, looked used and pallid. *We could all be ghosts, and we wouldn't even know.*

Both faces were still; both bodies moved with a kind of floating wariness, each seemingly ready to bolt at some mysterious signal no one else could hear. Then Lioness's face blossomed into a look that Joanna had never seen before on any face, and she sprinted the last few yards into the strange woman's arms. And color came back into the world.

They were close enough that Joanna and Lily could hear them talking, but the language was Greek, which Joanna recognized, but could not follow. What she could understand was that Lioness was positively chattering, as Joanna had never known her to do, while the other woman was speaking more deliberately, her voice low and level, with a curious quality that made Joanna think of sun-warmed stone. Beside her, Lily—too stunned for jealousy—was watching a wondrously new Lioness leaning back with the laughing confidence of a child against the arms that supported her. This time, when Joanna silently laid her own arm across her shoulders, Lily never noticed it.

Reunion past—for reunion it certainly was—the tone of the conversation just as obviously changed. The woman appeared to be admonishing Lioness in some way, holding her wrists and peering intensely into her face as she repeated the same two or three phrases over and over. The key to the context, for Joanna, was Lioness's astonishingly familiar reaction: she shut her eyes and shook her head fiercely, not merely saying no, but totally denying the possibility of ever saying yes to this person ever again.

The tall woman never raised her softly rough voice, nor tightened her grip, but Joanna could feel her growing agitation where she stood. Lioness suddenly pulled her arms free, crying what was plainly a refusal loudly enough that even Turk the hound looked up from trying to inveigle the rhythm guitar's guide dog to come and bark at fish with him. She began to turn away, but the woman spoke sharply for the first time—a single word—and Lioness stopped very still, stopped between one breath and the next, with one foot barely on the ground. The woman said the word again.

Lioness said clearly, "No." But it was a fragile denial, unraveling in her throat, just as her headshake was no challenge, but a raw shiver. The tall woman came to her, trying to embrace her again, making to stroke the desert-colored hair, but Lioness, now only whispering defiance, would not be touched.

Until Joanna smelled burning meat, she had completely forgotten the barbecue. When she whirled to it, she saw her guests still gaping in continuing slow-motion silence at the incomprehensible drama or farce taking place before them. She scraped furiously at the smoking grill, hearing Abe's dry murmur, "Could use a few subtitles around here." Then Twelve-Bar Billy was snapping orders to the band—Abe included—rounding them up like a border collie, and the tall woman was no longer commanding Lioness but pleading with her, unmistakably frantic to have her away from there. When she took hold of her shoulders again and began trying to haul her along by main force, Lioness easily broke free, gripping a wrist in her turn, and dragging the woman directly up to Lily and Joanna. Her voice was almost a whisper, but she was smiling with a shaky serenity.

"This is my mother," she said to them. "I thought you would want to meet her."

The tall woman no longer struggled, but stood silently before them, avoiding their gaze with what seemed an indifference beyond arrogance. Only when Joanna replied haltingly, "Yes, of course, we're so delighted," did the woman bother to look straight at her. The wide-set gray-green eyes, infinitely uninterested in her own, held them fast nonetheless: not by any liquidly sentimental appeal, but with a presence that hurt her so fast and so shockingly that she gasped aloud, and tried to turn away, and could not. Somewhere she heard Lily make the same sound.

For an instant, the woman's face—rounder than Lioness's face, but twinned in the bones, and in the dusty-golden skin—seemed to Joanna at once to be growing brighter and yet more distant: receding while the eyes came to fill all her sight, taking in the house, the barbecue, the hillside and everyone on it, the Sound beyond, Seattle beyond that, and the wide wild rolling and turning beyond and below, far beyond her understanding; and somehow including Abe's miraculous *Schwarzbier* as well, and Lily's Wallingford two-rooms-and-kitchen, with the cluttered futon mattress on the bedroom floor. Still standing by the grill, still attempting mother-to-mother conversation, Joanna felt herself swept off like a toy in the hand of a child, being zoomed and stooped over whatever caught an infant's interest, with no pattern or reason except greedy play. Only stubbornness kept her from doubling over then, sick with vision; and nothing but seriously idiotic pride made her ask politely, "Would you like some chicken? I'm afraid we're out of hamburgers."

Twelve-Bar Billy whooped, "Brace yourselves now!" exactly at that moment, and Seriously Blue roared into "Old Riley," playing as though they were on the deck of the *Titanic*. They were loud enough that Joanna almost missed the tall woman's equally courteous reply, in the deep, almost-guttural voice she remembered, "You need not fear me. My daughter speaks well of you." She paused, and the voice was barely audible when she added, "My foolish daughter."

"And for just that moment," she said to Abe that night, "we actually were mom and mom, that second time she really looked at me. Abe, the way she said it, my heart just turned over, you know? *'My foolish daughter'* . . . I'll never forget that, the way she said it. The sound."

"Mrs. Cleaver and Mrs. Brady," Abe grunted. "The mind reels."

"And then she just walked away. Back around the house, the way she came. I don't know if she had a car, or a ride, or what."

"Maybe she had dragons. Flew off in a dragon chariot, like Medea. Thank you for my birthday, cookie." He fell asleep abruptly then, and Joanna lay beside him in the island night, listening to the tide and recalling how Lioness had stood motionless, staring silently after her mother, with "Old Riley" blasting away all around her, the blind rhythm guitarist squalling and snarling the vocal.

> "Riley walked the Brazos,
> old Riley walked the water like Jesus . . ."

The memory brought her more fully awake, and she saw the Primavera face made plain by despair, and felt the tall woman's eyes snatching up her soul to show her something she did not want to understand. "Revelations are wasted on me," she said aloud to the darkness. "Wasted." Then she nudged Abe awake and asked him, "Hades is a place, isn't it?"

"Jesus Christ," he said. "What?"

"Hades. That's like the afterlife, right? She mentioned it a couple of times."

"Christ," Abe said again. "You know I hate being waked up. What about Hades?"

"When they were talking. It's the only Greek word I know, except moussaka and dolmas, but I'm sure I heard it anyway twice. And it scared her. Why would it scare her?"

"For that you woke me." Abe turned over. "It's an afterlife, it's the Underworld. The big heroes, the demigods, they go to the Elysian Fields, but most people sit it out in Hades. It's not hell, it's just mostly sad and damp and dull. Saturday night in Seattle."

"Oh. Well." Joanna sighed, shrugged, and finally curled herself around him, head on a bony shoulder, feet entwined with his perpetually cold feet. She was almost asleep herself when he mumbled, "Not just a place. Hades. A person." And no amount of nudging or shaking would get any more out of him that night.

# 10.

# AUGUST

They never saw Lioness's mother again, though Abe was quite certain that he once glimpsed her buying flowers in the Market. Joanna dreamed of the tall woman several times; indeed, within a very few days of the barbecue the whole encounter had become curiously dreamlike for her, fading into monochrome, its outline a fact without flavor or detail. Even the woman's eyes—and Joanna could not have imagined ever forgetting the swooping rush of their grip on her spirit—were grown in less than a week as distant and miniature as the glass buttons of a long-gone teddy bear.

For his part, Abe was alternately dismissive ("I was blowing with the band, I wasn't noticing anything but Zack being off the chord half the time") and thoughtful, suggesting diplomatically that Joanna might have been briefly overmastered by an undeniably powerful personality, seeing exactly—and only—what she was shown. "It's a form of practical mass hypnosis—you ask, I'll bet everyone else saw just what you did. Bayla, my first, she did it all the time. A remarkable woman." Joanna would have liked very much to believe him.

Neither of them expected ever to learn anything from Lioness about the incident at the barbecue; but when Abe, whom she was helping to lug a garbage can up the long driveway for the Wednesday truck, asked what she and her mother had been so obviously arguing about, the answer came calmly, "My husband." Abe almost dropped his side of the can, and Lioness laughed wryly. "I don't want to see him, and she thinks I should. No more to it than that. Mother can be very theatrical."

"I didn't know," he said. "Lily thought you might be married, but Del and I . . ." He shrugged, for lack of a dramatic gesture of his own. "We figured, if you thought it was our business you'd tell us. As long as he's not likely to maybe bomb the garage, or drop by with a shotgun." Lioness's face did not change. Abe said, "So where is he?"

"Somewhere," Lioness said. "Somewhere near. She would have taken me to him right then."

"But you weren't about to go. I got that much, anyway." They reached the top of the drive and set the garbage can down on the roadside together. Lioness turned away, but Abe said, "Look, we can help," and she halted. He said, "Lioness, if you don't want to see the guy, no one can make you do it. Injunctions, restraining orders, harassment laws—even I know a few things, and Del knows all that stuff, believe me. Stay cool—don't panic, or run off again, or anything. We can do something."

Lioness's response was unsettlingly quick and sharp. "Run off again? What do you mean?"

Caught off-balance, he gambled on impulse. "Well, you've done it once, so maybe more than once?" Lioness did not answer. "It's no good, you can't keep running. It's never any good. He always finds you, doesn't he?"

Her reaction surprised him even further; he had expected either silence or anger, but instead she said quietly, "Dear Abe," and touched his hand. She smelled the way she always smelled, of young grass and of nameless wildflowers. She said, "Abe, you have been so kind, you and Joanna, you have been better friends than I can tell you. But you don't know." He thought she seemed about to say something else; but instead she repeated, "You don't know, and you must not. I will deal with my husband. I have before."

"Well," he said. "If you need us." But she made no reply, and they walked back down the driveway without speaking. As he turned toward the house, Lioness said, "I did like your music. I wish I could hear it again."

"Say the word, and we'll play a command performance. I have some small influence." He patted her shoulder, savored her quick laugh, and watched her move away, bending to pull a few weeds in Joanna's garden before she went on to the garage. Returning to work, he slashed out entire paragraphs without bothering to prowl the ruins for salvageable sentences, and leaned often on his elbow to scratch his bald spot and brood over the notion of Lioness having a husband. He drank more of his own beer than he meant to that afternoon, and put most of the paragraphs back in.

Joanna's kayaking instructor abruptly broke her habitual silence one afternoon to say, "Time y'got down to it, girl." Joanna, seated in the bow, craned her neck to stare back at her. "Solo flight. While the weather holds."

The sweat on Joanna's back and shoulders turned instantly icy. She stammered, "I can't, I couldn't. I'm not ready."

"Ready as y're going to be," the New Zealander said. "Main thing's to wear a good hat and put sunblock on your lips. Last thing y'ever want, sunburnt lips." She relented slightly in the face of Joanna's incipient panic. "Look, y've learned everything I know to teach you. The rest of it y'll be teaching yourself—the water'll teach y', wind'll teach y'. Only way. Y'll be all right."

She said nothing further as they paddled back to shore; but

when they were stacking the kayak with the others on the dock, she advised Joanna gruffly, "Nothing drastic, not for the maiden voyage—not the San Juans or anything. What y'want, first time out, y'want something like the run over to Blake Island. Rent on Lake Union, launch at Alki Point, make an overnight of it, eat some salmon with the Indians. Y're up to that, easy-peasy." She tapped Joanna's fist with her own, added—firmly but obscurely—"Towels," and sauntered competently off down the dock. Joanna looked after her, forlorn as a child on the first day of school, watching her mother drive away.

She continued to meet Mr. Mardikian on the ferry, whether she caught the earliest boat at four in the morning or the last, just past midnight, but she never saw him disembark at either end. Jaunty as a cricket, effortlessly elegant as a Continental diplomat, he strolled the windy deck arm in arm with her, viewing the Sound as possessively as a gardener admiring his own new-turned black earth, yet somehow forever managing to slip out of sight moments before the first blast of the warning horn. Even when she offered him a ride to his destination, in Seattle or on the island, Mr. Mardikian still eluded her every time, always providing a perfectly acceptable reason for delaying or disappearing. "I am being met," he would tell her; or, often, "No, I prefer to walk, thank you, Delvecchio. Where I live, such enjoyments are most rare."

Once, watching streetlights and storefront lights going out as the dawn city neared, she heard him say softly, "Deceived, oh, deceived," and then something in another language. The words were clearly not meant for her, but there was such sorrow in them, such unparalleled regret—no feelings, right—that she held his arm tightly, causing him to smile down at her from what seemed a very long journey away. But he did not speak again.

Early autumn—though on the island it continued to feel stubbornly and absurdly like ripening spring—was invariably a busy period for her, between union meetings, training sessions for novice crews, and her regular flight schedule. She saw Abe infrequently at that time of year; it was purely a mischievous impulse that brought her to the island one afternoon, meaning to surprise him on his return from a research expedition to the university library. But she was the one to be stunned speechless when he walked in with Mr. Mardikian, both of them laughing immoderately at Abe's favorite fourteenth-century dirty joke. Mr. Mardikian was wearing, instead of his usual Edwardian tweeds, a leather golf cap, a blue polo shirt with a tiny brown bear embroidered over the heart, and a pair of perfectly creased blue jeans. He looked as though he truly belonged on Gardner Island, and Joanna found that completely unnerving.

On seeing her, Mr. Mardikian grinned joyously, slapping Abe's shoulder to announce, "Delvecchio, behold what I have found!" To all intents, he might have been the one returning home after long absence. "He was wandering the ferry, looking most forlorn, so I brought him home to you. Did I do well?"

Abe was managing to look at once embarrassed and slyly proud of himself. He said, "I figured he had to be the guy you've been talking about all this time. We were having a nice argument about Paracelsus, and I thought, now there's a man who'd appreciate a little real Russian stout. Only you said he never gets off the ferry, and here he trotted right along with me, no questions asked. So." He spread his hands and headed for the beer cellar, leaving Joanna and Mr. Mardikian alone.

"Well," Joanna said. "Isn't that something?" She felt shy, almost wary of the old man, as she had never felt in all their shipboard meetings, while Mr. Mardikian appeared to expand physically to fill the living room with his glowing pleasure in being in it. Joanna said lamely, "You know, you don't have to drink his beer if you don't want to. He won't be offended, really."

Mr. Mardikian's laughter warmed the room even further. "But I love beer! I love everyone's beer, ale, mead, metheglin, uisquebaugh, and I never get to drink any of it, years and years and years, never! This is wonderful for me, Delvecchio. I wish I had the language to tell you how wonderful." He took a step forward and placed his hands lightly on her shoulders. "But I take advantage. I should not have accepted your Abe's invitation. You do not want me here."

"No," she said. "I mean, no, it's not that, I'm glad to see you. It's just strange to see you, you know?" She fancied that Mr. Mardikian's smile somehow crouched like a cat, waiting for her next words. She said, "Because I'm right—you never do get off the ferry, do you?"

"No," Mr. Mardikian said. "No, never, until now. But, Delvecchio, you must understand. I am old and strange—yes, of course I am—and this place is more new for me than you can know. This city, the great water, the island, at first it was all overwhelming—is that what I mean? Too much for an old man, you could say?" His smile had grown more earnestly vulnerable.

"No, I couldn't say that," she answered him. "I don't think you've ever been overwhelmed in your life, and if anything's too much for you, I'd just like to see it, that's all. You're a very, very smart old man, and you've been manipulating me from the get-go, from the seagull and the sandwich. I didn't realize it until I saw you manipulating Abe." Mr. Mardikian continued to smile, but his lips were closer together than they had been. Joanna said, "What is it, what do you want from us? Because you want something."

For an instant, another light than twilight shivered far down in Mr. Mardikian's eyes. Joanna stepped back from it, though it was not menacing, but almost grieving, almost an appeal. Mr. Mardikian began, "Delvecchio, my kind, pretty Delvecchio, whom I like so much, what I want is not from you. It is not in the smallest to do with you, you must believe that, please." But just then Abe returned bearing beer in both hands, and Mr. Mardikian immediately began discussing hops and malt, barley and yeast, and specific gravity with him. Joanna stood watching them for a time, and then went to the kitchen to find crackers and cheese.

What was meant—Abe always insisted—to be no more than a brief between-ferries brewery tour extended itself (or was extended) into the evening, and so, inevitably, into an invitation to dinner at the Skyliner Diner. Mr. Mardikian declined graciously three times, pleading weariness, a rigorous dietary regime, and obligations in Seattle; but Abe had been at both the Russian stout and the *hefeweizen*. "I play there, we'll probably get a professional discount. It's a mortal sin not to exploit a professional discount." Joanna reminded them both of crowds and ferry schedules, but Abe brushed her warnings aside, and Mr. Mardikian at last shrugged and gave in.

They went in two cars, so that Abe could take Mr. Mardikian back to the ferry afterward. The restaurant was close to capacity, and plainly short-staffed, but Lioness was not working, which relieved Joanna for no reason that she could explain to herself. Their usual booth was available after a few minutes' wait, and Corinne herself showed them to it, which made Mr. Mardikian curiously wistful. "Imagine such a thing—to have people know you, recognize you, expect you, even to keep your own special place for you to take your meals. How enviable, to be welcomed." He stared around him with the awe of an immigrant.

Abe seemed gruffly embarrassed. "Mostly they're welcoming the twenty-two ninety-five for the house special. Or the eighteen bucks for the Australian Shiraz." But Mr. Mardikian declined to be disillusioned. Once they were seated he beamed at everyone passing the booth, complimented their harried young waiter on both his efficiency and his goatee, and chatted happily, first with the surly cook in fluent Russian, then in Spanish with Lioness's adoring flamenco guitarist, tuning up for the evening. When Joanna asked him about the conversations, he responded, "Journeys and mistakes, Delvecchio. The little madnesses that brought us each here, now." Both the cook and the guitarist sent wine to their table.

Mr. Mardikian ordered butternut squash soup and a salade Niçoise, while drinking as much red wine as Joanna had ever seen anyone consume and still remain alert and clear-spoken. He continued to address anyone who caught his eye, asking what they thought of the food, whether they were enjoying the evening out with their families and their friends, and—at utterly random moments—what they thought of living so far, and whether they were pleased, frightened, or disappointed to find themselves who they were at this moment. The questions were asked so openly, and with such buoyant curiosity that no one appeared at all startled or offended. A few patrons did plainly suspect that he might be an undercover agent of the county board of health, and stopped at the booth to assure him earnestly that the Skyliner toilets, kitchen, and grease trap were above reproach.

When the guitarist began to play, Mr. Mardikian insisted on switching seats with Joanna, in order to watch more closely, and promptly fell into a near-swooning rapture that would have done credit to a worshipful adolescent at a pop concert. Abe's scorn for dinner flamenco was lost on him: his eyes were wide and young, and Joanna heard him whisper, "Oh, deceived," as he had done on the ferry. She knew enough of the music to know that the guitarist was normally no more than competent; but the old man's passion seemed to have infused itself either into his hands or her ears, and whether or not he truly played any better than he ever had before, Joanna found herself on her feet and cheering with Mr. Mardikian when he finished a showy soleares. Abe stoically devoted his own attention to the house gumbo.

But it was at Abe that the guitarist suddenly pointed, announcing to the diners, "Ladies and gentlemen, I can't resist telling you that we have a local treasure with us tonight, the harmonica star of West Seattle's own Seriously Blue." Here came a slight drizzle of applause, as Abe froze with a speared scallop halfway to his mouth. Mr. Mardikian turned and bowed solemnly to him, clapping himself. Joanna patted Abe's shoulder. He said, clearly, *"Vey'z mir."*

The guitarist went on diffidently, "I know we don't exactly play the same kind of music, and I know it's a lot to ask right in the middle of your dinner—but if you wouldn't mind, maybe we could sort of jam a little bit together? One number?" The tentative applause grew stronger, and Mr. Mardikian chuckled with delight. Abe shook his head, waving his fork in protest, but Joanna murmured, "Come on, you've got two bites left—quit being coy. Get up and strut it for the people."

"I am not being coy!" he growled sideways at her. "I'm trying to eat my damn dinner in peace, okay? That still allowed?"

"Not for stars," Joanna told him, enjoying herself. The guitarist continued to coax Abe forward, urging him more loudly now. "I know you've got a harp or two with you, sir, harmonica players always do. One number—no blues, no flamenco, we'll just improvise something. How about it, sir?"

"Sir," Abe hissed. "Sir, yet." Raising his own voice, he replied, "Sorry, not in the mood. Old guys get cranky when they're eating." He dug back noisily into the gumbo.

Mr. Mardikian said, "I would like to hear you."

He spoke so softly that Joanna, across the table, hardly caught the words, but Abe stopped eating. Mr. Mardikian and he regarded each other, both mobile faces completely without expression, except that Mr. Mardikian's eyes had become all iris, and not blue anymore, but dark as the wind between worlds. Mr. Mardikian repeated, "I would very much like to hear you play." The rich woodwind tones closed Joanna's throat.

Abe put down his fork and stood up. Reaching into his inside coat pocket, he brought out a harmonica and walked toward the guitarist, as slowly as though he were moving in deep water. The applause began to patter uncertainly again, and the guitarist proclaimed, "Folks, we're in luck—I'm in luck. I hope I'm up to it, that's all. Ladies and gentlemen, Mr. Abe Aronson of Seriously Blue!" He flung out a hand to welcome Abe.

Abe did not take it. He said, "Key of A. You're up to that?"

"My best key," the guitarist answered. "What, a standard?"

"You just start," Abe said. "We'll see."

The guitarist grinned, accepting the challenge, and launched into a minor-toned ballad with a sinuous, arching melodic line, like a cat stretching itself in moonlight. Abe plainly did not recognize the tune: he let a full chorus and a half go by before he even lifted the harmonica to his mouth, and the low backup chords could scarcely be heard when he first eased in behind the guitar. Gradually the accompaniment evolved into an angular countermelody, bumpy as a country road, that wandered in and out of the guitar's key as it pleased, sorrowfully mocking, impudently tender. Exactly when the harmony hijacked the lead, the guitar stumbling after down lonesome, unexpected alleyways, no one could have said, least of all Joanna. All she knew was that all time but the music's time went away, taking ferry schedules and words and after-dinner liqueurs with it, and that when she could focus on Mr. Mardikian's face again, she saw that he was crying.

He made no sound. The tears left long tracks on his hard skin, glittering gray, but his mouth never twisted, his teeth never sank into his lower lip to bite back the surging grief. Only the tears: silent, unstoppable, endlessly shaping mountains, gorges, river valleys, deltas, and deserts. He leaned toward Joanna and said—his voice not choked or muffled, but quite clear—"Once. One other played so for me—only one other. I remember. It was long ago." He turned back to the music, still weeping peacefully and helplessly.

Abe and the guitarist played on, themselves as kidnapped and held for strange ransom as any who heard them. Whatever the melody had started out to be, it belonged to them now, and they to it as well, bound to follow as far and deep as it chose to lead them. No one listening moved; the waiters and the two busboys were leaning against the walls, while the cook sat alone on the bench near the entrance where people without reservations waited for tables. He had taken off his apron, and his head rested on his tented fingers. Joanna had begun studying him, slyly and guiltily, wondering for the first time who he was, when Lioness walked into the Skyliner Diner.

Abe saw her first. She was standing near the front counter, taking off her one old coat and chatting with Corinne, who welcomed her in a religious ecstasy of relief. When their eyes met, and she stood on tiptoe to smile and wave, the music broke violently from Abe's hands, raging so far out of key and tone and style that the guitarist literally gasped aloud in horror. Abe never looked at him. Gloriously derailed, the harmonica brayed its mad welcome only long enough for the cowering guitarist to give up completely on anything resembling accompaniment, let alone improvisation, and for Mr. Mardikian to stop crying and wheel toward the door, quicker than Joanna, too quickly, far too quickly for a tearful old man.

He saw Lioness an instant before she saw him. He became very still then, so still after that first fierce turn that Joanna, for the only time in her life, felt the earth spinning under her, under everyone and everything but Mr. Mardikian, whirling through space at eleven hundred miles per hour, as she had been taught in school, and never entirely believed, because wouldn't you feel a whole planet whizzing away like that? She felt it now, strongly enough that she caught hold of the table to brace herself against the terror of the raw, whizzing void, while Mr. Mardikian stood so impossibly still, the one comfortless solidity in a shifting, shapeless, real, too real universe. Then Lioness did see him, and she screamed.

Her scream was completely silent, never rattling a dish or a windowpane. What Joanna heard was a silence of hopeless recognition, and a rage and rebellion beyond hopelessness—all unmistakable in one moment's glimpse of desperate elm-leaf eyes. Then Lioness turned and ran out of the Skyliner Diner, coat and backpack forgotten, tawny hair as crazily chaotic as Abe's music, and her long, flowing body just as utterly out of control. Joanna remembered always how hard she banged into tables on her way to the door.

Mr. Mardikian did not follow her, or even move a step from where he stood. It was Abe who dropped his harmonica and charged after her, a frenzied, mindless rhinoceros, himself crashing blindly against tables and patrons. He would have trampled over Joanna's feet, if Mr. Mardikian hadn't scooped her out of the way. She clung to him for a moment, too bewildered to be frightened, thinking dazedly, *this is what was coming, this is what has come again. If I were flying, I'd know what to do. I wish I were flying.*

The only lights in the parking lot were those from the front window of the restaurant. Abe called aloud, but there was no answer, and it took him some while to distinguish Lioness's crouching figure, huddled almost fetally behind the front wheel of a camper truck. He knelt beside her, saying, "It's all right, it's all right, it's just me," but she cringed away from him, all but scuttling under the truck. He soothed her as best he could manage, repeating over and over, "Lioness, it's Abe, you know me, it's Abe," until at last she looked directly at him. Her eyes were wild, in the truest meaning of the word: unhuman, undomesticated, feral, glowing with defiance. He felt very old, and very different from whoever had been blowing up such wildness himself only a moment ago. He put his hand on her cheek and said, "It's all right, love. It's all right."

She answered him in the slow-sliding language that she had spoken to the stranded orca, and that he no longer thought was ancient Greek. "Lioness, I don't understand. Please tell me what's the matter," but she only stared at him out of her burning, frantic eyes. He gripped her shoulders tightly, wanting somehow to steady her in the world. She hissed with her mouth open, like a cat, and he let go immediately, even before she pulled away. She looked more beautiful than anyone he had ever seen.

On an impulse, he asked, "Is it him? Mr. Mardikian? Lioness? Is it Mardikian you're afraid of?"

Her eyes remained as terrified as ever, but the madness there, and in her body, began to fade. When she spoke again, her voice held the flat, unnerving calmness of exhaustion. She said, "That is not his name."

The words came so low that Abe was already repeating his question when the real answer hit him in the stomach. He whispered, "Jesus Christ. Jesus Christ. That's your husband."

Lioness looked back at him without replying. He wondered momentarily whether he were having a stroke, or a heart attack, for all his flesh and skin felt frozen, except for his face, which was painfully hot. "That's him, your husband," he said. "Tell me."

"He wants me to come back." Lioness's voice gave each word the same empty stress. "He will take me back with him."

"Jesus, Jesus Christ," Abe said. "And I brought him here." He felt, for the first time in a life spent studying the historical aspects of tragedy, like a piece in a board game, a little metal race car or top hat. He said, "But you don't have to. You don't—listen, I'll get you out of here."

"It will not help."

The resigned acceptance angered Abe more than he had thought possible. He shouted at her, there in the parking lot. "Listen to me! He doesn't know that you work here, he doesn't know you live with us. I'll take you home—tomorrow we'll think what to do. We can't think straight now, I'll just get you home."

She did not reply, but in his rescuing frenzy, he might not have noticed if she had. He dragged her, unresisting, to her feet and to his car, bundled her inside, and told her, "Wait, I'll be right back. You wait, okay?" He imagined a nod. "Wait," he said again, and hurried back into the Skyliner Diner. The guitarist and Corinne were standing outside, both asking frantic questions that he was too busy apologizing to answer. Most of the patrons were dazedly finishing their meals and calling for their checks, but Joanna and Mr. Mardikian were still in their booth. Joanna was on her feet, hands braced rigidly on the table, looking toward the door. Mr. Mardikian, appearing perfectly relaxed, was saying something to Joanna, but interrupted himself at Abe's approach to ask earnestly, "Is all well? Your friend is all right?"

"No," Abe said, "she's not." He did not trust himself to look straight at Mr. Mardikian. To Joanna he said, "I'm sorry I flew out of here like that. I'm taking her home."

"What is it? What's the trouble?" Joanna had been prepared to be upset, even angry; off-balance now, she lurched into anxiety. "What's wrong with Lioness?"

"I don't know. Panic attack of some kind. She's out in the parking lot, being sick. I'm just going to take her home."

"The clinic's on the way."

Abe shook his head. "I don't think it's anything like that. Panic, like I said. You'll get him to the ferry?" He tried to keep the italics out of his voice, but Mr. Mardikian turned in the booth to face him, eyebrows fractionally raised above amused twilight eyes. Beer camaraderie vanished with those eyebrows, and Abe knew it. "Put the bill on my tab—I'll come in and pay tomorrow. You can catch the nine-twenty-five, if you step on it." He headed for the door again without waiting for Joanna's nod.

In the car, Lioness at first sat frighteningly doubled-over, head between her knees, as if she really were ill, or about to be. Gradually, though, she brought herself upright, her face bloodless, her body moving as though she had suddenly grown much bulkier. When Abe spoke to her, she did not answer; she did not speak at all until they were nearing his house, when she said suddenly, "Put me out here."

"What?" he said. "What, put you out?"

Lioness's voice was that of a drowned ghost. "He will find me wherever you take me."

"Not alone," he snapped back at her. "The man's going to know you've got people on your side, that he can't just do what he feels like with you. You're going home tonight, tomorrow we'll figure out what we do next. But tonight you are damn well sleeping in your own bed." The absurdity of the statement struck through his bravura and made him laugh aloud. "Sorry," he said. "I saw *Cyrano de Bergerac* when I was really young, and I'm afraid it left tire tracks. Never mind. Here we are."

She looked so frightened still as they slewed down the steep drive that he half-expected to see her leap from the car at any moment, like a movie stuntwoman. But she stayed in her seat, and when he parked next to the woodpile, as always, and helped her out, she leaned against him with more weariness than he thought he had ever felt in a human body. He put an arm around her to guide her toward the garage; but when she fell twice, dragging him with her, he realized that her legs would not hold her up, and there was nothing for him but to carry her the rest of the way. He pushed the garage door open with his foot, stumbled inside, and all but dumped Lioness onto her air mattress. His breath sounded to him like his car trying to start on a winter morning as he groped in the darkness for her one bedside lamp. By the time he found it, he had knocked over two of her mason-jar houseplants, and he spent a guilty few minutes tidying up, while she lay silently watching him, her wide eyes unreadable in the flickering light. When he at last sat down uncomfortably on the very edge of the mattress, he told her, "That bulb's definitely about to go, you should have said. I'll bring you a new one tomorrow."

Her voice was so quiet that he had to bend close. "I will not be here tomorrow."

"Oh, yes, you will," he said, still a wheezing Cyrano. "Lioness, I told you, you can't keep running, it has to stop somewhere. Why not here?" She shook her head and started to answer, but he rushed on. "*Here's* as good as any—you know we'll face him with you, you won't ever have to be alone with him, because you're not alone, I told you. You're with us, we'll take care of you." And then, unplanned, unconceived, irrevocable, he heard the words lunge from him, "I'll take care of you."

Lioness's eyes changed. He had seen them do so once before, when she spoke of her fear of being cold, on the night when Joanna and he had first met her. Now they became, not distant, but so achingly focused on him that he felt himself lost among the elm leaves, himself the one far away, utterly embrangled in alienness. She said softly, "Take care of me?"

His face blazed up as painfully as any adolescent boy's shy, shamed, pitted face. "I didn't mean it like that," he mumbled. "You know what I meant." He reached for an instant to pat her hand, and then jerked his own hand back, blushing even more hotly. He said, "Look, we'll talk about it in the morning. You get some rest, okay? And you don't go anywhere, got that? Okay?"

He made to rise—an awkward matter from the scrawny mattress—but she reached out to him in her turn, and he froze where he stood, half-crouched, a cramped back muscle beginning to bite. Lioness said, very clearly, "Take care of me." This time it was not a question.

"I will. We will. That's what I was saying." He was babbling now, or so he sounded to his own ears. "You're covered, absolutely. No worries. We've got your back, Del and me. You sleep, come up for breakfast—believe me, we'll deal with your Mardikian. Sleep."

"Abe." She opened her arms only a little way: the gesture could have been, and well might have been, and definitely should have been, many other things than a summoning. But she said his name again, and he found himself kneeling by the air mattress with sweat running into his eyes. He said in a crumbling voice, "I am sixty-six years old."

"Take care of me," she said once more. She took his face between her hands, and he knew for the first time that he really was going to die, and he didn't care. He said that he would take care of her, yes, always, but no sound came out of his mouth. Lioness drew him down.

He had no memory of struggling out of his clothes, nor of unzipping the sleeping bag. He did remember thinking, *I have no right to see this, no right*; and in after years he never begrudged the fact that he could not quite call up that first image of her sitting up, laughing, as she tossed the green dress across the room. That seemed somehow proper to him; as though human eyes, which could look coldly upon any amount of horror, could only endure just so much beauty. Yet Lioness regarded his skinny, aged body with vast tenderness, and said to him, "Oh, my splendid Abe," and that he did get to keep.

In all the years of being "singly together," as Joanna sometimes liked to put it, there had never been a word of exclusivity between herself and Abe. It had simply come about, without promises or guarantees on either side, and with only a hiccup or two very early in the relationship, products of sudden panic at creeping fidelity.

Now, more than twenty years on—loving Lioness, mounting and mastering Lioness like an invading army, and being totally invaded, trampled, laid waste at the same time, destroyed by his own conquest—what guilt he felt had nothing to do with breaking faith. But even insanely triumphant, even aware that there was no one he would not have betrayed to know what he knew, even then he fought to keep himself from comparing Joanna and Lioness in any way. He was a bluesman; he knew a dream when it rolled over him.

Panting on her breast, speechless, aching with joy, he felt her hand moving in his hair—*God, she'll feel the bald spot!*—and then caressing his neck and shoulders, and he heard her voice far away, or felt it through her damp skin, murmuring, "So sweet . . . so sweet." After that the words came in that other language of hers, but it seemed, for some little time, always to have been his tongue as well. He lay still, listening to his heart, smelling Lioness, smelling them together.

When he could speak, he said again, "I am sixty-six years old. Had a birthday just a while back."

"Yes." She turned on her side to look down at him, her eyes not at all heavy after love, but fully open and full of his face. "I was there."

"No way in the world do I belong here with you. Not morally, not physically, not aesthetically. I just want you to know I know that." Her slow smile widened, but she did not speak; instead she tickled his nose with a strand of her hair. He said, "I mean, I really could be your damn father. You know that."

"No." The single word fell hard from a great height. "No, Abe. There is no way in the world that you could ever be my father." Everything inside him instantly turned to ice at the thought of somehow having offended her, but in fact she lay closer, slipping an arm under his head, her lips so close to his ear that he felt himself filled with her breath, and not his own at all. "Listen now. Listen, I will tell you a story."

He wriggled his cold feet shamelessly between her warm ones, marveling that she could ever have come freezing to his door. Lioness said, "Abe, once there was a girl, a child, who lived with her mother in another country. This was very long ago."

"Couldn't have been that long."

She hushed him with a kiss, smoke-light but lingering. "But it was. It was so long ago that there were no schools, and no day care, and no children's programs on television. And her father was—gone—and her mother worked, you see, Abe—her mother went away early every morning, and came home late every night. No weekends with her daughter, no holidays—" she tickled him again—"and no birthdays, never. Not ever."

"That's very sad," he said, still smelling and tasting more than listening. "What sort of sweatshop did her mother work in?"

Lioness answered him without hesitation. "She had to keep the world running."

When he turned in her arms, as though about to sit up, she said quickly, "Not the world, but the earth, the planet. She was in charge of bringing the right rain to the right places, making sure that the sun shone where it should exactly as long as it should. That the ocean currents always swept the fish where they were supposed to be, and the beautiful turtles and the whales, and the clouds of such tiny creatures they fed on—all of it just so, that was her task. The vineyards, the farms, the crops everywhere, in all the lands, and everything growing wild beyond the fences, that too. The ripeness, that was her task."

"Busy lady." He was busy himself, trying to memorize the long diamond-shaped hollows of her collarbones, the precise set of ears and tilt of nipples, the barely-visible spray of lighter hair at the nape of her neck. "Seasonal work, though, surely. She must have had a little time off in the winters?"

"There were no seasons then." Something in the sound of the words made him look up from grazing over her body, back to her urgent eyes. Lioness said, "It was all the same then, that long ago—one spring over all the world. Truly, Abe. It was just so." She took his hand and held it hard against her breast. It surprised him that her heart was beating as rapidly as his own.

"I believe you," he said, though she had not asked. "So the girl was alone a lot."

"Yes, but she never minded. She knew how important her mother's work was, and she was very good at keeping herself company. She loved to climb trees, and to swim in the pools and run around in the meadows, and she would make little playhouses out of leaves and branches, and she always sang, always." She was nearly singing herself by now, as she told him the story. "And there were animals—lions, even, and wolves, really—but she was never afraid. Nor were they."

She paused abruptly, shaking her head, and her voice returned to its normal rhythm. "Does all this sound animated to you, like a children's movie with talking mice? Oh, it was not like that, I promise you. It was just a child growing up, and she grew slowly, because there was so much time, time was such a very new thing then. And her mother came home to her every night and loved her enough for many, many days."

Abe gathered her in with an ease and dexterity that surprised him, and she pressed hard into him, as though into a dark, small, safe burrow. He said, "This has a bad ending, I can tell."

She was about to answer when she raised herself suddenly to glance sharply down his body. "Well," she murmured. "Well, my goodness. You are a startling person, Abe Aronson."

"I'm startled myself. I have to tell you, this is not normal."

She checked. "It certainly feels normal." She was laughing without making a sound; he could feel the laughter wherever he touched her. He said, "Maybe you should tell me the ending first. Me being sixty-six and all."

But she was already astride him, pinning his shoulders to the air mattress like a wrestler, laughing down silently. "And me being so very much older? We can wait."

She was sound asleep in his arms when Joanna walked into the garage, with Mr. Mardikian some way behind her, and she was still asleep when his harmonica whirled past his head and Joanna walked out. Mr. Mardikian lingered in the doorway for a moment, studying them—pinned and preserved in betrayal like butterflies in a glass case—with a kind of icy sympathy. He said simply, "A pity, that," and went away. Lioness never stirred—Abe's right arm was numb and useless for an hour in the morning—but he thought, all through the rest of the night, that she had heard.

When he got up to make breakfast for her, he stepped on the harmonica.

# 11.

# AUGUST

"We do not have to do this," Mr. Mardikian said. "The hell we don't."

"Delvecchio." Mr. Mardikian's twilight eyes were very nearly tender, or anyway less than usually cold. "Delvecchio, this is not love, this is not even honest lust. This is spite, simply. Even I know spite."

"No, it's not." They were facing each other on opposite sides of Joanna's bed, both fully dressed, although Joanna was trying to struggle out of her blouse, which was old and too small, and invariably managed to snag her hair or her nose on removal. She mumbled through fabric, "This is solace. I'm not asking a damn thing else of you, but I will have solace."

"No." Mr. Mardikian leaned across the bed and caught her fumbling hands, moving, as before, the least bit too swiftly for her to follow. "Delvecchio, my dear. There is no consolation to be had from me, and if you do not know that, you are not the Delvecchio I take you for. You do not want me at all, in any way." As he spoke, he was straightening the blouse and smoothing her hair, deft and deferential. "And I do have my pride."

"Since when?" Joanna glared at him, deliberately disheveling her hair again with both hands. "I thought you didn't have any feelings. You told me."

"Ah," Mr. Mardikian said. "Well." He looked startlingly embarrassed for a moment. "A very few, perhaps, of the most primitive—pride, surely, and hunger, and great anger. And I used to know lust myself, like—" he paused briefly—"like other people, but that is gone now. No more than those, Delvecchio."

"Well, you're a lot better off. Trust me." She had begun to feel irritatingly silly, standing in her bedroom at three-thirty in the morning, arguing with a strange old man who had witnessed her worst humiliation. *Or is it heartbreak?* she asked herself. *Am I actually heartbroken, at my age?* Aloud, she said, "You're right. I don't want you, I don't want to fuck anybody, for any reason, ever. I'm going to shoot some hoops."

Mr. Mardikian's baffled blink gave her a moment of the purest satisfaction she could remember. He stared as she took the basketball from its corner, and he trailed her hesitantly to the door, meek and mute. Outside, the night was still more black than blue; there was no moon, and no lights in any other windows. A single plane out of Sea-Tac twinkled overhead.

Joanna stalked down the little stairway that she shared with tenants above and below her, marched across the street to the empty schoolyard, and down the three steps that led into the basketball court. She poised the ball over her head and fired it blindly at the nearest hoop, barely visible. It banged into the backboard, rebounding almost all the way back to her, and she scooped it up, took a quick run, and yelled in triumph as she dropped in a hook shot that left the hoop buzzing violently, all but shaking itself loose. "Yes—the girl's on fire!" she announced, simultaneously wheeling and passing the ball hard to the astonished Mr. Mardikian. When it bounced off his chest, she grabbed it again and went in for a layup, which missed with an even louder clang. Mr. Mardikian said in thoughtful wonder, "This is what you do when you are unhappy."

"Or crazy-happy," Joanna answered. "Either way." Plainly able to sink a shot almost at will, she seemed to take much more pleasure in creating the loudest possible din smashing the ball as hard as she could against the rusty hoop, cheering herself on in the voice of a television commentator. She was sweating in the cold Seattle night, and her eyes were stretched wide.

"And Delvecchio going for the three-pointer!" she shouted, setting herself for the outside shot. The ball sailed over hoop and backboard alike, caromed off the school roof, and settled neatly into Mr. Mardikian's hands on the fly. He turned it a few times, examining it as curiously and respectfully as though it might be some odd alien form of life. Then he flicked it through the hoop from the foot of the stairway, without touching the sides or rattling the backboard. He said, "Ah" again, and smiled at her.

"Damn," she said. The ball rolled against her foot, and she picked it up without looking at it. She ordered, "Do that again."

Never moving from where he stood, Mr. Mardikian sank six shots in a row. The only sounds were those of the basketball's return bounces, and of Joanna's hisses of amazement as it plopped once more through the hoop. She said finally, "I think I could stand it if you at least bent your knees just a bit. If I thought for a moment that you'd ever played this game before. But you haven't, have you? Ever?"

Mr. Mardikian shook his head solemnly. "No, Delvecchio. I do not know how to play any games."

"Don't you, though?" For all the racket, there was no other sound on the street but the scrape of Mr. Mardikian's shoes and, fleetingly, the whumping bass of a car stereo coming down Queen Anne Hill. A small cat slipped by in the shadows, cautious and curious at once, not quite stopping. Joanna said quietly, "I told you before, you've been playing a game with me from the night we met. Mardikian, who the hell are you?"

"I am no more than I am," he answered her. "Only an old man, not really so smart, who grieved for your grief and thought at least he should see you home. So I will go, all right?"

Joanna stared at him. Mr. Mardikian smiled in an oddly tentative manner, looking rather like a child unsure whether his parents were buying his lie. Abruptly she shoved the ball back into his hands and crouched before him, spreading her arms wide. She said, "Try to score now."

A puzzled frown replaced the smile. "But I am taller than you. Delvecchio, this is not fair a bit."

"Try to score," Joanna repeated. "Play a game I know, for a change. It's my solace." Her voice cracked on the last words. Mr. Mardikian shrugged slightly, and raised the ball to shoot, and Joanna slapped it out of his hands. She snatched it up on the first bounce, dribbled it a couple of times, and headed for the basket, calling, "You have to stop me!" over her shoulder.

He caught onto the game almost immediately, though not fast enough to keep her from scoring early. His height and reach did make it easy for him to keep the ball away from her, but he proved to be a scrupulously clean player, and in one-on-one Joanna had never had a scruple to her name. Wearing her downtown-Palermo face, she stepped all over his feet; she elbowed, traveled, and held whenever she saw a chance, and even butted him viciously on occasion, though that only hurt her head. Mr. Mardikian never complained. When he leaned over her to intercept a shot, he would march imperviously back and forth between stairway and basket, paying no more heed to the furious little person dancing in his path than a rhinoceros would have paid a yappy Pomeranian. Neither of them tired; if anything, Joanna felt herself surprisingly stronger and quicker as the stars faded and the horizon began to show a thin pewter rim. The game went on.

Joanna was running with sweat, for all the dampness of the night, but Mr. Mardikian remained impassively cool and creased. Once, leaping to knock the ball out of bounds, she collided full-tilt with him, and he had to steady her against himself to keep her from falling. For the first time, she smelled him: a harsh scent, painful in her nostrils, like a forest fire burning a long way off, alarming and distantly alluring. That was when he asked her—conversationally, irrelevantly, breathing as placidly as though they were out for a nice walk together—"Delvecchio, what will you do now?"

She shook him away and was gone with the ball again, sprinting for the basket. He was up with her in two strides, easily blocking her shot, turning in the air as he came down with it, so that he was facing her, holding the ball out teasingly before he whirled again to drop it through the hoop. When she recovered it and paused for an instant to catch her breath, she could still smell him on her clothing.

Mr. Mardikian said, "I ask for a reason." Joanna lunged past him, dribbling like a machine gun. Again he snatched her shot in midair, but this time she leaped higher than she could have imagined herself doing and batted the ball out of his hands into the middle of the street. Racing after it as it rolled behind a parked car, she heard him insistently continuing.

"I ask for a reason, Delvecchio. I am older than perhaps I look, and in all my long life I have done only one thing for which I wish to be forgiven. And I never can be."

The faraway, all-but-impersonal sorrow in his voice made Joanna forget the basketball and whatever she had just stepped in, and turn to see him standing with his own hands at his sides, suddenly looking very tired. "What will you do, Delvecchio? I must know what is forgiveness. What is it that matters? How does it happen, what does it mean? Can you tell me this? I truly must know."

Joanna was shaking her head again, blinking rapidly, digging for the basketball lodged under the car as though for a dear one buried in earthquake rubble. Mr. Mardikian asked for a third time, "What will you do with what has happened to you? Tell me, Delvecchio."

Even when she retrieved the ball, she still kept her back to Mr. Mardikian. She said, "I'll do my work. I'll spend more time with my daughter, with my friends. I'll get somebody—" she stopped for only a moment—"I'll find someone with a truck, and I'll get twenty years' worth of my things out of that house. That'll be one serious pain in the ass, boy."

"Yes," Mr. Mardikian said behind her. "And for the pain in the heart?"

A car she had not noticed—and that had clearly not noticed her—passed altogether too close to Joanna's head, going up the hill. She turned, blinking into a dawn she had not noticed. "I'll shoot hoops."

Mr. Mardikian nodded. "Yes. Thank you, Delvecchio." He touched her shoulder lightly. "I will go."

"No," Joanna said. They stood looking at each other, with Mr. Mardikian's hand still resting on her shoulder. Joanna said, "Don't go. I'm sad, and I'm tired, and you're sad—or whatever it is you do—and I really don't care if it's lust or spite or what the hell. Don't go, please, Mardikian."

As they crossed the street, the condo sprinkler system came on, icy on her ankles. Joanna gasped, and they both laughed then, and Mr. Mardikian took her hand. As they started toward the stairs, she said impulsively, "Carry me."

Mr. Mardikian blinked at her. "Delvecchio?"

"I know it's silly, but I've always wanted to be swept up and carried into my house and dumped on the bed. He tried it once, but he sort of threw his back out."

Mr. Mardikian laughed again, and lifted her so effortlessly that she was not even aware of being off the ground until her back bumped against her front door. He loomed over her, blocking out the rising sun, and the smell of burning was all around her. Joanna shut her eyes and fumbled behind herself for the doorknob, trying not to drop the basketball.

At once evisceratingly greedy and boyishly grateful, constantly praising her body and her generosity, he prowled both with no more mercy than a sandstorm or an avalanche. Her own pleasure ravaged her more than his; he left her battered by a new knowledge of her capacity for delight, which frightened as much as it enchanted, since at the very least it had nothing at all to do with him. Spent, she lay apart, and said when she could, "That was the best. That always will be the best, I know that. But we are not doing this again."

He was instantly solicitous. "Have I hurt you, Delvecchio?" Naked, he looked surprisingly young, and was rather thinner than she had expected; otherwise, there was nothing especially unusual about him. "Please," he said. "I tried not to hurt you."

Joanna touched him, but moved no closer. "You didn't. It's just that you were right—there's no solace in you, none at all. No kindness. It's not your fault. You warned me."

"I am sorry," Mr. Mardikian whispered. He lay still beside her, looking at the ceiling, the fire-smell faint now. She noticed that his hands were clenched at his sides, the lean body almost grotesquely rigid, and she was moved by pity to say again, "You did warn me."

Mr. Mardikian did not answer her. Joanna closed her eyes, though she was neither sleepy nor embarrassed to see him beside her. Her heart had not yet slowed to its normal pace; her skin had not yet yielded place to her mind, but was still insisting on thinking and remembering and celebrating itself for itself. *Never again, never—not him, not that bloody damned old son of a bitch either. I can't afford it, none of it.* Behind the lids, her eyes began to ache and sting, but she thought, *no, you don't, Lily doesn't cry, be like Lily.*

"I still don't have any idea who you are," she said. "Usually, you make love with somebody, you know anyway something about them, afterward. You, you're just as much a stranger as ever."

"I am a stranger, Delvecchio." The woodwind voice was completely toneless. "There is nothing more to know."

Joanna opened her eyes. "Not to her, you weren't. I saw her face when she looked at you."

"Your Lioness." Mr. Mardikian sighed. "We know each other, yes. I am—I was, I used to be—an acquaintance of her mother's."

"Really? She came to our barbecue. The barbecue," she amended quickly, thinking, *Ah, Christ, I'm going to have to have a language garage sale.* "Tall Greek lady."

"She is not Greek. Nor am I." Mr. Mardikian turned toward her on his side. "It was all so long ago, Delvecchio—a thousand thousand worlds away." Joanna studied his face in as detached a manner as she could, giving up on expression and concentrating on any twitch of an eyelash, any deepening of a line, any slightest change of color in the stone-pale skin. Mr. Mardikian said, "Your Lioness is my wife. As much as theft could make her so, she is my wife."

Joanna opened her mouth, but no sound came out. Mr. Mardikian's sigh seemed to come from some further place than his body, and to go on forever. When he put an arm under her shoulders and cautiously drew her closer, she neither resisted nor responded. Mr. Mardikian said softly, "Delvecchio, I beg you, do not ask any more. Because I will lie if you do—I must, I have no choice—and there is no one I would less willingly tell lies to. Please, I need you to understand."

The fact that his arm and his hair and his smell all made her feel nothing but *not Abe, not Abe* infuriated her, and she snuggled grimly into his chest, still sullenly determined on comfort. "All right," she said. "At least you do keep warning me. For a man, that's something."

Mr. Mardikian caressed her body with a kind of graceful absence, a completely unsensuous courtesy. They lay together in detached peacefulness, until Joanna realized that she was writing her name on his skin with a fingernail, as she was used to doing with Abe. She said, "I wish I could cry the way you did in the Skyliner—endless, enormous, no sound, no shame. If I did it now, it'd just come out all whiny and spiteful and stupid. Not fair."

"No," Mr. Mardikian said, "no, Delvecchio, you could never cry like me." Again she peered intently into his face, searching despite herself for the towering, fiery formlessness that had carried her into her bedroom like a blind kitten in its mother's jaws, and finding only a sad and weary old man. He said, "I told you, I was remembering another music, remembering a man who played for me once, in that other world. He desired desperately something I alone could give him, and the music was a pleading, a prayer. I wept so then, and never again, until this time." He seemed about to continue, but did not.

"And did you?" she asked. "Grant his big old desire?" Her own sudden bitterness soured her mouth.

Mr. Mardikian sat up slowly, swinging his legs over the side of the bed. He did not look at Joanna when he spoke. "Yes, of course I granted it." He rose to his feet, still with his back to her. *Nice, trim for his age, but nothing that special. Kyle's probably got better buns.*

"But it did not help him. I could have told him. Nothing I do can help anyone." His voice continued low and even, no word holding more emotion than another. But the very small slump of his taut shoulders clutched at Joanna as if he had been her Lily, choking down one more defeat in a war without meaning or companions. She stretched to touch his hand, but could not reach him.

"I will go," Mr. Mardikian said. Joanna groped for her bathrobe. Making love with a stranger was one thing; being seen naked by anyone but Abe, quite another. She said quietly, "You helped me. You did. Thank you."

Mr. Mardikian began to gather up the natty clothes that had so startled Joanna when he wore them into Abe's house, literally ages ago. They went on as flowingly as they had come off: lintless, uncrumpled. Slipping the brown-bear polo shirt over his head, he remarked, "I tell you this, though you would never ask. They are not together. I do not know where she is, but they are not together."

"I don't care," Joanna said. Mr. Mardikian started for the door, then turned back to face her. "Delvecchio, I should kiss you good-bye. May I kiss you?"

Joanna shook her head. Mr. Mardikian bowed, the first awkward movement she had seen from him. But he smiled as well, in a way she had never seen on the ferry: a slow, hesitant struggle of a smile, as obstinately determined to be born as any bird pecking its way out of an egg. The smile chilled Joanna, not because it was evil or mocking; to the contrary, it was almost heartbreaking in its remoteness, its unhuman attempt at a human signal. It was the moon's midnight smile, shadows shaping a grimace across endless emptiness. He said, "It would do you no harm, Delvecchio, my kiss. Remember when I am gone—we have all touched each other closely, as even I never imagined, no more than you. And all touches change, and no touch can ever be taken back. Remember."

She followed him to the front door, locking it when it closed behind him, and leaned against it, saying aloud, "And that is by God that." Then she slipped down until she was sitting on the floor and cried, loudly and messily, for a good half-hour.

Abe called several times that morning, but Joanna did not

answer the phone. He left messages, each at once angrier and more pleading than the last. "Del, talk to me. Please, at least talk to me." "Del, I know you're there, pick up the damn phone. Yell, I don't care, spit at me, but pick up the phone." "All right, this is it, I'm not calling again. You call me when you come down from your tree." "Del, for shit's sake, can't we anyway talk like grown people? Del? Del, God damn it, *please*." She let the messages accumulate until at last he did stop calling, listened carefully to each one, and then erased them all.

Later, she called Lily and left her own message.

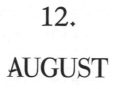

# 12.

# AUGUST

Lily did quite well up to the moment when the kayak was actually bobbing in the shallows by the ferry dock. Then she said, "Not in this life. Not a chance."

"We have a deal," Joanna said. "This is not negotiable."

"Well, I'm sorry, I have reconsidered. Until I saw it in the water, I never realized how frigging small these things really are. Put a foot in, you'd go right through the bottom. Sorry."

"These things are built better than we are. Heavier you load them, easier they handle." Joanna was distantly amused to notice that she had begun to talk in the clipped manner of the New Zealander. Saying, "Start storing the gear," she climbed down into the rear cockpit of the kayak, opened the aft hatch, and waited for Lily to begin handing her their supplies.

"No," Lily said. "I am not doing this."

Joanna said, "Lily."

"I am almost twenty-nine years old. I don't have to do what you tell me." Lily's tone was halfway between exasperated laughter and an adolescent's put-upon whine. "I don't."

"Tent first—then bags, then air mattresses, then the cookware.

Two compartments, enough space for everything. Let's go." Her own voice remained implacably serene.

"Look, I know you're upset, I understand if you suddenly feel like now would be a good time for us to do some serious mother-daughter bonding. And that's terrific, that's great with me. A teensy bit late, maybe, but hey, sisterhood is powerful. Just not in a scrawny little boat, all right? Believe me, I bond way better in a spa, a gym, a coffeehouse. I always do."

"The tent," Joanna said. "Lily, just at present I honestly would not mess with me if I were you."

"We're going to drown. We're going to capsize and sink and fucking drown." A protesting automaton, Lily picked up the neatly-folded pup tent and shoved it into her mother's arms.

"You can't drown in a kayak. If you capsize, you just roll right on over, the way the Eskimos do it. I'll show you. Okay, now the bags."

"Bag," Lily said. "One bag. Your bag. Are you listening to me?" She crouched on the dock so that her increasingly alarmed face was almost level with Joanna's face. "Look, just because you caught Abe porking Lioness—"

"Porking?"

"—that doesn't mean you get to enroll your daughter in a suicide pact—"

"You'll have to stick the pots and the water bottles in the forward compartment," Joanna said. "Just behind the seat."

Lily made a last forlorn attempt. "Damn it, I'm supposed to be working tomorrow. They won't know where I am, I could get fired."

Joanna was studying the rented paddles. "Wood . . . I hope there's not too much give in these. Kid, I know your schedule at the station as well as you do. We'll be back in plenty of time." She flashed Lily a sudden purely wicked grin. "Unless the weather kicks up, of course. Which I'm told it can on that stretch, but it's not supposed to. Or if we hit something."

The slow, heavy, profoundly theatrical sigh had been Lily's white flag since quite early childhood. She said, "All right. All *right*. Why have we got all these damn towels?"

"I was advised to bring towels. Don't ask." They had, as recommended by the New Zealander, rented the kayak that afternoon at a shop on Lake Union, somehow managed to mount it on the roof of Joanna's Jaguar, and driven with it to Alki Point, southwest of Seattle. Aping her mentor's brusque manner as best she could, Joanna had informed Lily that they would be crossing four miles of water to cruise the shore of Blake Island, and land on the west side, away from the marina and tourist complex at Tillicum Village. "No salmon dinner, no longhouse souvenirs, no Indian dances. Just two intrepid ladies having an adventure and a slumber party. On the way back, tomorrow, we just keep Gardner on our right and head for the lighthouse—couldn't miss it if we tried."

"Yes we could. What happens if we hit a ferry? And don't tell me there isn't a ferry, because there is."

"We won't hit it. And we won't get lost, and we won't get eaten by orcas. Would your own dear old white-haired mother lie to you?"

Lily had snorted without replying, and said very little for the rest of the drive. Only when the Alki Point lighthouse was in sight, looking, as always, like an ornament on a wedding cake or a model railroad, did she suddenly announce, "This isn't about us, this is all about you and Abe. Abe's the one who needs to be here, not me."

Joanna parked the car and turned off the engine before she said, "Abe who?" Lily looked back at her without answering. Joanna said, "Listen very carefully, daughter, because I'm only going to tell you once. This was always going to be a solo act. No Abe, no Lily, nobody but me—me, finally, finally alone on the water after all these years of looking down on the top of it through the clouds. You have no idea how much I wanted to be doing this—my little nothing baby trip—all by myself. No idea."

"But here I am," Lily said quietly. "Shanghaied."

"Here you are, right. Because this is important, and the last time you and I did anything important together, if memory serves, I was shoveling all kinds of disgusting crap down your throat to make you puke up all the crap you swallowed the night that lawyer bitch dumped you. While we waited for the paramedics. It comes back?"

"It does sound familiar." Lily smiled slightly, surprisingly. "Except it wasn't the lawyer, it was somebody else. You never knew that one."

"Really? Well, lucky me. You never knew how much shit I went through, talking the paramedics into reporting it as an accident, even though they knew. Let alone getting it past Abe. I'm still not sure he ever believed me."

"You never told Abe?" Lily's eyes widened as they had done when Joanna first told her that every single snowflake was different from every other. "Oh, I don't believe that. You tell him absolutely everything."

"Not that, I didn't. Not a whole lot of things, I damn well didn't." Joanna got out of the car and slammed the door. "I have never ever told Abe or anyone else that my daughter was enough of a pin-headed moron to try to kill herself over a lawyer, for God's sake—"

Another doorslam. "It wasn't the lawyer, I told you." Lily leaned on the Jaguar's roof, eyeing her under the precariously balanced kayak, challenging her with a curious hint of amusement. "So now you're going to blackmail me emotionally for the rest of our lives because you kept my shame a secret. You would, too."

"No," Joanna said. "This is a one-shot. Help me get this thing down."

The kayak was twenty-one feet long, and weighed a bit more than forty-five pounds. Joanna and Lily succeeded in lowering it from the roof without damaging either it or the Jaguar, and carried it easily enough all the way to the empty ferry dock. There were half a dozen boats already at the launching strip; and though the afternoon was overcast there were altogether too many joggers, rollerbladers, and volleyball games going on for Joanna's ease of mind. When their rented gear was finally aboard, the life jackets adjusted, and Lily was rebelling at stepping into the little aft cockpit, which kept dancing away from her feet, Joanna held the kayak steady and showed her how to insert herself snugly into it without so much as a splash. "Listen, that was the hardest thing I had to learn, just getting in the boat. Stretch your legs out, get comfortable, and stop saying, 'Oh, my God.' Okay? Okay—now sit still for a moment and look at the nice mountains. Here I come."

And Lily, for a wonder, did briefly lose herself in the clouded glory of the Olympic range. Against the dishwater sky, the mountains appeared much closer than she knew they were: a smudgy watercolor, glowing green and bright mauve, with no clear line or form to anything; only depth and dimension to lure the eye in and up and farther. She hardly felt the kayak shift as Joanna slipped in ahead of her.

"Now," her mother said. "Sit, don't do anything, I'm pushing us off." Lily gasped once as the kayak slid forward. The dock was gone, and looking down at the gray water, inches below, made her feel so dizzy and sickness so abruptly imminent that she shut her eyes. Far away, Joanna said, quite gently, "I know. Don't be frightened."

When she forced herself to open her eyes, Lily was in a stranger place than she had ever been. Everything was out of proportion: the water seemed almost level with her face, the land in every direction infinitely dim and distant; all sounds—laughter on another boat, the rattle of an anchor chain, the mad whoop of a waterskier, the splash of a plunging bird—appeared to come from random locations, completely disconnected from their sources. The kayak was angling toward the far humplet of Blake Island, slowing to a near stop as a loaded car ferry crossed their paths. The noise of the engines came to them only after they were rocking, not in, but somehow on the ferry's wake.

Joanna said, "Okay. Pick up your paddle."

"I'll drop it," Lily said. To her ears, her own voice sounded infuriatingly like a spoiled child's whine. More strongly, she said, "I don't even know how to hold one of these things. I'm scared it'll slip out of my hands."

"No, it won't. Don't grip it too tightly, that's one thing, your forearms cramp up. Nice and easy—if you lose it, it'll float. Pick it up now."

Light as it was, the paddle felt as unnatural as a shotgun in Lily's hands. Clumsy in the stiff life jacket, trying to summon up images of kayakers she had casually glimpsed, she waved the paddle vaguely over her head, then lunged it deep into the water on the right side of the boat, and almost did lose it pulling up for a stroke on the opposite side. Banging it down before her, she wailed, "This is crazy, give it up! I'm not Outdoorsy Girl, I'm sorry. Let's just go home, and you can be ashamed of me all you like, I won't say a word. Just let it go, all right?"

Joanna said nothing but "Watch me." Lily had little choice but to watch as her mother leaned forward, reaching out to plant the paddle in the water with her left arm straight and the right arm sharply bent. Rather than pulling back, as Lily had done, she pushed her body hard forward, twisting slightly at the end of the stroke. The effect was of levering, not of hauling or clawing, and the kayak glided ahead, more swiftly than it should have for the effort that Joanna seemed to be putting out. An unhurried flip of the paddle at chest level, and she did the same thing on the other side, moving as though she were poling the kayak through a muddy swamp. Over her shoulder, she said, "Try it. It's not hard."

Lily felt heavy with astonishment. "Where in hell did you learn to do that?"

"Watching a lady, same as you're doing. Only she was a whole lot more patient than I am. Come on, if I can do it, you can do it. Watch now."

The afternoon light was fading as the kayak moved on toward

the island—first, for some time, with one paddle; then with two, the tentative, lurching aft paddle constantly jarring the kayak off its path as Lily attempted to mimic her mother's lazy-looking rhythm. It took her a considerable while, but she fussed less and less once she began to grasp the principle of the pushing, levering technique, and Joanna only snapped at her twice. Despite the grayness of the sky, the Sound began to assume color with the sunset, so that the kayak flowed through oil-slick-bright patches of maroon and viridian and near-orange water. To the east, Seattle came on like a flickering neon sign, with some bulbs missing where Gardner Island blocked the view. Lily heard a woman calling to someone, and the single bark of a dog.

The moon was rising behind the Space Needle, which had always reminded Lily of the great striding towers of *War of the Worlds*. Now it seemed to have grown a head as golden as a dandelion, as fierce in its flat brilliance as the face of a dragon. When Lily turned her head reluctantly away from the Seattle skyline, the suddenness of Blake Island astonished her. She had been so occupied for most of the trip in battling her paddle to a draw that their destination had lost whatever little reality it had ever had for her. Now it came near filling her vision: even in the dusk she could distinguish the marina and the longhouse; then, as Joanna headed the kayak southwest, the powerboat docks and picnic shelters began to be replaced by massy woods above thin, rather uninviting strips of beach. She smelled fish cooking.

"We made it," she said. She was not aware that she had spoken aloud until Joanna turned around and grinned at her. Then she said, as she had earlier, "This is crazy. We made it."

"Four entire miles. Open water all the way." Lily realized that her mother was trembling uncontrollably; even the smile was as quirky and shaky as though she were about to weep. "Okay, not really open water, not really the sea. A little nothing baby trip, no big deal. Anybody with a rowboat could make it."

"But it was us." A quick cold breeze found its way under the life jacket, and Lily felt suddenly farther from home than four miles. She asked, "So we're camping out?"

Joanna gestured toward a point indistinctly farther ahead. "West Beach. It's on the map, I'll find it. Fire pits, bathrooms, the lap of luxury. A mile or so, I can find it, don't worry." She began paddling again, and Lily, having once again mislaid the push-pull technique, flailed muzzily in her wake.

Joanna did find the western shore, flying blind when it grew too dark to read the map. Lily, too weary and chilled for triumph, expected her to take the kayak directly in, but instead Joanna shipped her paddle and said, "I want to sit still for a little. Just a bit."

The night closed around them as the kayak bobbed on the small waves. A ferry horn lowed somewhere behind them, off Bainbridge or Gardner or Vashon; on a passing yacht, a news broadcast proclaimed the evils of the day. A sudden swirl off the bow might have been only a vagrant current, but Lily wished it into a dolphin. She became aware, in the same muffled way, that she was hungry. She asked, after a decent silence, "Is it all right if we park now?"

"I was thinking," Joanna said. "How long it took me to travel such a short way. Yes. We'll go in."

They ran the kayak up on the sand and lugged their gear to the empty campsite on the berm just above it. Erecting the tent was nearly more of a campaign than the voyage itself had been, but between them they convinced it to stay up, and Lily herself built a fire to heat their dehydrated soup and cook their vacuum-sealed crabcakes. Too tired to talk much during dinner, they struggled fully clothed into their sleeping bags, and lay without speaking for some time. The wind did not drop off, and the air was growing steadily colder, but Joanna, on her back, looking out at the stars and the water through the open flap, felt quite warm and wide awake, and could not stop smiling.

"Thank you for coming with me," she said at last. Lily did not reply for so long that Joanna thought she might have already fallen asleep. Finally, as she was beginning to wander away herself, she heard the soft question, "Why did you really bring me here?"

"What does it matter?" As close as they were lying in the tiny tent, she could not see Lily's eyes. "I'm just glad you're here."

"Abe," Lily said. "Abe and Lioness. If not for that mess, you wouldn't even have told me you were taking off. I may do a lot of stupid stuff, but I'm not stupid."

"What are you talking about? Didn't I call you right away?"

"Right, you told me we were going on this kayaking thing, no questions, no argument. You didn't ask, you just fucking told me—just left a message on the machine, that's that. Nothing like maybe, 'Daughter, I'm really hurting, I really need to talk, I really need your company.' You never ask me for help—not real help, never. Not once in my entire life. Do you realize that?"

"Oh, come on!" Joanna was up on an elbow, by turns hot and cold with indignation. "That is simply not true—"

"It's always been true. Always." Lily groped for their Coleman lantern, found it, and got it lighted, after a brief, raging period of alternately breaking matches and smoking up the tent. Her face was pale, and her mouth was twitching. "I never wanted cuddling, petting from you. I swear, I never even wanted approval. All I ever wanted was to be able to have silence with you. Not shutting up, not leave-me-alone, but the way friends can be silent together. Because it's all right, you know?"

Joanna's belly turned to lead. She said, "Honey, you *are* my friend. You're my best friend."

Lily said, suddenly almost gentle, "Abe's your best friend. All the people you know, all the people you work with, and he's the only one you've ever allowed the whole way in. That's why all this. Tell me I'm wrong."

Joanna did not answer her. Lily reached through the yellow light to pat her arm awkwardly and heavily. "How do you think I feel? Thinking of the two of them together? I know it's not the same thing—that's why I haven't said word one about any of it. I've known her—what?—a few months, half a year, whatever. And she never promised me a thing, I don't have any kind of claim on her, not like you and Abe. But I feel just as bad as if I did—idiot, idiot . . ." She broke off, still trying to keep her mouth under control, and presently resumed. "I thought maybe we'd talk about that."

"There's nothing to talk about." Joanna attempted to return the touch, but succeeded only in singeing her wrist against the lantern. "I don't have any claim on your old Uncle Abe, either—nobody's got any claim on anybody. He just did the dirty on me, and it shouldn't matter so much—not at our age, in our time—but it does, and I don't want to see that bastard ever again. Absolutely nothing to talk about."

"Then what am I doing here?" Lily abruptly ripped open their forgotten packet of high-fiber chocolate-chip cookies, shoved three into her mouth, and still managed to demand clearly, "What am I doing here?" She pointed a nonfat-chocolate-stained finger across the flame at her mother. "What the *hell* am I doing here?"

Joanna sat up, ignoring the wind. She met Lily's eyes, holding them with her own. She said levelly, "You're here because I can't swim. That's why."

Lily's cookie-filled mouth fell open. Crumbs dropped out. Joanna continued, "I'd way rather have gone alone, I told you that. Nobody to look after, nobody to explain to, nobody to make me feel ashamed because I couldn't keep my man in my bed. But I can't swim, and you can, and this is the first kayak trip I've ever made. And I'm not suicidal, I'm just pissed. So I asked you along."

"Jesus bleeding Christ," Lily said, and the whispered words might easily have been a prayer. "You think I can swim?"

"Think? I know you can swim—I paid for the lessons, remember? Tuesdays and Fridays at the Y. Wait, I know the name. Don Something, big blond UW student. Tuesdays and Fridays."

"Oh, my lord," Lily said softly. "Oh, my lord," and suddenly she was knuckling at her eyes. "I never did learn to swim, I sank like a damn stone, every time. They just pocketed the money and told you I was doing fine. And I never had the guts to tell you." She kept rubbing her eyes, though Joanna saw no tears, and at the same time she was beginning to laugh, spluttering absurdly. "Trust me, I can't swim a lick better than you. If you're counting on me to preserve you from a watery grave, we are fucking doomed."

"Oh," Joanna said. "Oh, for heaven's sake." She was laughing herself, hiccupping helplessly, bending her head to her knees. "He was so cute, old Don. Don Whoever. 'Coming along, Lily's coming along really well.' What did I know?" She glared at her daughter. "And you looked so cute in the pool, hanging onto the edge, smiling up at me. You were part of it, you were just as fraudulent. Didn't we bring any vodka or anything?"

"No, we didn't. And yes, I was. But I wanted to be swimming, I wanted to learn for you, so much, and I thought maybe I really was learning, and just didn't know it." Neither of them could stop laughing. Lily wheezed, "You better show me that Eskimo thing, the roll, before we start back tomorrow. Just in case."

Joanna threw her arms wide and flopped back into her sleeping bag. "Well, it's my fault, shanghaiing you under false pretenses. But I am glad you're here. I am." She glanced sideways, waiting with a certain coyness for Lily's response.

"I'm not," Lily said. "My feet are freezing, and my damn mattress keeps losing air, and I didn't bring a pillow, and I forgot to charge up my toothbrush. Frankly, I could have skipped the whole thing, if it weren't for the bonding."

"Is that what we're doing?"

"Must be. It's aggravating enough. There are two, three cookies left."

"Yours." Joanna turned off the lantern. For some while there was no further sound, except for Lily's munching, and her fretful squirming in her sleeping bag. Once something large crackled the twigs of a nearby bush; twice the wind carried faint voices from other campsites to their tent. Joanna's own air mattress lay on a slight slope, and no matter how she rearranged it or herself, there was no escaping the sense of skidding gradually downhill. Her nose was increasingly stopped up, and she was bleakly certain that she was incubating a yeast infection.

Lily said, suddenly and fiercely, "I wish it hadn't happened. I don't want to be mad at Uncle Abe." After a silence, she added, "I can't be mad at her. I can't be."

"Your business. I'm mad enough for both of us." Joanna sneezed, felt around for a tissue, found none, and wiped her nose on an edge of the sleeping bag. "So you think I should keep up appearances. Go on with him, same as always, nothing changed at all. Everybody's perfect couple, growing old practically together. Like that?"

"No, of course not like that! I don't know, it's up to you. I just can't think that his doing it with Lioness has to be the end of the world. Forget fresh air, I'm closing this fucking flap." She crawled to the entrance and began to lace it shut, saying over her shoulder, "Even if it is. The end of the world. Even if it is."

"Nothing to talk about, I told you. Goodnight." Joanna burrowed as far down as she could into her sleeping bag, even covering her head. Then, abruptly, as impulsively as she had ever done anything, she sat up again. She said, "She's married."

In the darkness, she could feel Lily's silent shock like a living thing—a large, unfriendly animal crowding into their tent—and feel the pure physical effort that her daughter's silence was costing her. Lily finally said, in a quiet, toneless voice, "Lioness is married."

"Yes. Get back in your bag, you'll freeze." Joanna heard the slow rustling, and reached out for Lily, but could not find her. "You were right, all that time ago. His name's Mardikian, and she's been running from him since before we met her. That night, at the Skyliner, he finally caught up. That's what happened."

She felt the silence crushing her into the farthest corner of the little tent. Lily whispered, "Her husband."

"Mardikian. Don't know his first name. Older guy, very elegant. I've been meeting him on the ferry now and then . . . we got to be sort of friends. He was with us when she walked into the Skyliner. She panicked and ran out, and Abe went after her. Said he'd take her home." Even with her nose stopped up, she managed a creditable snort. "And so he did."

Even with the tent flap closed, the wind forced her back down into her own sleeping bag, wrapping her arms around herself. The coldness of her feet reminded her unwillingly of Abe's. Lily's voice continued, soft and flat. "She must have been so frightened."

"I guess Abe took care of that." Joanna was trying to keep her own voice as level as her daughter's. "She never even woke up when I threw his damn harmonica at him. Sleeping like a baby."

"I'm glad. I mean, I'm sorry, but I'm glad she could sleep peacefully."

"After what she did? Whose side are you on, if I may ask?"

"Not if you don't want an answer." For the first time since hearing of Lioness's husband, Lily's voice had taken on a living edge. "Right now, this isn't about you, it isn't about Abe—it isn't about who did what with whom. This is about Lioness, and the hell with the rest of it. Where is she? Do you know where she is?"

"No, I don't!" Joanna flared back at her. Knowing exactly how childishly sulky she sounded, she still could not keep from mumbling, "And thanks for making it clear who matters around here. Thanks a whole bunch."

"Mom. Stop it." The word, so rarely used, caught at Joanna's throat. Lily said, "I know you're really in pain, and I'm really sorry for it—I *am*. But you're not alone and on the run, and Lioness is. I have to find her, and I have to help her, and as soon as we get back, that's what I'm going to do. And it'll make me feel bad if it hurts you, but I have to do it. Please. I'm sorry. I have to."

After a time, Joanna said quietly, "Then you do what you have to. Goodnight."

Cold and uncomfortable and wretched as she was, she was almost asleep when Lily asked quietly, "You awake?" Joanna did not answer. Lily leaned close over her to say, "This is like when we went camping, remember?"

"Don't remember." Joanna was not sure she had even spoken aloud.

"When I was nine, ten. You, me and . . . and the three of us. When it rained, and the tent fell down. And he cooked those awful sort of waffly things."

"You woke me up for that," Joanna said.

The long, mournful sigh. "I cannot believe I forgot my pillow. I can't sleep without my pillow."

"Here." Joanna shoved her own over, laid her head on her folded arms, and was asleep before Lily could thank her.

The sun was already high in a startlingly clear sky when they were awakened by the sound of waves and the voices of hikers crashing along the trail toward East Beach and the visitor center. Joanna made questionable instant coffee while Lily located a restroom, and they took turns washing and brushing and despairing. Lily came back saying, "I look like a crocodile," and Joanna told her, "Mirrors lie—this is a scientific fact." They were shy and silent with each other during their breakfast, which was bananas. Afterward, Joanna roused herself to ask, "You want to schlep over to Tillicum? Real coffee and postcards?"

Lily shook her head. "I'd just like to go home."

"Me too." Joanna was scrunched small in a corner of the tent, hugging her knees. "I'm sorry, I knew I should have done this alone. I should never have made you come with me."

"But then we couldn't have bonded," Lily said. She came over and crouched in front of her mother. "I'd have missed that." Joanna touched her hand, and they looked at each other in half-smiling silence. Lily said, "One thing. If we ever do this again—and I am not saying we will—if we are *ever* to do this again, we have got to lay in some serious gear, okay? Like an air mattress that actually holds air, and sleeping bags that don't smell funny. And warm socks. Lots of socks." She stood up again, wincing as a joint cracked. "Damn, my hip was on some kind of boulder all night. Let's do it."

They rolled up the sleeping bags and stowed their cookware, working almost in harmony. When they took down the tent and stood for a moment in its absence, Joanna realized fully just how quickly the wind was rising. Carrying sand, it stung her face and filled her hair with grit; it was also beginning to whip up ominous little rollers on the Sound. Lily cast a dubious eye at the water, and then at Joanna, who said, in her best New Zealand voice, "Shallow far enough out, we can get off. Keep Gardner on the right, head for the lighthouse, home in time for *People's Court* reruns. Easy-peasy. Come here, you've got your life jacket on wrong."

They pushed the kayak straight into the chop and held it steady for each other to get aboard. Almost immediately Joanna became aware of the difference in the day. The wind had scoured away any overcast, leaving the sky and the Sound troublingly shiny, even to a novice eye, and the waves were already three feet or more high. She turned her head to tell Lily, "Dig in, make for deep water. Hit a rock and we've got trouble." The wind carried off Lily's reply, which Joanna thought was probably just as well.

For all the height of the waves, they were not breaking, and for some while Joanna, if not Lily, actually enjoyed managing them.

Paddling was far easier than on the outward journey, for they were going with the current, sliding smoothly up one side of a roller and then down into the trough, hardly shipping water. Joanna, in the bow, her face lashed raw by the wind and by her own blowing hair, found herself yowling wordlessly as the kayak flowed to the top of a wave, and brandishing her paddle at airplanes passing overhead to cry, "I'm flying! I'm flying!" Whether Lily heard her, she could not tell, but once or twice she thought she heard her daughter laughing.

Behind them, when Joanna had a moment to look back, the Olympics and the Kitsap Peninsula seemed truly to dance on the horizon in exultant salute and celebration. Ahead lay Gardner Island, properly close on the right; beyond, bone-white, the toy Alki Point lighthouse. The waves' rhythm became her body's rhythm, and brought back the words of her instructor: "Water'll teach y', wind'll teach y'. Only way." Joanna yelled her gratitude to the Sound, and angled the kayak sharply toward the lighthouse.

At that moment, the wind shifted, blowing now almost directly offshore. Joanna felt it first not on her skin, but in the seat of her pants, as the boat instantly lost way, staggering gracelessly over the crest of a wave and crashing down the other side with a tooth-cracking jolt. At first she blamed herself for somehow having fallen out of step with the water, and concentrated on once again finding the beat; but when the kayak continued to plow drunkenly into each roller, rearing until its bulbous nose pointed to the sky, and then belly-flopping across the grain of the wave, she understood the situation with a grim clarity that rather surprised her. *Don't look back, she'll see you're scared.*

The waves were smashing over them, pushing them sideways, most frightening in their pure weight. She could feel the shock in her legs, feel the kayak flexing, literally bending under her with each blow, *Well, that's good, isn't it? You give so you don't break. Christ, what if we split a seam?*

Even in the pogie mittens, her hands were frozen around the paddle. The kayak had a foot-operated rudder, but it was locked in place, as the New Zealander had advised her to leave it in calm water—"Y'll just get dependent on it, mess up y'r paddling"—and Joanna was too disoriented to free it now. The empty innocence of the sky added to her loneliness, the more so because she was convinced that the lighthouse was growing smaller, that they were being driven farther and farther from Alki Point, and that no one on shore could see or help them. She thought of Abe.

The thought was a tender one, which outraged her in the midst of her panic. She did turn her head then, to shout back to Lily, "In case we die—I slept with Mr. Mardikian!" Lily's white face was blankly bewildered, though notably less terrified than Joanna had expected. "What?"

"Mr. Mardikian! On the ferry—I told you about him! I slept with him!"

A four-foot wave that the kayak could not surmount buried them both before Lily could answer her. When they surfaced, Lily was still looking slightly confused. "The guy on the ferry?"

"Lioness's husband, for God's sake! I told you—"

Lily cut her off. "Later! Dig in! We can make it!" And Joanna, all but convulsed with cold, at once soaked and desperately thirsty, her entire body feeling battered beyond responding, screamed, "No, we can't!" from the bottom of her soul, and dug in.

Everything she had so painstakingly learned from the New Zealander had long since abandoned her completely. Far from paddling efficiently, she was clawing at the water like any beginner, at times missing her stroke altogether when a breaking wave dropped the kayak out from under her. She was grabbing for breath as well, nauseous with fatigue, wallowing limply from side to side. Ridiculously she thought, *oh, shit, never did show Lily that Eskimo roll*, and actually laughed through a strangling mouthful.

For all her mockery of her body's decay, she had always been proud—vain, even—that at fifty-six, the body still did what she asked it to do, whether shooting baskets, rollerblading, making love all night long, or spending an entire flight on her feet. Now, almost between one feebly thrashing stroke and another, all of that was over. Ordering her back to straighten, a leg to brace harder against a peg, an arm to reach even a little farther forward made nothing happen: it was as though her body had gone deaf to her, as though her commands were echoing through an empty house. The worst of all was the curiously casual realization that she no longer cared, and seemed not to have cared for a very long time.

Summoning the strength to turn her head one more time, she saw a strange thing. Lily had stopped paddling, and was sitting quite placidly in a curiously meditative fashion, eyes closed, lips moving soundlessly. When Joanna managed a cry, she opened her eyes and smiled in a way that Joanna had not seen since the day her daughter first set off for school.

"All right," she said. "We're all right now."

Joanna had to read her lips, and her calm eyes; she had spoken too quietly to be heard through the clamor of the waves. She leaned back now, still smiling, trailing one hand in the water, like a parasoled pastel lady being rowed grandly down a painted stream. Joanna, bonelessly exhausted, unable even to sit erect, dimly felt the wind beginning to fall away, the breakers gradually dwindling to blue rumples on the sparkling face of the Sound. She began, slowly and heavily, to paddle again.

"You don't have to do that," Lily said behind her. "She'll take us home."

"Maybe," Joanna said, "but the current will take us to Vashon if we don't watch it. Sit still."

---

Joanna threw up on the beach, effectively ending a volleyball tournament. Lily dried them both off with most of their stock of towels, and used the remaining few to cover Joanna while they rested together. Dozing and waking, it was more than two hours before they recovered enough strength to carry the kayak back to Joanna's car and strap it on the roof. That done, they sat in the car for a time, Joanna still too tired to turn the key in the ignition, and Lily too tired to remind her. At last Joanna said, "Lioness."

"She said she'd always come if I really needed her." Lily was staring ahead, speaking evenly, but with long pauses between words. "If I called inside myself—you remember?" Joanna nodded. Lily said, "And I really tried not to need her, not to call, but I really had to. I mean, if I hadn't . . ."

That pause went on until Joanna finally started the car. Beside her, Lily whispered, "I hope she knows I tried not to need."

Joanna drove back to the Lake Union shop very slowly, both of them as silent as they had been the day before on the way to Alki Point. Once Joanna volunteered, "My legs still don't feel connected," and once Lily mumbled, "Think I paddled some better on the way back." Beyond that, they hardly spoke until the kayak had been returned and they were on their way to Wallingford. The silence was oddly companionable, rather than cold or withdrawn, but separate even so, as though they two had leaped from the same burning airplane and were now floating to earth, side by solitary side. Joanna thought, *Well, bonding's what you make it*, and tried to concentrate on moving into the exit lane.

She double-parked in front of Lily's apartment house, cut the engine, snapped on her blinkers, turned to face her daughter, and said, "Thank you for saving our lives. Much obliged."

"It wasn't me," Lily protested. "You saw what happened. You saw what she did."

"Yes, well, would you mind if I'd rather owe my life to you than to somebody who betrayed me with my old man, the son of a bitch? Whoever she is, let's just say that she came to help you, and I just happened to be there at the time. Can we say that, and let it be, and I go on thanking you? I'd find it so much easier."

"And we don't talk about what's really been going on? About your little payback fling with her husband, your Mr. Mardikian? Or does all that have to wait until our next near-death experience?" Lily gripped her mother's shoulders with both hands, and Joanna could feel her forearms trembling with the effort of not shaking her. "Mom, I don't know who she is, or what's happening to us, but it's real—she's real! That's all I know, that's all I can deal with—that's all I *want* to deal with! If she's running, then I have to help her run—if she's hiding, then I have to find a good place for her to hide. Do you . . . can you understand?"

Joanna covered the hands on her shoulders with her own. "No. I don't understand a damn thing. I'm not sure I'll ever understand anything again. The one thing I'm sure of is that Mardikian's not someone you get away from. He'll find her, baby. I know this."

A delivery driver, unable to get around them in the narrow street, was banging rhythmically on his horn. Lily reached for the door handle, shaking her head. "No, he won't. I won't let him." She got out of the car and started toward her house, then wheeled abruptly to ask through the rolled-down window, "You want to do something like dinner tomorrow?"

"I'm not planning to eat ever again in my life. But I could come along and watch you." Lily nodded, flipped a hand to her, and turned again to enter the house. Joanna cleared her throat. "Lily."

Lily stopped. Joanna said, "About Lioness. I'm not ordering you not to see her, anything stupid like that. Just be . . . I guess, just be really careful."

"She's gone," Lily said, with her back still to her mother. "She went away right after she helped us. See you tomorrow."

She walked into her house as the driver trapped behind Joanna began to descend from his van. He was not at all calm, and Joanna drove away quickly, almost hitting a parked car because she was weary and flustered. It took her a long time to make her way home to Queen Anne Hill.

# 13.

# SEPTEMBER

A be began leaving messages on Lily's answering machine. "Lilsville, will you please tell your mother to call me?" "Lily, you think you could maybe spare a little *rachmones* for your suffering Uncle Abe? You heard me, suffering. Pass it on." "Lily? Lily, you nagged Del into sending you to horse camp, you can nag her into calling me." "Lilsville? Thuglet, you there? Would it help if I reminded you who put your goddamned seventy-nine-dollar bicycle together on your ninth Christmas Eve?"

None of the calls were returned; not even the last and quietest, the one that said, between long pauses, "Lily, I'm not offering excuses, I'm not expecting forgiveness. Not ever. I did what I did, I have to live with it, that's all. But a lot of weirdness has been happening around all three of us—you most of all, probably—and I just think we ought to talk about it . . . uh, dispassionately . . . and try to figure out what exactly it is, and what we can do about it. Dispassionately, okay? Call me. Please." But she never did.

Twelve-Bar Billy would have been delighted to help—jealous women being a staple of his personal and professional repertoire— but, as he said himself, "Daddy, short of tracking your lady down, roping her, and hauling her home on the hood, ain't a thing in the world I know to do. My experience, she'll be in touch, if only to call you some really juicy names she forgot last time. You got Caller ID?"

He had rather expected Lioness to be gone when he came back to the garage with breakfast. She was, and he never bothered looking for a note or any sort of romantic keepsake. "Dreams don't stick around for coffee and toast," he reminded himself aloud, sitting on her sleeping bag while the meal got cold. He admitted to a certain amount of wistful relief, chided himself for it, and spent that day, and each day following, trying to get Joanna Delvecchio to answer her telephone. But in his dreams he searched for Lioness.

Asking at the Skyliner Diner, he discovered that she had not shown up for work since their night together. Corinne had heard nothing, nor had any of the other waiters—nor, for that matter, had the flamenco guitarist, and it showed. "He sort of lumps there on his stool, playing like his hamster just died." She cocked her head and focused shrewdly on Abe with one half-closed eye. "What the hell happened that weird evening, when she walked in and took right off again? And you went after her? Did you do something?" Abe did not reply, but simply held his wrists out for handcuffs. She slapped them away. "Get out of here. I never did trust old men. You see her, tell her to stop fooling around and come back. Customers are asking for her. Tell her I'll give her ten more than she'll get anywhere else on the island. Anywhere else."

"There's a Jewish joke," Abe said to Twelve-Bar Billy.

"Ain't there always?" The cowboy was squatting on his heels in an empty rehearsal room, rolling a cigarette while they waited for the rest of Seriously Blue. He lost more tobacco by this method than he ever smoked, but he said it was his way of cutting down.

"It's about a rabbi who's always, always wondered what bacon might taste like. He obsesses so much about this that finally he can't stand it anymore, and he turns up his coat collar and sneaks into a deli and orders a BLT. Which he likes well enough, but when he comes out the weather's turned really nasty: the sun's vanished, the sky's full of great black clouds, rain's starting to come down, there's lightning and thunder—the works, okay? The rabbi cowers in the doorway, and the only thing he can say is, 'Can you imagine it? All that fuss over one little piece of bacon!'"

Twelve-Bar Billy laughed around his ragged cigarette, but said nothing. Abe said, "Excuse me? You do see my point?"

"Oh, I surely do. Three whole women gone, vanished out of your life overnight, and here you are, saying, 'All that fuss over one little piece of pussy?'" The clear, cold blue eyes made Abe lower his own. Twelve-Bar Billy said, "But that wasn't hardly ordinary pussy, was it? I saw that girl at your barbecue. Trade two ordinary women for her any time, and throw in a set of dishes."

Abe felt his eyes actually swelling in his head, and his vision fogging red. He trusted himself only to say, very quietly, "Those two aren't ordinary."

Twelve-Bar Billy slapped his own face, hard enough to leave a palm print. "Well, sakes, was that me roused you up all mannish, daddy? Apologies are in order, mea maxima whatever." But the blue eyes were still alight with mockery. "Ain't you the one, though? You want all three of them, am I right? Little Butch, and your old lady, and Herself too—don't plan on leaving nothing for nobody else. Damn, and they say trumpet players got ego." He attempted a smoke ring, but the tobacco flakes on his lip got in the way.

"Right now," Abe began. He had to stop, because his voice was shaking, and it took him a while to speak again. "Right now, all I want is for Del to speak to me. I don't care what she says."

"Oh, I believe you. Far as it goes." Twelve-Bar Billy regarded him somewhat less sardonically. "Question is, just how far will *you* go?"

Before a puzzled Abe could respond, the other band members began straggling into the room, and Twelve-Bar Billy immediately turned to berating them all for their lateness and their lack of professionalism. He and Abe never did pick up their conversation, but Abe wandered home to Gardner Island in an oddly thoughtful state of mind.

Joanna never understood how she could have missed him. Granted, the whole boarding process had been a howling horror, from a check-in computer malfunction to a jammed hatch, a baggage-loader breakdown, and a woman trying to smuggle a toy poodle aboard in her purse. Grace and Heather, the two youngest flight attendants, both arrived so late that she had already called for standby replacements when they finally showed up. Granted, the delay and confusion had even caused her to miss the first passenger count—an event none of her crew could remember—but she had caught the second count, and done the walk-through herself as well, and it was simply impossible that she could not have seen him there in a fucking aisle seat in first class, sipping a gin-and-ginger-ale, thumbing through a Dorothy Dunnett concordance, and smiling at her with just as much warm old knowledge as though he weren't dead and rotting and frying in hell. She stopped in her tracks, and Grace bumped into her from behind, and Joanna came as close as she had come in fifteen years to spilling a tray of drinks.

"What are you doing here?" Her voice sounded to her like the scratching of a ratty broom on a dirt floor; as constricted as her throat was, she had no concern about Grace hearing her. "What are you doing here?"

"Going to Chicago," Abe said. "Hear some good blues."

"In first class? You never fly first class! You can't go first class!" The two passengers across the aisle were showing a certain smiling interest, and she moved on quickly, taking drink orders and handing out menus. When she looked back, Abe was calmly reading his Dunnett, even making notes in the margins. *He always does that, every book in the house* . . . Over the P.A. system, the pilot requested the flight attendants to prepare for takeoff. Joanna went to buckle herself into her accustomed jumpseat, which faced Abe directly, separated by only two vacant seats. He went on reading, never once looking up.

Not until the plane had leveled off did he catch her eye, holding out his glass for a refill. He said, "Nice to watch you at work. Not one wasted move."

"You can't do this!" Joanna leaned toward him, keeping her voice as low as she could. "You have no business on this flight."

"What, I can't visit all my nieces and nephews in Evanston?" He nodded at an empty aisle seat. "Sit, we'll discuss this."

Joanna remained standing. "I'm the one with family in Evanston, and every one of them has a contract out on you. Here's your drink, here's a *Times*, enjoy your flight, watch the movie, leave me the hell alone." She walked away into the galley and leaned against a bulkhead.

Little Grace came up to her to ask timidly, "What's the matter? Can I do something?" She was Vietnamese, with huge eyes and a built-in concern for old people. Joanna patted her shoulder and mumbled something about a migraine, which was a mistake, because Grace spent the rest of the flight constantly watching over her. But it helped, too, since it meant that she was almost never alone when she passed Abe, and he did no more than smile occasionally and praise the meal. He did not look at the movie.

Only when they had begun the descent into O'Hare did he speak directly to her again. "You good for dinner? How about the Indian place by your hotel?"

"If you come near me," she said. "Do you understand? If you come near me . . ."

"Okay. So maybe not dinner." He made a show of checking

his appointment diary. "Well, you've got the whole day free tomorrow—I could make lunch. The Palmer House, my treat?"

Grace was beside her almost on the instant, reminding Abe to return his tray to the locked position, and asking Joanna under her breath as he obeyed, "Is he bothering you?" Joanna did not reply to either of them. She dealt calmly with the landing, and with the deplaning afterward, and looked over Abe's head as he ambled by with the other first-class passengers. *Still trying to walk like that hillbilly bandleader. I am not impressed.*

She half-expected him to follow the crew bus to their hotel, and was braced to confront him in the lobby; but in fact she never saw him during the layover. On the following day, however, he was in the same seat for the return flight, again engrossed in Dorothy Dunnett, again sending his compliments to the microwave. Apart from his one gesture toward the still-unoccupied window seat and her silent refusal, they had no contact during the journey. Leaving the plane in Seattle, he was too busy struggling with his coat, his briefcase, and his overnight bag to look at her at all.

Since the kayak trip, she had worked every flight her crew made, even on weekends, though at her level of seniority she was entitled to almost any time off she cared to take. Lily remonstrated with her, but was told, "I have to stay tired. If I'm not exhausted right through, inside and out, then I can't sleep, and when I can't sleep I lie there and think about just exactly how upside-down my life turned in one night. I have to work. Right now it's what I've got."

Lily regarded her pensively over a pistachio ice-cream cone. "You surprise me, you know that?" They were sitting in Steinbrueck Park, at the Market, watching the courtship dance of lacy Asian kites, circling and weaving and bowing to each other in a chilly autumn sky, so blue that it seemed to swallow the highest kites, leaving the children below looking up as though they had tied their strings around clouds. Joanna said, "Surprise you how?"

"Well, the way you've been dealing with all this. I don't know—I guess I expected you to be a bit cooler about everything. A bit more . . . sophisticated, is that the word I want?" Joanna turned to face her, and she added hurriedly, "Not that I'd do any better, probably—I mean, hey, look at my track record. But I can't help wondering."

Joanna studied her without speaking until Lily lowered her eyes. "So I should suck it up and move on? That's what people say these days, right? *Move on.* Everybody moves on."

"No, that's not what I meant." Lily took both her hands, getting ice cream on one of them. "What I'm trying to say is, I don't really understand why you can't give him another chance. It's not like he ever made a habit of chasing around, the way Dad . . . I mean, it was just with Lioness, and just that one time—"

"That I know of," Joanna snapped. "One time that I know of." She pulled her hands back sharply, and then caught herself, patting Lily's hand half-apologetically. They were both silent for some while before she spoke again. "I don't know if I can explain this to you." Her voice was low, but quite clear. "It isn't about him being in bed with another woman—even that one, that woman who was some way special to both of us, though I can't say why or how. To you too, I'm sorry, I know." Lily nodded, looking away again.

Joanna said, "It was the way he looked that night, at the Skyliner, when he ran out after her. When he came back to the table to say he was taking her home. You weren't there, you didn't see. Twenty-two years, and suddenly I never saw him before. His face, the way he moved . . . twenty-two years, Lily, and he's somebody I don't know anything about, somebody I'm a little scared of. More than a little, damn it. If he can change like that between one minute and the next, maybe I never knew him—maybe it's twenty-two years of total misunderstanding. It happens with people."

She paused, and Lily realized that, for all her apparent calmness, her mother was almost fighting for breath, like an asthmatic. "If I don't know Abe, I don't know anybody. That's what I mean about my life being upside-down. I feel like I have to start everything over, kid, everything absolutely over. A bit late, yes?"

"Well," Lily said. A beautiful scarlet-and-gold kite crashlanded just in front of them; a small Asian boy exploded into violent tears; a shabbily-dressed old Aleut man comforted him, helping him gather up the ruins. Lily moved closer to Joanna on the bench, awkwardly settling an arm around her shoulders. "Well," she said. "You know me."

Joanna smiled then. "There's that. I could start with that."

Lily hesitated briefly. "And Mardikian? Do you know him? Was he any help when you were with him? Any little comfort there at all?" The voice was coyly teasing, but the arm embracing her mother was taut enough to tremble.

The sun was sinking now, and the wind growing colder. The children were going home. Joanna sat motionless, still gazing out toward Gardner Island. Joanna said, "No comfort. He warned me there wouldn't be. He's very . . . honest."

Lily said abruptly, "I can't find her. I've looked everywhere." Her eyes were old with loss. Joanna did not respond. Lily said, "I even called to her, inside, the way I swore I wouldn't. But it wasn't for me—it wasn't to help me—I just want to help her, that's what I kept saying. But she hasn't answered. I can't feel her answering." Her right-hand fingers kept flexing hard against her left palm, a habit she had had since childhood.

"Well, maybe that's why," Joanna offered. "Because she knows you don't need her that way." Lily nodded without replying. They stood up together and started away from the little park toward their cars. Joanna said gently, "She's not with Abe. And she's not with Mardikian, either."

"*How do you know?*" As quietly as they had been speaking, the cry was doubly startling when it ripped out of Lily's throat. She stopped walking, and turned to face her mother. "Maybe he caught up with her and took her back with him, and I'll never see her again!" The anguish in her voice was, suddenly and finally, more than Joanna could bear.

"No," she said firmly. "He could just have taken her right then, when we walked in on . . . on her and Abe. But he didn't—he walked out, same as I did. So no, that's not where she is. That much I do know." She tucked Lily's arm through the crook of her own arm, and after a moment they moved on.

He was there on her next flight, in an aisle seat again, nodding as she passed on the walk-through, but not looking up until she stopped beside him while the safety video was running. "This is stalking," she said. "You know that. I really will call a cop."

Abe put down his book and leaned an elbow on the arm of his seat. He said carefully, "Del, I'm not harassing you. I'm not following you around, I'm not leaving messages anymore, I'm not even speaking until spoken to. I'm just flying back and forth, Seattle to Chicago, because that's my idea of a good time. Slice it any way you like, I don't see how that counts like stalking."

"Whatever you call it, you can't afford it." A tidy, fretful-looking young man was sitting next to him, already tapping rapidly at a laptop computer. The effort of keeping her voice down made her throat hurt. She said, "You can *not* keep this up. You can't."

"Why not? I've got enough books." He patted his briefcase. "People are always telling me, as a historian I should read Dunnett. So far, not bad." His beard was looking ragged, and the fact that she noticed it angered her all over again. She stalked off to check safety belts, as he went back to his book. On her way forward he asked for a glass of merlot.

In Chicago, the next night, she went out to dinner with Grace and another crew member, and got drunk enough that when she tried to telephone Lily from her hotel room, she called Abe's number instead, from force of habit. She banged the phone down as soon as she heard his voice on the answering machine, and promptly heard it again when she checked her own machine for messages. "Just in case, I'm staying at the Voyager, the one by the lake. They've got cable and coffee and everything." She hung up, missed her other messages, and watched old Godzilla movies all night.

He was there on the return to Seattle, and on her next run, and the one after that: maddeningly tranquil, never staring unduly at her, never addressing her, except to request a drink or an extra bag of snack mix, contentedly reading through an apparently endless series of historical novels. She did her best to ignore him, to censor him out of her vision, attempting a kind of psychic Wite-Out; but he loomed larger and larger with each flight, so that often when she surveyed the first-class cabin she literally saw nothing but an immense tumbleweed beard, a book the size of a spade, and a pair of half-raised eyebrows like barbed-wire entanglements. She would go away then and hide in the lavatory, until little Grace knocked anxiously to make sure she was all right.

Joanna was at times tempted to confide in Grace, but always resisted the urge. Grace would have glowered dutifully at Abe, but would also have considered the situation impossibly romantic. So would Joanna have done, she knew well enough, if it had been Grace's situation, or Lily's, or anyone else's. Abe was neither threatening nor importunate: he read his Dunnett novels, watched the movie once in a while—though he invariably went back to reading before the film was over—and spent his Chicago nights in a cheap chain motel, well away from the crew's usual base. All of which she found so transparently calculating, so shamelessly manipulative, that it further hardened her resolve to have no contact with him beyond the unavoidable.

Once, when the window seat was empty, she paused beside him to say, consciously quiet and reasonable, "This has got to stop. You'll go broke in another month, and it won't help. Give it up."

Abe lowered his book, regarding her with a placidity as staged as her own. "Isn't my bank account my business? I could have sworn."

"You are living on your pension and Social Security. You have some savings"—she told him the amount almost exactly—"and a little-bitsy income from that textbook you wrote with Max Connolly and Joe Whoever. You couldn't fly first class on a cropduster."

"Actually, I could. I know this farmer in Puyallup." He gestured for her to sit down, and started to shift to the window.

"Stay right where you are." The beard looked better this time, but he needed a haircut badly, and the ancient corduroy jacket looked like a bald tire. She wanted very much to hit him. "I don't want you to bankrupt yourself just to aggravate me. It won't prove anything, and it won't change anything. It's just stupid, cut it out. Quit, Abe."

His head was turned away from her as he marked his place in the book and set it down beside him. When he looked at her again, the teasing was gone from his eyes, and the careful mildness as well. He said, "So much time, so much history, and you still don't know my one real talent, my one gift. I don't ever quit. Not on John Ball, not on black beer, not on 'Midnight Hour Blues.' I joke about it—I say, I surrender, this is silly, no point making a complete idiot of myself, but I never really do. I thought you understood that, after I learned to samba."

The passenger across the aisle had cleared her throat twice before Joanna turned hurriedly to see what was wanted, while Abe went back to Dorothy Dunnett. When they landed, he invited her to lunch once again, but she managed to be too occupied to reply, and he went on his way to his motel. He left no more messages on her answering machine—she was furious to discover herself half-expecting one—and when he was late for the Seattle flight, having missed his shuttle bus, she became, if not apprehensive, something enough like it to plague her sleep on Queen Anne Hill that night. *No, he doesn't. No, he doesn't. He is not about to turn me against myself.* On the next run, she did not speak to him at all.

But she came to the Voyager motel in her flight-attendant's uniform at one-thirty in the morning of the return flight, knocking until he stumbled to the door to snap on a light and let her in, and taking a certain unpleasing pleasure in the sagging slitted eyes, the white stubble, and the threadbare pajamas. She walked past him and looked around at the room: altogether functional, sensible, barren, stinging with the smell of industrial carpet cleaner; an unexceptionable lodging for a bed, two vinyl chairs, and a nineteen-inch television set. "Boy," she said. "Early bus-station."

"Decor entirely by Greyhound. Cozy, though." His voice was the ragged morning scrap that always took at least two cups of coffee to lubricate. "To what do I owe this visitation?"

She pointed to the two vinyl easy chairs crowding the coffee table. "We're going to talk."

"Now." It was not a question. He scratched his head and took his faded blue terrycloth bathrobe from the second chair. "How come all the times I wanted—?"

Joanna cut him off. "Because my Aunt Carlotta used to say, 'Don't waste time talking to somebody you want to kill. Next thing you know, they'll talk you out of it.' I needed to wait, you understand?" Abe nodded, and she said, "I'm glad," and slapped him then: a full-arm swing from the shoulder, with nothing held back. He grunted and plumped down hard on the bed, rubbing his cheek and nose. Joanna said, "I don't want to kill you anymore."

"Oh. Good." He dabbed at his nose with a tissue, saw that it wasn't bleeding, and said with his usual thoughtful interest, "I don't suppose that comes anywhere near making us even."

"Of course not. Nowhere near." She sat in one of the chairs, her face as smooth and unyielding as vinyl itself, smiling calmly at him. "Not even me sleeping with Mr. Mardikian. Which I did that same night, by the way." Abe's sharp, rasping intake of breath was more balm to her than anything that had happened that night, or since. "He was right—that was just spite and sorrow, and it doesn't count. Absolutely nothing like what you did."

"Mardikian." Objectivity gone, rational reflection out the window, he was on his feet: a paragon of injury, the rest of his face as red as the slapped cheek. "Mardikian? Do you know . . . do you have the least idea. . . ?" He stood gaping, stripped of language, as well as of breath, detachment, and dignity, while she smiled and savored. At last he managed to say, "Jesus, God, you are an idiot. You are such an idiot, you don't even know how much of an idiot you are."

"Perfectly right," Joanna said serenely. "I can't tell you how much I'm enjoying being unreasonable. Better than sex." She considered that for a little while, and then added, "Some sex, anyway." All the same, his intensity began to rouse certain alarms, not so much in her mind as in her skin, where she usually felt the big ones first. She had known him too long not to know when he was completely serious.

Abe sat down eventually, and they regarded each other in a tired, pettish silence, as though they had already had their talk, and mended nothing. The headlights of occasional passing cars on Lake Shore Drive turned them both into tallowy ghosts with faces like burned-out candlewicks. Joanna said in time, "Lily tells me I'm making too big a deal out of you fucking Lioness. I am, too. I know I am."

His voice was quiet again, ruminative, dispassionate. "It happened. It's not going to happen again, but it's never going to have not happened either. If I could snap my fingers right now and make it not have happened . . ." He stopped abruptly, running his hands over his face, then looking wonderingly down at them. He said, "But you don't understand. I know that's the worst thing I could possibly say, just at the moment—"

"You're right," Joanna said. "That really is the very worst thing you could have said. But it does make things easier." She stood up and began undressing.

Abe's eyes went round, and he actually backed away from her. "Del, whatever you think, I'm no more than half-crazy. We are not going to bed here."

"You're the one who doesn't understand," she said. "This is not even an issue—this got decided the first time you set foot in first class. You're figuring to shoot every last dime you have, until I'm finally won over by your devotion, and forget everything I can't possibly forgive. And I need more than anything to clear my head, and clear my desk, and put a nice, sharp, *clean* end to twenty-two years"—her voice faltered only for a moment—"and the only way I know to do that is with a last round of vengeful goodbye sex. And I've got a plane to catch in six hours, so let's get to it. One for the fucking road."

On the thin, rutted mattress—dazed, humiliated, and hopelessly limp at first; then absurdly, almost comically rigid with outrage—he drove himself beyond himself, determined to overpower her scorn and regain her attention, if nothing else, by pure will and stamina. He would have hurt her then, deliberately, if it had been in him to do, just to own her notice for that lone moment, to ravage the same twenty-two years' worth of assumptions that she was simultaneously trying to shatter as she bucked and clawed against him. They were not fragile human beings now, but heavy machinery—bulldozers, backhoes, railroad cars coupling—until she pulled away suddenly, crying out, "No, not like this, not like this!" Her eyes were full of tears, and her face was the known, known fifty-six-year-old face that had so often burrowed blindly into his chest in search of sleep, whose worn, worried lines had faded into a child's trustful assurance time and again on his cramped arm. The madness left him too then, and he whispered, "No, not like this, no, cookie, no," and held her.

They dozed murmurously together for a small, sweet while, until Abe woke, sitting up with a sudden violent shudder to say, "Mardikian. Lioness." Joanna sighed and opened her eyes. Abe said, "Listen, Del, you have to listen. The two of them, they aren't . . . Del, this is going to sound really nuts. I know who they are. It's nuts, but I know. Lioness started to tell me . . ." He caught himself, and Joanna saw him catch himself, and smacked him across the chest with the back of her arm, but he hardly noticed. "She's not human," he said. "You know it, and I know it, and Lily knows it best of all. Lily always knew, some way. She talks to orcas, and they dance for her—she shows kids how to dig for blossoming flowers, only when you put them back they disappear. She's the Clam Liberation Front, she's the Weather Witch, she's the Fruit Juice Sorceress. Del, Del, she's Persephone!"

When Joanna only stared and said nothing, he grew impatient, scrabbling desperately for words. "Come on, you know the legend! Daughter of the earth goddess, Demeter. She got stolen away by Hades, he's the king of the Underworld, didn't I tell you about Hades?" A minuscule acknowledgment. "Ages ago, all of it—I mean ages, forget science, forget reality. And her mother wandered all over the earth, looking and calling for her, and generally letting the planet go to hell. Floods here, droughts there, deserts that used to be gardens—the lot, total worldwide catastrophe. Any of this ring a bell?"

"Lily's third-grade reader," Joanna said. She stretched sleepily, still trying to pretend to herself that they were home in a better bed and time, and he telling her a favorite story. "But the other gods, they made him give the girl back to her mother, right?" She fumbled, blinking, for her watch on the bedside table.

"Right, but he'd gotten her to eat a—what?—a pomegranate, half a pomegranate, in the Underworld, and she swallowed some of the seeds, five, six. And for every one of those seeds she had to spend a month in the Underworld with him, and that's why we have fall and winter, because her mother's missing her so. Never mind that PBS stuff—the earth's rotation, the tilt of the axis. That's really how it works, Del. It's all true, and God knows what else is true. And your Mr. Mardikian—"

"Wait a minute—*wait* a minute!" Joanna was sitting up herself now, hugging her knees. "In the first place, he's not *my* damn Mr. Mardikian—I just borrowed him briefly, for good and sufficient reasons. In the second place—"

"He's Hades," Abe said. "She's left him—just run away—after God knows how many million millennia. And he's come after her."

"Oh," Joanna whispered. They were staring into each other's eyes, and her own were blinking rapidly. "Oh, poor Lily."

"Try *poor us*, while you're at it." Abe's voice was harsher and colder than she had ever heard it. "Del, we've made love with gods. You and I, we've fucked the fucking Infinite. Do you imagine anything's ever going to be the same?"

"Excuse me? Just hold it right there, my insignificant other. No-body made you take off with Lioness and jump her bones in the first bed you could find. I had to force myself on Mardikian—practically raped him, if you want to know. Altogether different, damn it."

"No, baby. It's not." The endearment was one that she herself used only to Lily. She could not recall Abe ever speaking it to her, or she to him. "You do it with a god, it happens because it's what the god wants. Not you. Reasons, circumstances, they don't figure—nothing matters but the god's desire. If Lioness had wanted you, if Mardikian had chosen me . . ."

"If it had been Lily with Lioness . . ." Joanna was suddenly cold; she pulled the ratty bedclothes around her shoulders. "Abe. You don't really believe this."

"Gods riding the Seattle ferry? Unimaginably ancient fertility spirits dropping by to catch some barbecue? The Queen of the Underworld waiting tables, living in my garage? What's not to believe?" When he smiled, he looked younger than she had ever seen him.

"A fundamentalist Greek," she said. "You couldn't just believe in UFOs, or Reverend Moon being the Messiah. Not you. Not my crazy old Abe."

"Makes crazy sense. Explains the endless spring on Gardner, when it was way down in autumn everywhere else. Because she was there." He interrupted himself, waggling a forefinger. "Explains about the orcas, about the flowers, not to mention the Yandells' tap water. About the way she looks—I'll bet you anything she actually posed for that Botticelli *Primavera*. I'm right, Del. For once, I really do know."

"Lily in the wind," Joanna murmured. "Lily knew we'd get home." Her eyes widened. "So, at the barbecue—"

"That was Mama, all right—that was Demeter herself, come to bring Lioness back to her lord and master, a deal's a deal. And you saw what happened."

Joanna did not answer, remembering her one terrifying moment of sharing a goddess's vision, and hearing again the deep voice saying, "You need not fear me. My daughter speaks well of you . . . My foolish daughter." She put her fingertips to her mouth.

Abe was saying, "This time . . . after all the years, *this* one time, the world was too beautiful, she couldn't hold it close enough, like in the Millay poem. She couldn't go back to the Underworld—to *him*—not this time. So she ran away, and he followed. And he found her—of course, he found her. How could you not find Persephone, in this world?"

"How could you not love her?" Joanna's voice was all but inaudible. She got up slowly from the bed and began to dress in the dim, stuffy little room. "He loves her." Abe did not move, but sat watching her. She seemed further away in that moment than all his lost certainties and expectations. "It's cold there," she said, like a child muttering in her sleep. "It's so cold there, where he lives. He only wanted her sunlight, he didn't know she couldn't bear the cold. He didn't know, really."

Abe said, "I'll call you a taxi." He padded naked to the telephone and dialed a number from memory. Waiting, he looked up to add, "Wonder it never happened before."

"Maybe it did." Joanna had her uniform blouse on, and was picking up her skirt. "Maybe she did run, and her mother talked her into coming back, doing her duty. Mothers do things like that."

"Hi, I'm going to need a cab right away," Abe said into the phone. He covered the mouthpiece then to tell her, "You go, I'll get a later flight. I'll call you tonight."

She dropped her skirt and stared. "Did I miss something? A little sweet talk, a little mattress mambo—all shall be well, all's forgiven, so it's back to flying coach? The canapés aren't all you'll miss, Aronson."

"Five minutes." Abe picked the skirt up and handed it to her, gently gripping the hand that closed on it. He said quietly, "Del, I have no idea what's passed between us tonight, and neither do you. All is not well—maybe it shall not ever be well, I don't know. What I do know is that you need to think, and you aren't going to need me winking at you and rolling my eyes at you like a fool in heat all the way to Seattle. I will, too—I can't help it—and it'll just embarrass you in front of your crew, and you'll hate me all over again. Turn around, you've got it on all wonky."

Obediently she turned to let him straighten her skirt and do up the hidden top button, which she could never reach. She said, "You really don't know where they are? Either one of them?"

"No idea. Halfway back to the Underworld, could be." He smoothed the skirt with his usual mock-lascivious courtesy, and added, "But I don't think so. We'd know if they were gone. We're connected to them now."

The taxi horn sounded outside. Abe opened the door and stepped back. "Catch your plane. I'll call."

"All right." They looked at each other for a moment longer, neither quite risking an expression or a gesture. Joanna very nearly touched Abe's bruised cheek; when he stroked the emptiness just above her hair, a tiny spark stung his hand. Then she was in the cab and gone, and he was standing naked in the motel doorway, looking out at a drizzly Chicago dawn, already sucked cold and colorless by the vampire wind.

# 14.

# SEPTEMBER

The weather changed.

Within days of Lioness's disappearance, while Seattle was enjoying its usual benign September, the skies over Gardner Island turned cold and sullen. Rain fell almost daily, most often in vicious sheets, blown almost sideways by Alaskan gusts. The Seattle-area papers all ran learned and comprehensive articles on the inexplicably sudden ending of the inexplicable endless summer of Gardner Island. El Niño came in for a lot of criticism. Mr. Nakashima came back from Spokane, happily vindicated. Lily spent more than one useless weekend following up unlikely stories on improbable regional Indian summers. A piece in a free bus-station handout led Abe and Joanna to Mount Rainier, tracking a rumor of a remarkable late blooming season on one particular western slope. But though they caught the earliest ferry, managed actually to find their way to the strange flowering, and plodded calling until near nightfall, there was no suggestion, beyond an undeniable overabundance of lupin, wild lilac, and California poppies, that Lioness had ever walked those high fields. They returned in silence, and Abe—as lately happened more often than not—left Joanna at her apartment and went on to Gardner Island alone.

When Joanna did visit, they were generally quiet and thoughtful with each other, neither accusing nor confiding. She did tell Abe about her kayak voyage with Lily, which prompted the comment as they sat at the top of his beach stairway, late one afternoon, "Well, at least with the weather back to lousy, you'll be staying off the damn Sound for awhile. One good thing, anyway."

Joanna was silent for a long time before she answered him. "Lily would know."

Abe blinked at her. Joanna said, "If Lioness—Persephone—if she were really back on her throne in Hades, the Underworld, whatever, my kid would feel it. She would."

Abe shook his head. "Look there." He pointed off across the creek, to Janice Yandell's favorite rhododendron bush. The astonishingly long-lived flowers had fallen, all of them, overnight, and the leaves themselves were rapidly dying back, as should have happened more than a month before. "Look over there," and he directed Joanna's attention to her own proud and treasured fuchsia, whose blossoms were literally crumbling to pink dust before their eyes. "Like that girl in *Lost Horizon*," he said. "The magic's all gone. She's gone. He's got her."

A day of fitful storm had, ironically, blown itself into the kind of gloriously tasteless sunset only clouds can provide, brazen orange all the way to Seattle. Presently, with the orange blaze beginning to fade to a pale, soapy yellow, Joanna said softly, "If we could find him. He liked me." Abe slanted an eyebrow at her. "Don't go there. He liked me. If we just knew where they were—"

"We'd what? Snatch her to safety at the last minute—smuggle her away over the border? Del, there's no way we can rescue her—there's nothing to rescue her for, or from. I keep telling you, it's just the deal."

"Why is it the deal?" Joanna's eyes had darkened; when Abe touched her hot cheek to calm her, she pulled her head away. "Where is it written that she can't stay on in this world? She belongs here, and she makes it so beautiful where she is. Why can't she ever stay?"

"Because she's a damn goddess. Because if she isn't coming and going with the seasons, everything's out of balance, everything. Perpetually perfect weather on Gardner Island really isn't the ultimate purpose of the universe. The world needs winter, the world needs volcanoes, the world needs floods, storms, bloody hurricanes, because you cannot have Primavera without nasty. Demeter has to grieve for Persephone when she's away in the Underworld, and Demeter has to rejoice when she returns, never mind if they get along or not. And Demeter knows it—that's why she came to the barbecue, to tell Lioness that it's time and way past time to go back with your Mr. Mardikian. Because she belongs there, too."

He fell silent, reaching out for Joanna's hand, not seeming to notice when he failed to reach it. His eyes were closed as tightly as when he played his harmonica with Seriously Blue, and he did not open them when he continued. "The others—Zeus and Poseidon, Athena, Aphrodite, all the rest of that horny, spiteful, childish, wicked, unfair, inconceivably beautiful gang—they don't matter so much anymore, wherever they are, in this world. But Hades, Persephone, her mother—light, dark, spring, autumn, life, death, rebirth . . . they go on together. They're how things are."

The sky was fully dark now, except for a few vertical streaks of cloud that looked like claw marks, with a strange bright sliver showing through the rents. Joanna said, "I want to say goodbye. That's all."

Abe's voice was heavy and distant. "Funny. Traditionally, people are always supposed to feel empty, devastated, when a god leaves them. Nobody ever seems to wonder how the god might feel. Leaving the only people who almost understood."

"She might miss us," Joanna said. "Miss Lily, anyway."

"She knows where we are."

Joanna spent most of her free days that fall riding the Gardner Island ferry, back and forth, like Mr. Mardikian, on the impossible off-chance of meeting him again. She never told Abe or Lily about this.

Lily haunted Abe's garage almost literally, touching and turning over everything that Lioness had left behind, often spending the night on the worn sleeping bag. One afternoon she flew up to the house, her eyes and face lustrous with joy, to tell him, "The stone I left for her, the pretty black one, it's gone—I couldn't find it anywhere! She took it with her, she must have taken it! Lioness kept my stone, isn't that utterly fantastic?" She looked about eight years old.

Abe himself hardly worked at all on the John Ball book. He now played the blues with his eyes wide open, constantly scanning the audience at every performance of Seriously Blue that Twelve-Bar Billy kept lining up in unlikely clubs in obscure crannies of Washington and Oregon. At times he would abruptly break off in the middle of a solo to peer through the roaring dimness at the face of some late arrival, or at some slender form half-glimpsed in the shadows crowding a far corner. Billy had to speak to him about it.

In the end, Lioness came to Lily.

She had slogged home from working late on a chill night swollen with imminent rain, dropped her coat, kicked off her shoes, stood forlornly for awhile at the bedside of her moribund African violet, and finally wandered to her open refrigerator to debate the virtues of two-day-old Albertson's roast chicken against those of reheated vegetarian lasagna. When the light knock sounded, she said aloud, "Terrific, the Mormons, all I need," and stumped mumbling to the door. Lioness was standing in the dingy hallway, smiling slightly, shoulders a little slumped, looking a bit tired and faded for the sum total of all loveliness.

All Lily knew to do in that moment was to take hold of Lioness's hands and Lioness's shoulders and drag her inside, crying, "Oh, please, oh, come in—oh, please, please come in!" And Lioness Lazos, Queen of the Underworld, Consort of Hades, walked for the second time into her two rooms, looked around, and said thoughtfully, "You've changed the curtains. It's nice here, Lily."

"No, it's not," Lily said. "It's the pits and the shits, and even you being here doesn't change that. But I'm so happy you're here."

In her home, at the sudden end of her despairing search, she asked no questions. Instead she brought Lioness to the ancient blue-corduroy window seat that was her one true pride, after which she made chai, and sat with her there, saying little, looking down at dark Wallingford Avenue as the rain began to fall. By and by— also for the second time—Lily put her head on Lioness's knee, and Lioness stroked her hair.

"I don't know who you are," Lily mumbled into the familiar flower-print dress. "A myth, a fairy story, someone I made up. It doesn't matter. I never ever know who anybody I love is, anyway."

"Even in my own tongue, there is no real word for what I am." Lioness's voice was calm and uninflected. "In yours . . . well, old is as good as any. Very old."

"I want to ask where you've been, but I'm sort of afraid you'll tell me." Lily felt her hair reaching out to curl around Lioness's fingers.

"With him. Even when I was not." *She smells like herself . . . oh, she smells just like herself . . .* Lioness said, "He delays strangely in your world—he lets me run a little free while he wanders himself. It is not like him."

"We'll hide you," Lily said. "I'll hide you. I know all kinds of places, backcountry, way up in the mountains—Oregon, Idaho, you wouldn't believe. I've got friends, they knew places. I'll make some calls right now."

Lioness said nothing, but only quieted Lily's desperate prattling with a finger across her lips. She began to sing, very softly, in a language Lily did not know. Lily was terrified of falling asleep, and fought against it, trying as hard as she could to inhale the voice and the song, but she did doze a little. Lioness did not move at all. When Lily's eyes snapped open she said immediately, "I snored, didn't I? You can tell me." Lioness laughed and shook her head. Lily said, "I've been told I snore."

"Hush," Lioness said softly. "Hush, sweet Lily. You could never imagine how long it has been since I sat with anyone like this."

"It'll be a lot longer before anyone else ever calls me 'sweet Lily.'" She turned her head awkwardly to look up into the still face and the long, tilted dark-green eyes. "You're going with him."

"Tomorrow. I asked him for one more day. He doesn't really understand about days and nights, so it was a little hard to persuade him. But he tries to be good to me. He has always tried."

"And you came to me. On your last day." Lily tried to keep her voice steady, and almost did. "It's all right, don't worry, I'm not going to cry. I never do."

Lioness smiled, and Lily reached up to touch the smile and then pressed her fingers against her own cheek. "It is not so dreadful, my Lily. I was very frightened at first when I knew he had found me. It brought me back to that terrible moment I still dream . . . so much unimaginable time, and once again my mother's earth is tearing apart under my feet, and he is there, driving, lunging upward, exploding into the light, all cold night shaped into a black chariot, black horses, a man . . ." Lily felt a single long shiver against her body. "But then . . . then I thought, *Ah well, I am only going home, after all.*"

Lily sat up sharply. "It isn't your home! It was never your home, it was never where you were meant to be! He stole you, he stole half your life—he dragged you underground into prison, for God's sake! Nobody has to just walk back into a prison!"

"Even a prison can become home," Lioness answered her. "If enough of yourself is there with you. Even free on the beautiful earth . . . even then, half of me was there beside him, always." She took Lily's face between her hands. "And perhaps that is where I was always supposed to be. Perhaps it was always planned so from the beginning of beginnings—not by him, not by any of the gods, but by something greater than they, something that holds some power yet, when they are shadows lost in the alleys." She gave Lily's head a small, gentle shake. "Besides, it's not really underground, that place. Not under this ground. Truly, I promise you, it is not so dreadful."

"I couldn't stand it," Lily whispered. "I couldn't live thinking every day about you being back in the dark and the cold. It's too long, I couldn't live."

Lioness turned to look out of the window. Directly below, on the rainy street, a man with long, thin white hair and a bad leg was trying to maneuver two balky grocery carts stuffed with green plastic trash bags into a shallow, narrow doorway. There wasn't room for himself and the carts, no matter how he arranged and rearranged the three of them. At one point he uttered a wordless wail of anger and fear and frustration, and folded to the sidewalk in an oddly graceful movement, like a dancer. But he was up in a moment, once again battling doggedly with the carts and the rain and his leg. Lily heard Lioness say something softly to herself in the language of her singing.

Letting her head fall back onto Lioness's knee, she again forced herself to ask what she did not want to ask. "You won't be here when I wake up, will you?"

"No."

The single word fell like a soft hammer on Lily's heart. The hand in her hair stopped moving for a moment; then slipped down to rest lightly against her throat, so that Lily felt her pulse beating wildly in Lioness's palm, like a bird. Lioness said, "But I will leave with you all that I can leave. Sleep now."

"No." It was Lily's turn at the word, and she said it with all her strength. "I won't. You'll just have to go while I'm watching, I'm not about to miss one lousy minute of you. Go on, then, just go on, any time you like—I can deal." She kissed the long fingers fiercely, one by one. "One thing, just tell me this one thing. I'm special to you. I know I am, but I couldn't really say it until now—now, when I've got nothing to lose." She did not dare to look up, but she could feel the slow half-smile through Lioness's hands. "Why? I can't give you anything, I can't do anything in the world for you. Even if I even knew what you needed, which I never will. Why am I special?"

"Why you?" Lioness did not answer immediately, but seemed to be translating her words carefully from that other language. "My Lily, where I come from—where I came from, so long ago—there are children who belong to the gods from the day they are born. Sometimes the parents make a promise, they bargain—the first daughter for a good corn crop this year, the second son if the fishnets are full all winter, if the wolves stay away. Those children, later they become the priests of the gods, and never mind if that was what they wanted or not. Do you understand me?"

She paused for a little time, plainly expecting no reply. When she continued, her voice sounded like the rain ruffling softly at the window, driven by a wind from across the world. "But some, a very few, come to the gods all on their own. They find their way—long and far it is, sometimes—and they wander up to the altars, shy and clumsy and embarrassed and alone, and when they can get the words out, they say, 'Well. Here I am.'" Her laugh was almost a sigh, and Lily felt that also through the hand on her head. "They never become the priests, those, never, but they are greatly beloved."

"And I'm like that? Like them?" Lily could hardly breathe.

"You are like that. And more, which you have yet to discover." Lioness laughed sadly again. "But oh, Lily, my dear, you have made a poor choice of goddesses. This one has no altars, no priests or acolytes, no secret scriptures, no sacrifices in smoky caverns, and definitely no mysteries. Even those who follow her have no idea that they do so, and would not ever call it by such a name as worship. Prophet, sibyl, oracle, Pope—choose your appointment, name your rank. Believe me, you have the field almost to yourself."

"I just want this. This moment, this now—I just want this to go on forever, that's all. Forever and forever and forever." Lily let her eyes close, seeing through her lashes, not a familiar face, nor even a human form, but a forest: a green tumble of vines and leaves and green earth, at once coursing with life and just as gloriously vibrant with death and decay. Seeking Lioness in that verdant drowsiness, she announced, clearly and truculently, "But you better keep that stone, you hear me? Only thing you ever let me give you. You hear?"

Lily woke with a blanket over her and a cushion under her head. The first thing she focused on was Lioness's shabby stuffed camel lying beside her pillow; the second was her African violet, blooming in fullest proud velvet, as though all the sprays and fish emulsions and time-release fertilizers had at last taken hold simultaneously. She got up realizing in a cloudy way that she had not eaten since breakfast, and thinking heavily that she might not eat again.

The rain had stopped. Blinking hazily down through the still-streaked window, she saw the old shopping-cart man asleep in the doorway, with his head on one of his plastic bags. As she began to lower the living-room blinds, he woke abruptly and looked directly up at her. He had an angular, high-boned face, and eyes of a curious shifting color, like snow in shadow, and a deep and harshly commanding voice as he called her name. "Lily Delvecchio! Come to me now, Lily Delvecchio!"

The street was dark and empty under a cold crust of stars; she saw only a couple of late shoppers, themselves laden with department-store bags, who detoured into the street to avoid the shouting old man. But Lily, without hesitation, moving with the moonlit sureness of a sleepwalking child, turned from the window to her door, and came down two flights of stairs to meet him where he waited for her between his shopping carts. He wore ragged jeans, a sweater foul beyond color, and sopping carpet slippers; his white hair looked as sticky as old soap, and his eyes glittered as heartlessly as the stars, but she was not afraid. She said, even before she reached him, "I know who you are."

He bowed formally, as no one had ever bowed to her before. "And I know you. Even though you look nothing like your mother."

"People tell me that a lot," Lily said. "What do you want?"

"The sea," the old man answered quickly and seriously. "The sky. But those were claimed and taken long ago. So I must be satisfied with a moment of Lily Delvecchio's time."

"Just a moment?" she asked. "You took all of *her* time. You stole her whole life, and I hate you for it."

The strange eyes flashed briefly at this, as though her voice had struck sparks against steel, but there was midnight amusement in them as well. "Accuracy, child. It was half of her life I stole—and if I had not done so, you would never have known her. Would you truly give that time back to her, and forget forever her hand on your skin, her sweetness in your mind? Perhaps not? So. Listen to me."

Lily became aware that her legs were trembling, which infuriated her, but her head was clear, and she faced the old man with as much challenging pride as she could muster. "Listening isn't believing. Talk."

The old man shook his head in apparent censoriousness. "Your mother is also a far more mannerly woman, Lily Delvecchio." His abrupt laugh had the sound of breaking glass, and as much self-mockery as humor in it. "And here I am, infected and contaminated by her mortal manners, lingering vainly on her earth, possessed to do her daughter one small, thankless grace. Oh, I have surely no business in this world—may my lady queen please to fly to some other, some more tractable creation, should she forsake me ever again. But now"—and Lily felt the sudden crack of power in the single word burn across her throat, exactly where Lioness had touched her—"now you will be silent and hear me. If you wish to see her even once more, and bid her farewell, you will hear me."

They faced each other silently over the plastic bags, which in the freezing starlight seemed to Lily to be transforming themselves into great, slow, cheese-green waves, poised to crush and drown her if she looked at them too directly. She said at last, quietly. "I do wish to say farewell."

The telephone finally broke Joanna free of an endless dream of a howling dog. Her daughter's voice, at once astonished and chagrined, babbled in her ear, *She was here.* Joanna's mouth tasted, appropriately enough, of dry kibble. She had no chance to respond before Lily went on, her voice now so tensely controlled that Joanna could feel the strain in her own throat. "She was here. She was here. Him, too."

Joanna sat up, knocked her bedside radio to the floor, and switched on the light. Lily said, "She's leaving, she's going back there with him. Today, she said today, he's coming for her." The voice was shattering like a double-paned window: a spiderweb of cracks spreading everywhere. "And I'm going with her."

"What are you talking about?" Joanna was already fumbling on the floor for yesterday's clothes. "Lily, talk, make sense. What are you saying?"

"She wants me to come. I know she does."

Clicks and crackles on the line terrified Joanna with the thought that Lily might be about to hang up. "Wait! Lily, *wait*, talk to me!" The underpants ripped, as they had been threatening to do for months, and she stepped on something small and sharp. "Lily?"

"Mommy, I'll miss you. I will." She did hang up then, and Joanna stood balancing precariously on one foot, holding torn underwear in her hand and crying her daughter's name over and over, while the dream-dog howled.

# 15.

# SEPTEMBER

"Lake Union. *Lake Union?*"

"Lake Union. Because you and I heard the same dog howling all night long."

Joanna stared at him in a way that she had not done since walking in on him with Lioness. He took a curve, returning her glance without expression. "Because we had the same dream, the one about the house in the tree. Or the treehouse, if you like—I'm easy. Buckle your seat belt."

Joanna took a deep breath, very consciously, and let it out very slowly, like an archer taking aim. "You can't know that. There is no way that you could know that."

She had been shivering on the dock in the soft, cold rain for half an hour when the ferry pulled in, loaded to capacity with the earliest commuters. If she had not told Abe to park on the right side of the car deck, there would have been no way for them to find each other; as it was, his momentary stop for Joanna to scramble into the old station wagon almost caused a pileup, and did set off a frenzy of honking and veering as the cars behind tried to swing around them. Abe grunted, "Buckle the damn belt, cookie. Why do I always have to nag you about that?"

"Lake Union." She had somehow managed to dress herself after Lily's call, dragging one garment at a time onto a body that seemed to belong to someone else, and even to clench herself tightly around a core of hysteria as she waited out the night until it was time to meet the first predawn ferry from Gardner Island. "Right. *Right.* I'm the God of the Underworld, and I've been having a high old time chasing after my wife—my consort, my teenage queen, my prisoner, whatever, *whatever*—and now I've rounded her up, got the cuffs on her, and it's home again, home again, jiggety-jog. Along with somebody's crazy, crazy daughter." Her voice did not break on the last words, but as clear as they were, Abe could barely hear them. "And naturally—naturally—my port of departure for the great beyond, at five o'clock on a very cold morning, is Lake Union, where the condos roam and the fancy new restaurants cling together like Velcro. But of course, Lake fucking Union. I should have known."

Abe leaned forward to wipe the windshield with a sleeve. "I don't know *what's* wrong with the damn defroster. Rear one works fine. You notice a really weird thing about that howl?"

Joanna did not answer him. Abe said, "It sounded almost like three dogs howling together—practically harmonizing, you could say." Joanna felt the blood leaving her face. "Or just maybe like one dog with three heads?"

"Cerberus," Joanna whispered. "The Guardian . . ." She shook her head violently, as though to dislodge the thought. "Oh, no. No, damn it. We had the same dream—it's happened before, a couple of times, remember? It happens to people when they live . . . people who've been together for a . . . while. And the dog was in the dream, just part of the dream—I stopped hearing it the moment I woke up."

Abe said, "You didn't sleep at all. No more than I did." His eyes were filled with an immense, weary pity. "We'll get her back, Del. The kid's not going anywhere."

"She called me Mommy," Joanna whispered. "You *know* she hasn't . . . not since she was *little* . . ."

"Ah, Del. Del, the kid's always been calling you Mommy. She just couldn't hear herself."

"The house, the house in the tree . . ." She fell silent, never taking her eyes from him as he piloted the station wagon down streets grown unfamiliar with darkness and fear. But when, without turning his head, he reached out to touch her hand, she pulled her whole body away, pressing against the car door. "It wasn't really *in* the tree . . ."

Abe nodded. "It's a houseboat. It just looks that way because of the angle, the way we always see it from the road. We've driven by it a lot, visiting George and Nancy on Fairview, remember? Actually, it's probably a floating home, moored permanently in one place— no motor, no steering, not going anywhere. Sort of a bell tower thing on top, a cupola? Come on, you're the one who always points it out to me."

"And that's where they are?" She could not keep the mockery out of her voice. "In our dream house? So Lily dreamed the dog too?"

He made a wrong turn, swore at himself in a chagrined mumble, and spun the old car into a U-turn on the empty street. But his voice was as calmly matter-of-fact as she had ever heard it. "The gods send dreams. They come through the Gate of Ivory and the Gate of Horn, and I can't think which gate is supposed to give us the true dreams. I should remember, but I never do. Very aggravating. But, Del, I can feel it in my *kishkas*, this is exactly where we're supposed to be right now. You're just going to have to take my word on this one."

"I don't have to take your word for shit!" she cried out. "I don't have to take your word on anything, not ever again. I want my daughter, and I don't give a damn about the rest of it. Him—*her*, what you did with her—whatever Lily thinks she's doing . . . none of it, none of it. I just want it all done with, gone, and Lily home, and everything back the way it was, and that's never going to happen, is it?" Her voice was ragged and hiccupy, but she was not crying. "Where are we? Is this Eastlake?"

"'Patience, bedbug, the night is long.'" It was his favorite Spanish proverb, often deliberately employed to tease a restive eight-year-old Lily into mimic—and sometimes quite real—fury. "Okay, *now* we're on Eastlake. It's a way along—you'll know it when you see it." Beyond the lake the darkness was thinning slightly, but there was as yet no suggestion of dawn. Joanna could feel a coming storm crackling in her hair.

Abe said, "They'll be waiting for us. They sent that dream to say goodbye."

Her voice was as level and consciously expressionless as she could keep it. "And Lily?"

"I . . . don't know." The words came as slowly, as though he were being charged a bitter toll for each one. "I can't tell you, Del."

"They wouldn't kidnap Lily? The way *he* did *her*?" Instead of retreating from his hand, she grabbed it in both of her own. "They wouldn't. . . ?"

"No, no, of course not, what are you *talking* about?" *The same snuggly authority in his voice, the same comfort in his hand, as when he assured me absolutely that Lily's little dead sister was going to live.* "This isn't mythology, love. Lily isn't mythology."

"There!" she said. "Pull *over*, Abe—right there!"

The old car promptly lurched to the right, and skidded into a shallow roadside ditch, and stopped. Abe cut the engine and the headlights, set the parking brake, and looked at her from very far away. He said, with a slight hint of hesitation, "Del. I don't know how it's going to go. I don't know what's going to happen."

"Well, *there's* a change." But she softened more than she meant to, seeing the fear and exhaustion in his face. She got out of the car, and he followed, and they stood together on the roadside, hands in their coat pockets and their heads lowered against the cold mist. There was no moon, and few stars were visible; yet from where they were Lake Union appeared to pulse with its own sullen light, strangely angry and alive. Joanna said, "It's the last one on the left, right at the water's edge, see it? And that's not a cupola—it's a fancy coop, practically a bird penthouse. I guess the owner keeps pigeons."

"Wonder how he gets away with it. Houseboat people sue each other because one of them's been dumping used Depends over-board." He took her arm, gently setting her behind him. "It's likely to be wet and icy and slippery, so be careful. If you slip, you'll fall into me, and I'll catch you. Ready?"

"Yes," she said. "Funny . . . I used to think that you'd always catch me, no matter how far and hard I fell. Seems so long ago now, doesn't it? Another world."

"A world in which you didn't feel quite so sorry for yourself? I remember that one, too." He became truly angry so rarely that it always took her by surprise. "For God's sake, lady, whatever you think of me right now, your kid's the nearest I'm ever going to come to having a kid of my own. I'm not here for Lioness—Persephone—I'm here to get Lily back, same as you are. Beat me up later, you got that?"

He led her down the stair to the wooden walkway, and slowly between the structures, pausing now and then to whisper over his shoulder. "Yeah, these are all floating homes, you can tell. Some of them, it'd be like sailing a city block." Packed as closely together as cars in a parking lot, the homes were generally bigger than the houseboats: beyond that, even in the predawn darkness that rendered them all monochromatic, they were engagingly dissimilar, constantly distracting Joanna from her mission. One might have been a miniature high rise, glassed in almost entirely on three sides; another was a nearly perfect replica of a railroad caboose, except for being bright white. A third looked like a country cottage, its front door half-smothered by roses climbing out of pots the size of feeding troughs, while a fourth home had a deck expansive enough for a picnic table, a barbecue grill, and a wet bar. There were futuristic homes, seemingly constructed of unrelated colored blocks from a kindergarten play set, while others were traditional enough to have fitted comfortably into a New England fishing village or a 1950s television comedy. Two had child-size plastic swimming pools on deck; one actually had a swing and a tiny sandbox. There was a dead crab in the sandbox.

The soft, cold rain had stopped, and the water of the lake was largely calm, but even so Joanna felt as though the walkway were rocking slightly under her feet, and the buildings swaying alarmingly the moment she looked away. By the time they reached the floating home with the cupola, moored at the very end of the walkway, the lights across the lake appeared no brighter than fireflies, blinking on and off with the thickening mist. Joanna could not even make out the planks she stepped across, and was grudgingly grateful when Abe reached back and took her hand without speaking. She heard a boat start up nearby—a good-sized one, to judge by the cough of its slowly-warming engine—but could not see it, not even as a shadow among gray shadows. The men on deck seemed to be speaking in shadows as well, and she could not make out a word.

The house was two stories high, not counting the cupola, itself surmounted by a motionless weathervane in the curious shape of an Ourouboros, circling a globe and mouthing its own tail. There was a miniature deck, and a landing too small for anything but a skiff or a canoe to tie up to; by contrast, the arched doorway looked too high for its setting, slightly skewing the building's proportions. It stood partway open, but there was no sign of a light within.

Abe called "Hello?" but the mist muffled his voice, and Joanna's "Lily?" sounded no less lost and hesitant. They stood in silence, staring at each other, while the mist rolled in and an oar or a jumping fish splashed out in the lake. A breeze coaxed a hoarse grumble out of the Ourouboros, but the vane hardly moved at all.

Then the dog began howling inside the house.

*Cerberus* . . . It was the sound that had torn Abe from sleep on Gardner Island, a world ago, shredding the night and his faith in his own sanity together, and leaving him crouched naked and whimpering on his bed, too frozen even to cover his ears, too eviscerated to notice for some while that the terrible sound had finally ceased. In his soul, it never really had, even when he at last rose and dressed and called Joanna.

Joanna whispered, "Lily," and hurled herself through the open front door. Abe, knowing perfectly well that the three-headed dog who challenged all living who dared the Underworld was unimaginably far from a floating home on Lake Union, hesitated all the same before following her. *He knows Master and Mistress are coming home at last. He's just excited, that's all. Turk next door does the same thing.*

Once he closed the door behind him, the darkness was almost total, except for a faint glimmer upstairs, at the end of the winding stairway curling up like smoke from the farthest corner of the big room. Abe bumped hard against a bookcase, bruised his shin on a low table he never saw, lurched into a glass-fronted cabinet, sending a number of tinkly objects to the floor, and promptly followed them there when he skidded on an equally invisible carpet. Nursing his leg, hoping that whatever he was sitting on wasn't broken, he demanded loudly, "Del? Del, where *are* you?"

"Keep it down, Uncle Abe." The answer came in Lily's toneless voice, startlingly close by. "There's somebody dying upstairs."

As his eyes became partially accustomed to the dimness in the room—the two tall windows on either side were almost totally blanketed by wolf-gray mist—he made out her form, seated between two unlighted lamps on a narrow-backed chair that looked like garden furniture. As though out for the evening, she was wearing her favorite ensemble: a multicolored India-made light jacket over a maroon linen blouse and dark-gray denim pants, with a treasured red-and-gold scarf—a long-ago birthday gift from Abe—around her throat. To her left Joanna perched on the very edge of a long couch, as awkwardly as though she had fallen on it, like Abe. Turned sideways, facing Lily, she asked, in a child's voice, "Dying? How do you know?"

Lily said, "I went up to him. I gave him water. He's alone, he's waiting, like me." Her own voice was strangely tranquil. "That's why they chose this house."

"You had the dream," Joanna said. Lily looked back at her without answering. The dog who welcomed the dead had fallen silent, and the only sound Abe could hear was the complaint of the frozen weathervane. "Baby, they aren't here. They aren't going to be here, they're gone. Come home with me, Lily."

"No." *Her favorite word when she was two. Only then she used to scream it out—now it falls on the air like a closing door.* "They're coming. They are."

As though in answer, the air began slowly to brighten, although the light came neither from outside, nor from any of the untouched lamps in the room. Distracted momentarily from Lily, Abe turned and turned to marvel wryly at the efficient sleekness everywhere around him. As far as he could see, everything flowed seamlessly into everything else: the living room into the white kitchen, into a white hallway with a blue bathroom beyond, and the open white door of what must have been a guest bedroom beyond that. The crushed-velvet chairs and couch complemented each other affectionately;

the paintings were all soothingly nonrepresentational, and the magazines on the coffee table seemed to deal entirely with home decoration and cooking for large groups of people. The high ceiling had a pale blue tint that made it appear almost transparent.

Joanna saw them first, reflected in the glass door of a bookcase, given body and color by the gaudy jackets and leather covers. Mr. Mardikian appeared to be just behind her own shoulder—Lioness glimmered in his shadow—but when Joanna, instantly on her feet, turned to confront them both, she realized that they were actually at a farther distance: present and not quite present, poised between this and that, here and gone. Beside her, Lily made a low sound that haunted Joanna ever after, long after she had forgotten—as all who hear it must do—the howling of Cerberus.

Lioness said, "Joanna. Abe. My Lily."

Even Lily had no words for them. It was Mr. Mardikian who spoke. "I too wished to see you again, Delvecchio."

"Yes," Joanna said.

Abe said, in a voice he himself did not recognize, "I should never have let you stay with me." After a moment he added, "With us."

Lioness looked down and away, oddly like a punished schoolgirl. "No, my beautiful Abe," she answered him very softly. "No, you should not have let me stay. For my sake, as well as yours."

Lily stepped forward, "Lioness," she said. Her voice was remarkably clear and steady. "Lioness, I'm coming with you."

Joanna understood an instant too late. Clutching at her daughter, she tripped over a hassock, and fell flat. Abe lunged, but Lily was past him, stretching out her arms to the half-real figures beyond. Something in her right hand glinted like a candy wrapper, and Abe and Joanna cried out together as she turned it toward her heart.

"I'm coming with you," Lily said again. "This is all I have to do, and then I can come with you."

Joanna's nose was bleeding. Abe moved to raise her, but she

waved him away frantically, unable to make a sound, yearning helplessly toward Lily. Abe took a step, and then froze when Lily looked at him. "It's all right, Uncle Abe. It's really all right. I know what I'm doing."

"No, you don't," he answered, wondering in a distant manner where he found the air to make words. "You die, your mother dies. That is really not all right, Lilsville, and I won't have it. Put that thing down." He pointed at the knife, and added, "Besides, I gave it to you when you moved into that apartment. A whole set, five knives in a teak butcher block. Put it down."

Lily smiled at him. It was a kind, peaceful smile, but it went very strangely with the dark glint of the kitchen knife, and with the eagerness of the mist pressing against the windows. "My mother's tougher than you are. Way tougher than me. She'll do fine." Lily's tone was gentle, but there was no mercy in it; nothing but serene certainty. Abe thought wildly, *Christ, I'll bet Joan of Arc was the same way, exactly the same.*

Lily turned back toward Lioness and Mr. Mardikian. Neither one had moved since she had brought out the little knife.

"I'm not scared," she said. She was still smiling. "I don't mean about the thing, the doing it—I mean, I'm not scared of Hades. I'll be with you, and I'll see you all the time, forever, so how bad could it be?" The knife was touching her now, the tip just under her left breast.

Mr. Mardikian said, "Child, it is not your time." But there was a hesitancy in his voice, and Lily caught it. "My time's when I choose," she told him. "I'm a human being, we get to do that." She closed her eyes.

Joanna felt it then: the small, silent jar under her feet that neither Abe nor Lily appeared to notice. She saw that Abe was gathering himself for a clumsy, desperate spring, and knew that it would fail. She knew also that Mr. Mardikian could stop Lily as effortlessly as he sank baskets, and understood that he would not.

Lioness moved. She stepped away from Mr. Mardikian and lifted a hand: not in a grand sea-parting, time-freezing gesture, but as though she had recognized a friend across the street, one whom she was not quite sure would remember her. But however close or faraway she truly was, the elm-green eyes were seeing in and down, down and only, and Lily instantly opened her own eyes wide to the Primavera gaze. Lioness said, "If you do this, you will never be with me again."

The words came gray and hard as the lake water. Joanna would not have known the voice. Joan of Arc vanished as Lily demanded, suddenly shrill, "What are you saying? When I'm in Hades, you'll be there, that's the one thing I know for sure—"

"You will never see Hades." Lioness took a step nearer—only one, but it brought her somehow close, at the same time that it seemed to move Mr. Mardikian farther away, barely discernable now, a shadow among antique shadows. She never looked at the knife, which she could have captured easily; instead she held out her hand, and the knife fell from Lily's fingers. To Joanna, the hand appeared no different from Lily's, except for the suggestion of an iridescent shiver where the two met. Lioness spoke, in the low, almost-accented, almost-laughing voice of the Skyliner Diner. "Oh, Lily, my Lily, whatever made you think that you were to end as a thirsty ghost forever wandering the shores of that night river? Don't you know that you will go straight to the Elysian Fields when you die? My Lily, don't you *know?*"

Lily stared at her, far beyond speech, a world beyond comprehension. "Heroes," Lily said finally. "Heroes go to the Elysian Fields. Even I know that. Everyone else—"

Lioness actually snorted, the sound almost shockingly human. "There are heroes and heroes, as there are battles and battles. And there are choices, always, even after the battles are over. Listen to me now. You would never spend a single moment in Hades, because you would surely never choose to set foot there. Not you—not my Lily." She took hold of Lily's hands, holding them both between her own. "Oh, love, you made that choice long ago."

"Will you be there?" The voice was that of a small girl, and Joanna found her eyes aching much more than her bruised nose.

Lioness shook her head. "*He* has nothing to do with the Elysian Fields." She made no gesture toward Mr. Mardikian, but Abe thought he saw the tall old shadow flinch, as though an old wound had fleetingly pained him. Lioness said quietly, "I have never seen the Elysian Fields."

"Oh," Lily said. "Oh. Then . . . well, then I won't either. I've changed my mind." She bent to kick the knife away, but Lioness held her fast.

"Lily, there is little time." Joanna sympathized profoundly with the distinct vexation in Lioness's voice. "You may change your mind, but you cannot change your soul. You cannot ever come where I am, however you come, and I grieve for myself, but not for you. Trust me now, and listen."

*We're moving. We can't be, but we are. Doesn't anyone notice?* Mr. Mardikian seemed closer also, though Joanna had not seen him move at all. When he looked at her she could not read his lean old face, but she felt his impatience, and beyond that a certain genuine bewilderment; and, to her own wonder, she sorrowed for him.

"Listen," Lioness said to Lily. "If you choose to live—and, yes, that choice is yet yours—then you will know me each spring, and feel me beside you, and know that I feel you, and feel your love, every moment that I walk this earth. My mother could be no nearer. Do you understand me, sweet Lily?"

Lily was crying, for the first time that Abe could remember. She made almost no sound, but her body was shaking as though some terrible creature had her between its jaws. "But I won't ever see you again. I won't ever see you."

"Abe." Joanna got his name out somehow, but he did not hear her. She said his name again, louder. "Abe, the boat—the house, whatever—it's come loose."

"What? What are you talking about?" His own face changed then, and he turned to stare, not out of the windows at the flowing, hungering mist, but toward the door he had closed.

Lioness reached into a pocket of the new green dress she had bought in the spring—or had it become in some manner a mist-colored gown?—and brought out a small, rather plain cologne bottle. To Abe the whisper of scent that arose from it brought him a frail near-memory of storm and flowers. Lioness pushed the bottle into Lily's hand and firmly shut the slow fingers around it. "You wore me once. Wear me again whenever you forget."

Lily's skin had tightened and paled over her cheekbones. "Forget?" She could barely get the word out, and then only in a desert whisper. "You think I need . . . I don't need anything to make me remember you."

Lioness smiled. It was not the near-smile of the *Primavera* painting, enticingly sly, elusively mischievous; rather, this smile was utterly mortal, crooked and irregular, even a little tremulous, uncertain of its own beauty. It was the last smile of hers that any of them ever saw, but it might as well have been the first.

"When you forget yourself," she said. "When you forget that you are Lily . . . Lily . . . *my* Lily, and no stupid, ugly dyke freak." To Joanna, the words Lily had so bitterly called herself sang like harp notes in Lioness's voice. "When you forget that Persephone loves you. Wear it then."

"We're drifting," Joanna said. "Abe, we *are*."

"No, we're not." But he was already moving to the door, constantly looking over his shoulder, for all the world like a thief slipping away with his swag. No one but Joanna paid him any attention.

Mr. Mardikian made no sound, but Lioness turned her head.

"Yes, I know." Joanna heard him too, though she could never have said exactly how, or exactly what she heard. The call had no more words than whalesong, but it held the same ancient undersea longing, as well as a power that momentarily halted the blood of her heart—as she discovered when she touched her nose. *He does love her. More than Lily does.*

Lioness said, "Goodbye, sweet Lily." She held one hand out to Abe, one to Joanna. She said, "My dear ones, my teachers, thank you for keeping me warm."

Lily's lips were moving, but no sound came from them. Mr. Mardikian's voice was clear and human. "Delvecchio. Remember me also, a little." Joanna felt the sting of tears, and as if that pressure had opened others, the warm coppery taste of blood as her nose began to bleed once more.

Abe opened the door.

Beyond were no lights, no boats, no warehouses, no waterfront restaurants—not even the lake itself—only the mist, and the rising awareness of a darkness on the farthest side of the dark: a shadow at once looming and luring, whispering sweetly in Joanna's skin as it neared. The mist smelled to her like Mr. Mardikian's tears, those he had shed in the Skyliner Diner, remembering someone who had once played for him. The howling had begun again, as close as her stumbling heartbeat now. There was no other sound. There never had been.

"*The Styx.*" The two words came out of Abe like arrows being plucked from wounds. "We're crossing the goddamn River Styx."

"No," Joanna said, but only to be saying it. She had known the far shadow of the river between the living and the dead before Abe himself recognized it, though she could never have said why. *Have I been here before, drifting on this same water under the rusty gaze of a serpent eating its own tail? Have I been in this house that I dreamed was in a tree—already tossed doggie-treats into those triple jaws? What is it I should know?* The shadow was swimming almost into shape on the farther shore—Joanna glimpsed what she first imagined might be towers, and then re-envisioned them as a horizon of hemlocks. *God, I've always hated evergreens!* But then they decided to be bleak blood-red hills, and after that nothing more than colorless blurs that made her eyes ache. *Objects in the hereafter may be less visible than they appear.*

A man in blue pajamas came down the stairs. His feet were bare, and never quite touched the steps. He looked to be in late middle age: tall and round-bellied, his soft cheeks unshaven, his thinning hair disheveled and his eyes puzzled. He seemed about to speak, but only kept shaking his head.

Mr. Mardikian put his hand gently on the barefoot man's shoulder. The confusion went out of the slack face, taking with it—to Joanna's eyes—both terror and memory. Lioness spoke to him in a slow, murmurous language, words that Joanna knew she would only hear once again. Lioness took the man's hand, and turned away toward the open door with him and Mr. Mardikian, and she never looked back.

Mr. Mardikian did, for a single moment. He said Joanna's name, soundlessly, "*Delvecchio* . . ."

Then they were gone, followed only by Lily's rending wail of loss, and Abe put his arms tightly around a weeping Lily and Joanna, and held them so, until he felt the soft, impossible jar of a boat that could not ever move from its moorings settling home from a long journey through waters as deep and cold as the eyes of Mr. Mardikian. He saw the dawn, heard a motorboat go by, heard laughter as light as the waves that made the floating home stir dreamily in the cruiser's wake. Then he took Lily and Joanna out of the tall house with the weathervane of the serpent eating its own tail.

# 16.

# OCTOBER

"He's cleaned it all out," Lily said. "Bedroll, the heater, her flowers, all her things. There's nothing left, nothing of her."

Joanna shrugged. "Why not? That's what I did. Took me a whole lot longer, let me tell you."

"He'd just finished when I was over there. He was taking the Miss Piggy calendar down."

"You went to see him? How nice. How awfully nice of you." Joanna's eyes and voice softened alike as she regarded her daughter across the quilt they were folding together. "It was for her, wasn't it? You were looking for something she might have left behind." She reached for Lily's hand and squeezed it gently.

Lily shook her head. "No, I went to visit with Uncle Abe." She used the term deliberately, spacing the two words with precision. "I went to see how he was doing—what she left for him." She faced Joanna unflinchingly, even smiling slightly. "You'll never ask, so I'll tell you. He's sitting in the house playing the harmonica. No beer, no book. Just playing blues harmonica in an empty house."

"That's nice too." Joanna took the folded comforter from her, set it neatly on a hall closet shelf, and shook out a crumpled red sheet with a Persian-rug print. "Come on, you said you wanted to help. I've got another union thing at five."

Lily put her hands on her hips and grinned fully, shaking her head again. "Look at you. Look at *us*, look at women. Change your hair, change your life. The time I broke up with Colleen—no, you never met that one either, this was before . . . I mean, I did that, and right away I cut my hair, *colored* my hair, changed my damn *toothpaste*, for God's sake. Had my ears pierced—got that tattoo you hate—"

"I don't hate your tattoo, I hate where you had them put it. Anyway, I haven't done any of those things, not a one. *Lalalala, life goes on*, right?" Impatient with her own edginess, she began folding the sheet single-handed, glowering back into Lily's smile. "Nothing's changed, except I'm busier than ever, with a lot fewer distractions. The *money* I've been saving on ferry fares, you wouldn't believe—"

"Yes, I would, I do believe you. That's the trouble. Give me that." Lily took hold of the red sheet by two corners, tugging it smooth. "For God's sake, he's been part of our lives since I was six years old. I don't care what he's done, what you feel—you can't just go along as though he never existed. That's crazy, I mean it. That really is crazy."

"Walk toward me," Joanna said. They met with the doubled sheet hanging between them, like neighbors gossiping over a backyard fence. "What do you want me to tell you? I'm not mad at him, not the way I was—I just don't have anything to say to him. Yes, I'll miss him for awhile—maybe quite a while, I'm not going to fool myself about that. But I'll tell you something, I missed your father too. You didn't know him, so you got off easy, but I missed him longer than I ever said. But I got over it, and I can't even remember when I realized that I was over it. I really can't remember." Abruptly she leaned forward across the sheet and kissed Lily's cheek, startling her. "Baby, life is mostly getting over stuff. One of the very, *very* few things I know for sure."

"I'm not buying it," Lily said loudly. "I'm *not*." She let go of the sheet, which dropped to the floor. Joanna did not stoop to pick it up. "And I'll tell *you* something—I'm going to go on seeing Uncle Abe any time I feel like it. Just so you know."

"Cool." Joanna looked around the bedroom and sighed pointedly, rubbing her chin. "The drapes have got to go. I've made up my mind."

Considering such circumstances as the bassist having been arrested on a morals charge while Seriously Blue was setting up, and his hastily recruited substitute turning out to be the drummer's drug connection—neither of which seemed to have much to do with the lead guitarist physically assaulting Twelve-Bar Billy during the first set—Abe thought that the Bremerton gig could have gone a lot worse than it actually had. Billy had suffered a blackened eye as well as the loss of a back tooth, but his embouchure was intact, and in the second set he played "Columbus Stockade" as fiercely and inventively as Abe had ever heard anyone do. The guitarist had a noticeable limp and two sprained fingers, but he gripped a flatpick as though it were Twelve-Bar Billy's throat, and managed a remarkably fluent solo on "Pure Religion" and got through "The Devil Went Down to Georgia" without once tripping over the lyrics. Their listeners were rowdily enthusiastic—easily the band's noisiest audience west of the Cascades—yet Abe's own version of "You Don't Know My Mind," accompanied only by the sweating dealer/bassist, brought them, first to utter stillness, and then to stamping, bottle-banging pandemonium. It was then, as Billy immediately launched the band into the first scheduled encore, that he saw Joanna.

She was not at one of the tables, but standing alone in a far corner, her back to an oversize Buddy Guy poster. He had long since given up on the fantasy of having her appear at one of Seriously Blue's performances, and she had clearly not come to be seen. The only way he could be sure that she had noticed him noticing her was that when he looked again at the Buddy Guy poster, she was gone.

There was no going after her in what amounted nearly to a third set, but the instant they were done with the very last encore, he was out in the dark street, looking and calling for her. The bright twilight was warm for a Northwest October, and the sidewalk was full of strollers, including people who had been cheering him and the band on moments before. Spilling out of the club, plucking at his sleeve to praise his playing, their kindly, friendly, enthusiastically drunken bodies kept blocking the view everywhere around him, and he was not capable of elbowing and snarling his way through such a crowd. By the time he was finally clear of them, he was rumpled, sweaty, and exhausted—as he had not ever felt onstage—and was no longer sure that he had ever seen Joanna at all.

He walked slowly back into the club. Picking up his coat, he bade goodnight to his bandmates and picked up his share of the take from Twelve-Bar Billy, mentioning that they ought to have twice the gate tomorrow, once word got around. Billy snorted darkly, and promptly winced, muttering, "Yeah, we likely will, daddy, no question about it. And they'll just as likely be expecting that crazy sonabitch to show up with an AK-47 and a fire ax. Show business, you got to keep topping yourself."

Abe promised to be in Silverdale in time to help set up for the Wednesday night gig, and left wishing that he had remembered to bring the LeCarré audiobook to play on the long drive home. *Nothing to listen to this late but PBS repeats. Damn.*

She was in his car, sitting in the passenger seat, holding out the keys to him as he got in. "The house key's with them."

"You might want to hang onto them," he said without expression. "I'm traveling a lot these days, and you might need to get in for something."

"Nope. I'm done." They stared at each other, neither speaking, but neither looking away. Joanna said finally, "I could use a lift to the ferry."

Under a down vest, she was wearing a gray silk blouse that he had bought her on one of their two vacations out of the country, and a ratty and cherished pair of black jeans. Abe started the car and backed it around to head for the Bremerton docks. "Lily?"

"Could be worse. She holed up for a few days—didn't talk, didn't go to work, pick up the phone, didn't answer the door. Just a few days." The car stalled, being cold, and Abe snarled at it and started it again. "She sleeps holding that perfume bottle. Like a teddy bear. She told me she sleeps better."

They spoke not at all of themselves, but of Lioness and Mr. Mardikian—it still took a near-physical effort to refer to them by any other names. Joanna sat closely enough beside him as he drove, yet managed to keep a distance: a demilitarized buffer zone of air that definitely had its own area code. After a while, she asked hesitantly, "Where do you think they really are right now? They wouldn't actually be underground, would they? Lioness said—I mean, Lily *told* me she said . . . ah, the hell with it, what do you think?"

"I don't know," he said. "I don't think the gods ever lived on Mount Olympus—or on Mount Rainier, for that matter, or Shasta, or Kanchenjunga—anyplace with a name and address. Hades might be in some other dimension—some other time, even. We'll never know, cookie."

He used the detested endearment deliberately, hoping to spark her traditional reaction. Joanna seemed not to have heard it. She said softly, "I've been wondering if she'll even remember us, where she is. She told Lily she would, always, but I keep wondering."

The road was almost empty, and he slowed down, turning to look at her. "What *I* wonder," he said, "is whether we'll ever see each other again after I drop you off at the ferry."

She occupied herself in worrying a loose thread on the cuff of her jeans. They drove on in silence for some time. When the ferry lights came in sight, she finally spoke.

"They changed us. We're different now. I don't mean from what we were—I mean from everyone else in the world. You've had a goddess living in your garage, I've shot hoops with the King of the Dead, we've both made love or something with people—with creatures—whom everyone else knows don't exist. It's too different. It's lonely."

"Do you wish it hadn't happened? If we hadn't gone to the Skyliner, that one night?"

"Oh, no." She actually put her hand on his forearm; then drew it back, almost before the touch, looking at him from somewhere as far away as Lioness. "Oh, no, I couldn't ever wish that. But I don't know what we're supposed to do now. Who we're supposed to be."

"Well, I'm surprised that you're taking the ferry, for one thing. Lily says you're kayaking everywhere now. Bought your own two-holer and everything."

She laughed for the first time. "Hardly. But I've made Bainbridge and Vashon already—and Gig Harbor last week, if you'll believe it—and I'm working up to Orcas Island next summer. Probably take a friend along on that one—Orcas is a biggie." She turned her head away slightly, and then turned back to look directly at him. "It's what I've always wanted, Abe. I didn't know just how much I wanted it until I went and did it. Like with you and the harmonica. You've gotten really good, by the way. Really, really good."

"Yeah, me and the harp," he said. "The Yiddisher Little Walter. We'll be playing Vashon ourselves, a couple of weeks. After Silverdale. Surprising, the changes." The soft grayness over the

Sound was uniform now, sky and water all but indistinguishable, pressing together like lovers losing identity in each other for a little time. "I miss you, Del."

"You miss *us*. You miss the usualness, the unsurprisingness. *I* miss me, usual old me, just the way I was." For a brief moment there were tears in her eyes; he fancied that he could actually see her willing them back. "But that's gone, Abe. Page turned. Whatever comes next, that's gone."

The Seattle ferry hooted as it approached its berth: not the long and aching cry of a night-train whistle, but the deep challenge of a kraken. Joanna said, "Got to go. Flying tomorrow."

"I haven't forgotten. Zip your vest, it'll be cold on the water. Last thing she said to us, that we kept her warm."

She smiled fully then. "We did, didn't we? It took all night, but we got her warm." Her hand was on the door latch when she stopped suddenly, turning back to face him. "Do you ever think that she might not have been a goddess at all? Or maybe a goddess, okay, but maybe not quite right in the head? You told me she said that all the old gods were like on the street, gaga, mumbling to themselves. Maybe she was the same way, only"—she halted for a moment, until her voice was steady again—"only beautiful."

"I can live without knowing," he said. "I always could. Goodbye, cookie."

"Goodbye, old man. Goodbye, my old man."

The cars were already rolling off the ferry as she closed the door behind her and walked to join the handful of late passengers waiting at the barrier. She looked back once and waved. He kept the engine running, to stay warm.

# ABOUT THE AUTHOR

Peter Soyer Beagle is the internationally bestselling and much-beloved author of numerous classic fantasy novels and collections, including *The Last Unicorn*, *Tamsin*, *The Line Between*, and *Sleight of Hand*. He is the editor of *The Secret History of Fantasy* and the co-editor of *The Urban Fantasy Anthology*.

Born in Manhattan and raised in the Bronx, Beagle began to receive attention for his artistic ability even before he received a scholarship to the University of Pittsburgh. Exceeding his early promise, he published his first novel, *A Fine & Private Place*, at nineteen, while still completing his degree in creative writing. Beagle's follow-up, *The Last Unicorn*, is widely considered one of the great works of fantasy. It has been made into a feature-length animated film, a stage play, and a graphic novel.

Beagle went on to publish an extensive body of acclaimed works of fiction and nonfiction. He has written widely for both stage and screen, including the screenplay adaptations for *The Last Unicorn* and the animated film of *The Lord of the Rings* and the well-known "Sarek" episode of *Star Trek*.

As one of the fantasy genre's most-lauded authors, Beagle is the recipient of the Hugo, Nebula, Mythopoeic, and Locus awards, as well as the Grand Prix de l'Imaginaire. He has also been honored with the World Fantasy Life Achievement Award and the Inkpot Award from the Comic-Con convention, given for major contributions to fantasy and science fiction.

Beagle lives in Richmond, California, where he is working on too many projects to even begin to name.